THE WILLOWDALE CONSPIRACY

A RORI CAHILL NOVEL

by Thomas D. Linehan

LP Publishing

119 Long Pond Drive
Denmark, ME 04022

The Willowdale Conspiracy

A Rori Cahill Novel

Written by Thomas D. Linehan

Copyright ©2014 by **Thomas D. Linehan**

The Willowdale Conspiracy by Thomas D. Linehan
is available on Amazon and other online
booksellers, and as a Kindle ebook

Cover by damonza.com
Layout by Laura Ashton (laura@gitflorida.com)
Rebecca T. Dickson, Editor
www.rebeccatdickson.com/write-raw

ISBN: 978-1500190736

Library of Congress Control Number: 2014911136
Create Space Independent Publishing Platform
North Charleston, SC

First Printing

Printed in the United States of America

Dedicated

to my wife Judy who has supported me and has had to endure
reading and reading my novel several thousand times. Love you.

and

to my other best friend, Mark Graffam.
I will miss all that we enjoyed together. RIP.

Todd

Thanks for your
generosity.

Thomas D. Boucher

Chapter One

On her thirteenth birthday, Rori's present from Aunt Charley was a Ruger 9 mm handgun. It came with a card that read, "To my daughter. Love, A.C."

Aunt Charley took Rori in more than two years ago and had been teaching her about life—something her father had never done. Rori devoured everything Aunt Charley offered. She was like a buzzard on a carcass on the desert floor.

Part of that teaching was protecting herself. Rori had already passed safety certification, as well as concealed weapons training, using Aunt Charley's gun.

"I didn't get the laser. You won't need it with the three dot sight and besides it might jam up in a holster," Aunt Charley said.

Aunt Charley lived just outside of Syracuse, New York. She was forty-two, single, the sister of Rori Cahill's father. A hundred years ago she would have been called a spinster, which would have suited her fine —as long as no one controlled her life except her. Any loves she had fell by the wayside once they tried to oversee her. Her life before Rori was exactly the way she wanted it.

When Rori moved in after both of her parents were killed in a car accident, it changed everything for Aunt Charley. Rori was left alone for three days before Aunt Charley showed up. She had more than saved Rori after the accident. She rescued the girl from the little town of Scantville, New York, where nothing ever happened, except another pregnancy and another fourteen-year-old father.

When can we go shooting?" Rori asked.

"As soon as you eat and get ready."

Rori wrapped her hands around the gun, as though it was a baby.

Checking to make sure it wasn't loaded, she stepped out of the kitchen door onto the deck, followed by Aunt Charley.

Bringing the gun up, she aimed it at a mocking bird on a branch of a nearby bush.

The gun had no bullets in it, but she wished it had. She hated mocking birds with their ten thousand songs waking her up at three in the morning.

She turned to her aunt. "Can I name it?" she asked.

"Rori, let's get things straight. Whether it's naming your gun or making a life decision, it's you and no one else that decides."

"I'm going to name him after my old tomcat I use to have."

"What's that?" Aunt Charley asked.

"Jack," Rori said. "Jack is my new friend."

Chapter Two

Twelve Years Later

An older lady in her mid-seventies opened the door. She had a refined appearance and was not unattractive, but her face looked as though she had spent too much time in the sun. It made no difference to Dr. Moskowitz. He was there to entice another rich person.

"Mrs. Eisenblatt?"

"Yes."

"I'm Dr. Madison Moskowitz, from the Maryland Life Rehabilitation Center."

"Please come in. I've been expecting you. Follow me into the library." Her voice sounded much younger than she appeared.

They walked but a few feet and turned into a spacious room. A gas-burning fire added a blanket of comfort on the cold February morning. The room was neat and opulent. In the corner hung a Degas, *After the Bath*, as well as Asian artwork and sculptures. Dr. Moskowitz made a mental note of the valuables. It would come into play when his final charges were dispensed.

Mrs. Eisenblatt took a seat on one side of the fireplace and directed Dr. Moskowitz to a wingback chair opposite her.

"You have a nice place here, Mrs. Eisenblatt. This fire feels good on my old bones."

"Well, thank you very much. It does feel good. And you may call me Emily. Would you like some coffee?"

"That would be fine," Dr. Moskowitz said.

Emily stood to pour, but the doctor jumped up.

"Let me do that. Will you join me?"

"Please. Coffee is one of my pleasures these days."

"I know what you mean. Mine are coffee and popcorn. I love popcorn. I guess it goes back to my childhood."

Dr. Moskowitz let the small chat go on a bit longer. Once he felt he had successfully wooed his client, he decided it was time to get to work.

"You mentioned on the phone your husband has a problem. How may I be of assistance?"

Mrs. Eisenblatt bit her upper lip, stared down at her lap. "Let's not beat around the bush, Doctor. My husband has become a drug addict. The pressure of his work has finally gotten to him. I don't know if it was the deadlines or the failures that affected him more. He has turned into someone I no longer know. I don't mean to make excuses—he has a brilliant mind, and it just all got to him."

Mrs. Eisenblatt stopped fidgeting with her fingers, took a deep breath, and looked up toward Dr. Moskowitz. Her lips parted and she released a deep breath, like a deflating balloon.

Dr. Moskowitz looked her directly in her eyes. "There are no excuses or apologies needed. Life gets to us all. That's why there are places like MLRC, and people like myself. I'm here to help."

"Thank you, Doctor."

"Please, call me Madison. If you let me take charge, I will take care of everything. You will have your husband back in no time and life will be as it once was."

"Tell me more," she said.

Reaching into his satchel, Dr. Moskowitz pulled out his tablet. He tapped a couple of times on the screen, then stood and moved over to Mrs. Eisenblatt.

"Here, look at these photos of the facility," he said, handing her the tablet.

Emily stared at the screen a few seconds. "I'm sorry, but other than my phone, technology is one of those things I don't care to spend my time understanding," she said. "That's more my husband's business."

"Here, let me show you. I'll just turn this into some split screens so you can see the entire facility." Tap. "This is our beautiful living room. Here's our spacious bathroom, and this would be your husband's bedroom. We want our clients to feel as though they are at home. Our bathrooms have marble floors and counters, plush carpeting in the living areas, and if what you see doesn't suit you, in minutes you can pick out exactly what you'd like for your husband."

"You have put some thought into this," Emily said.

Moskowitz smiled. "You have no idea how much work I have put into this. I wanted to make everything perfect."

Emily continued smiling.

"Excuse me just a minute." Dr. Moskowitz returned to his chair and started tapping on the screen of the tablet once more. He entered his password and pulled up the site for booking patients.

"I'm looking at my facility's availability, and I have a private villa open. May I book it for tomorrow?"

"Can you assure me none of this will get into the papers? That some second-rate snoop won't destroy my husband?"

Madison's face tightened and he glared at Mrs. Eisenblatt. "Let me clarify your husband's situation. From here on, Mr. Eisenblatt has pneumonia. Everyone knows my reputation for protecting our clients, including our employees. No one breaks my rules. You came to me because you heard good things. Your friends recommended me. Whatever the reason, I'm here because I care about people. Isn't that true?" he said, nodding.

Dr. Moskowitz was a professional mind manipulator. He was like a bear waiting upstream for the salmon to swim into his giant paw. Some would escape, but the ones he really wanted never got away.

"I suppose," Emily said.

Dr. Moskowitz let her settle into her own thoughts as he started to tap on his screen again. Emily assumed he was making arrangements. Moskowitz was not even paying any attention to Emily. A couple more taps and a password and he was in direct contact with a former Russian spy. He entered a coded note, telling General Vitaly Kenchinkoff to deposit $2 million into his Cayman account.

Dr. Moskowitz extracted information from his bed-ridden clients by injecting them with truth serum. It would put their mind in a relaxed state. It didn't always work on every patient, but Moskowitz had learned over time how to trick the tougher patients by increasing the dosage. The problem was it took longer for the patients to recover from their inhibited state. His canned response was any side effect came from the other medications he prescribed. It was his job to extract information, based on questions Vitaly provided. Vitaly would then sell the information around the world. They stole military and corporate secrets from their drugged patients. Vitaly had buyers putting up money before a question was ever asked.

Dr. Moskowitz wanted to alert Vitaly he had a new client. It was time to find buyers, and deposit his share of the cash up front. Any additional money Vitaly negotiated would be his. Signing out, Moskowitz returned his gaze to Emily.

"Just to make you feel more at ease, I want you to know I will be the only attending physician. I have special personnel who will attend to all his needs with the utmost confidentiality. And as I said before, no one will speak of him outside the walls of the facility."

"What do we do next?" Emily asked.

"Let me take some information here." Tap. Tap. "Just a few more minutes," he said as he completed the admission papers and waivers for the MLRC.

Dr. Moskowitz stood up and then handed the tablet to Mrs. Eisenblatt.

"Sign here," he said, handing her a stylus. "This is a contract stating what we will do for you and the cost, and it allows me to access your insurance. It also states you will pay for whatever the insurance does not cover."

"I understand," she said, "and there's nothing to worry about. We're good for any cost."

"Just let me make a couple of taps. One … two … three," he said. "Just like that and we're done. This goes straight to my associate, Laura. She will have everything set up by the time I get back to my office."

"That was a lot easier than I thought," Emily said.

"There are two more things. First, I will have a nurse come over this evening. She'll stay at your husband's bedside the entire night. Where is he right now?"

"He's sleeping. His physician gave him something. I wanted him out of the way. He would have made it impossible to speak with you this morning."

10

"Very well. Does he know what's going on—that you spoke to me?"

"Yes we talked … and talked … and talked. I told him he's got to do something or I'm going to expose him and then leave him."

"None of that is going to be needed, I assure you. The nurse will give him another sedative to keep him asleep for the night until the ambulance comes in the morning. I'd like his doctor's name and number, as well as any medications he's taking."

"I'll get that for you."

"As I was saying about the ambulance, it will be unmarked and discreet. But I'm going to have it here at 4:30 a.m. That way none of the nosy neighbors will be up to bother you or us. Is that fine with you?"

"That's fine. It'll be a relief not having him here—I mean until he's better."

"You don't have to get yourself up, either. Our nurse will allow the attendants in and lock up on the way out. You've been through enough," he said, and made his way to the door.

* * *

"General, did you receive my message?" Dr. Moskowitz asked.

"Of course," General Vitaly Knechinkoff said.

"I have Dr. Eisenblatt coming to my facility in the morning," Moskowitz said.

"The laser weapons developer?" Vitaly asked.

Dr. Moskowitz set the price on most patients without even telling Vitaly who he was admitting. There were times Vitaly would come back to him and say the demand price was too high and they would agree to a new price. Dr Moskowitz had learned certain patients were more valuable than others. Vitaly could no longer lie about the value of patients.

"The one and only. We should be able to ascertain much information during his stay," Dr. Moskowitz said. "I'm having him picked up in the morning."

As a young man, Vitaly was part of the KGB. He was, at one time, a close friend of Luchen Sachoff, who wanted to become the supreme leader of the Soviet Union. That was before the breakup of the Soviet Union and its Eastern Bloc. As Luchen moved up the Soviet ladder, people seemed to disappear. Vitaly felt he needed to distance himself before he did too. He decided to have himself transferred to opposite postings, just to maintain a safe distance from Luchen. It worked. Luchen died of a "lead heart attack" from another ambitious soldier's bullet. His name was Vladimir Putin.

Now, all Vitaly could think about was what information could be obtained and sold. It would be a generation before others would learn where the leak originated—if ever.

"What do you think would be a fair price?" Dr. Moskowitz asked.

"That depends on the information we get from him."

"It depends on nothing, General. You saw my message. Either there's $2 million in my account by 5 a.m. tomorrow, or I'll be making a call at 5:01 to General Chen Wung Ho."

Dr. Moskowitz had no intention of going to another operative, but it was good once in a while to let Vitaly know he was not the only one who would pay for information from his patients.

The phone was silent for a few seconds, then Vitaly asked, "What's wrong with Eisenblatt? I don't want to be purchasing damaged goods."

"He has pneumonia."

"Likely story," the general said, and then gave a little laugh. "The money will be there, and I will stop by with a list of questions to ask."

"Have a nice day, General."

Chapter Three

"Laura, we have a patient coming in tomorrow around 6:30 a.m. It's about a two-hour trip from their home. I want the ambulance to pick him up at 4:30 a.m. It seems he has been experimenting with some illegal drugs," Moskowitz said to the nurse on the other end of the phone.

"I received your information, and I have the villa all set. A Dr. Dietrich Eisenblatt, is that correct?" Laura asked.

"That's correct."

"I've listed all the usual medications associated with pneumonia on his public file, and I listed the ones you normally use with our rehab patients on his personal file," Laura said. "Are there any specific medications that I should list besides the norm?"

"No," Dr Moskowitz said. He never let on to the nurses about the use of sodium pentothal. Whenever he used it he only recorded it on a record in the HR office, something the nurses never saw. "Have you placed that file in the bookcase drawer?"

"Yes sir," Laura said. "He's in V7, as you asked. I've notified Nurse Lexington. She'll be in later to pick up the sedative and any other instructions. Is there anything else?"

"No. As usual you've done a fine job," Dr. Moskowitz said.

Laura Gorham was the lead nurse for all of the villas. It was her job to see that everything was set up for each patient, per Dr. Moskowitz's instructions. The villas were under his strict control, and *his* patients were the *only* patients that went to the villas.

The MLRC's main building was an old mental institution. The brick building was built to last, and although it was in need of refurbishing and general plumbing and electrical updates, it was perfect for what Dr. Moskowitz and the investors planned.

In the government's efforts to eliminate drug use, tax breaks were created for medical facilities that treated addicts. Many politicians thought it was a wasted effort to try to turn them back into productive citizens, but pretended they cared. Because of the tax breaks, the investors would have zero tax liabilities for the next ten years. They added a new building onto the backside of the facility, which housed side businesses, a clinic and a minor surgery room.

The facilities were divided up into three units. The first was the old brick building. It handled drug abusers who were in state-mandated (and paid for) recovery programs. The second was the modern add-on which provided services covered by private insurance. The third set of units, the villas, were completely detached and reserved for the wealthy. Entrances and patios separated each villa. Every convenience was attended to, and patients in the villas had their own dedicated staff. Well-manicured hedges, fencing and a long, winding driveway separated the disjointed villas from the rest of the property. A gatehouse stood at the end of the driveway to keep nosy people from the area.

When the villas were first opened, Dr. Moskowitz was approached by General Vitaly Kenchinkoff, who explained the opportunity. The doctor would gather information from patients and Vitaly would make sure he was well-paid for that information.

Vitaly had read an article about the work being done at the rehab center, and about Dr. Moskowitz. He invited the doctor to his house for cocktails. Moskowitz thought it was about another addict. At first the doctor didn't seem interested. Vitaly gave the doctor one million dollars to take home with him. A few days of staring at the money changed the doctor's mind.

When a patient was admitted into the villas, the doctor would notify Vitaly. Vitaly would then research the patient and put feelers out to his worldly contacts for a buyer of information.

Chapter Four

Laura accidentally switched on the camera in Dr. Eisenblatt's room. Cameras were normally off when the patient was being attended.

She turned to shut the camera off when she saw Dr. Moskowitz already in with his patient. Her hand nearly on the switch, she stopped and observed for a bit.

The doctor walked into the living area, went over to the end of a walnut bookcase, which was specially built with drawers on the bottom section and an area for books on the top. It had a latch and a button built-in at one end that released a set of filing drawers at the other. Moskowitz reached down to release the drawer that opened the bookcase. When it didn't open, he walked down and touched the drawer, and it popped open.

"I've told them before to use the button to close the damn drawer. Sonofabitch, do I have to do everything around here?" the doctor mumbled.

Laura watched and listened. *I'm going to get hell for this.*

The doctor returned to the patient and reached into his medical bag and retrieved a small vessel of sodium pentothal.

Eisenblatt had been a patient for three weeks and had given the doctor technical information on laser weapons Vataly had asked about. He had told them where his sketches and mathematical calculations were stored. Vitaly entered the house when Mrs. Eisenblatt had gone to the hospital to attend a family therapy session. The doctor sent a limousine to pick her up to control her time. He already received another million dollars and assumed Vitaly had done a lot better.

Dr. Moskowitz hadn't noticed the red light indicating the camera was activated. He turned back to Dr. Eisenblatt, still lying in bed, and injected him with the sodium pentothal, waiting for it to take effect. Laura watched as the doctor stood at the edge of the bed, looking over a list. At first she thought it was the records she prepared, but then she saw those were still hanging on the end of the bed.

Dr. Moskowitz looked at his watch. He pulled out a small recorder and proceeded to read off questions from the list.

Laura listened as the doctor asked questions about a laser weapon. She didn't know what it was, but she knew it had nothing to do with the patient's illness.

Laura rolled her chair back. *Something is wrong here.* She reached down and shut the recording off.

When the doctor turned his head, he thought the light was on, but it went off so quickly he wasn't sure.

He kept his eye on the camera as he finished up. When he was through with the questioning, he returned the medical file to the drawer and then pressed the button. The drawer closed.

Stuffing the list of questions and responses into his satchel, Dr. Moskowitz took one last look at his client, turned, looked at the camera once more, and stepped out of the suite.

Laura saw the doctor coming. Her stomach knotted. *Should I be honest and tell him it was an accident, or bluff my way out?* She froze when he stepped up to the nurse's station.

"Laura, did you put the file away in the bookcase?"

She took a deep breath. "Yes, I did."

"Please remember the drawer may appear to be closed, but it must be closed with the button only. Is that understood? I don't want to have to speak about this again."

"Sorry about that. It was my fault, and I'll make sure everyone knows about it in the other villas, too."

"Very well." He turned to leave, and Laura let out a slow breath.

"Oh, one more thing."

"Yes, Doctor?"

"I thought the camera light was on in Eisenblatt's suite."

She hesitated. "I'm sorry, doctor, but no one has turned the camera on. I've been here the whole time you were with the patient."

"Just you?" Moskowitz asked.

I should have said I flicked it by accident. "Yes just me."

"Very well," Dr. Moskowitz said and stepped out to the open air. He pressed speed-dial on his cell phone for Lieutenant Snedicker.

Snedicker was in charge of security for the hospital. It was his job to make sure both the staff and visitors were kept out of the rehab areas, especially the villas. His constant checking and reviewing the employees' movements kept everyone from breaking rules and regulations.

"Lieutenant, Dr. Moskowitz here. Do me a favor and check the length of time the camera was on in Eisenblatt's suite."

"I'll get back to you in a few minutes. Do you want me to call you?"

"No, I'm on my way back up to my office. Just bring me the results."

Chapter Five

Lt. Snedicker knocked on the door then entered Dr. Moskowitz's office. The knock was a courtesy. He was a full partner with the doctor.

At one time, the lieutenant was one of the doctor's clients, from the brick building. His care was from the state mandated area. Dr. Moskowitz sat in private sessions at the hospital listening to the Snedicker explain why he was on drugs. The doctor knew no matter what he said his patient would never fully recover. It was just too much to overcome. His father forced him to shoot his mother after she was dead.

The doctor, recognizing a particular need and knowing the lieutenant's history, made an offer when he was leaving the hospital. Moskowitz wanted someone to keep a watch on workers and take care of problems he had no stomach for. He needed someone without a conscience. An agreement was made, but the doctor failed to understand who exactly Simon Snedicker was. After his recovery, the lieutenant decided to up the ante.

In one of their meetings, Snedicker used his phone to record the doctor talking about a patient that died using a new drug, Medifinne.

"Make sure you sit with Nurse Laura. Tell her to refer all comments from authorities to my office and make sure she feels a bit threatened."

Moskowitz was willing to share money but knew at some point he would have Vitaly get rid of Snedicker.

"It was on for six and a half minutes," the lieutenant said.

"Six and a half minutes is a lifetime," Dr. Moskowitz said.

"Could it be an accident? Maybe no one knew it was on."

"I don't think so. There's a light that comes on at the nurse's station, too. You'd have to be blind not to see it." Dr. Moskowitz tipped back in his leather chair, his hands behind his head. "I think Nurse Laura needs to find another job, if you know what I mean."

"That's what you pay me for. Should I question her about the camera?"

"Don't bother. She'll lie or make accusations. No, I think this should be taken care of permanently. Pretend she's going to get a huge severance. Make something up. Just take care of it."

* * *

Laura Gorham pulled into The Black Sow with the thought of having a quick drink and getting on with her life. She had just been fired at the MLRC, but was given a more than adequate severance. The Black Sow was a bar she frequented a short drive from the hospital, and she wanted to say goodbye to Bertrand Bean, the bartender. Over the years Bert had become a friend on her weekly visits with her girlfriend.

"A little early, aren't you," Bert said.

Laura looked at Bert with only a half-smile. "I just got shit-canned at the hospital."

"I wouldn't have thought they would do that to you," Bert said.

"Me either."

"What happened?" Bert asked.

"I did a stupid thing and didn't admit to it. Not worth discussing," Laura said.

"What are you going to do?" Bert asked, as he popped a cap off a beer and passed it to a customer.

"Not sure. But I've put some money aside, and they're going to send me a six months' severance."

Bert slid a Bud Light to Laura, without her asking.

"Thanks, Bert," she said.

"Sure going to miss you," Bert said.

"Not trying to rush you, but are you going to want another?"

"No, one is enough. I just came in to take the edge off and say goodbye. It's not the end of the world."

"It's on me," Bert said.

"Thanks." Laura tipped the bottle up and took a big swallow and set it back onto the bar. Waving to Bert she headed out to her car.

* * *

The lieutenant sat off to the side of the road in his Ram pickup just past The Black Sow. He only drove it on special assignment days. It was older, heavier, and looked like it could use a little TLC. He had conned it off of another addict. It had been patched up in several places with metal welded to cover rust spots. The rivets were never sanded and still showed, as well as never having been repaired. Its beat-up appearance was only a front. It had unique features, like a high, thick maple wood front and rear bumpers, a special suspension to keep from rolling, and extra power to use when needed.

The lieutenant could feel adrenaline start to pump through his body. It was as much of a high as any drug he had ever taken. A big smile came across his face as Laura stepped into the open air.

It was unusual she wasn't working during the day, in the middle of the week. She leaned up against the door of her black Altima, tipped her head back, closed her eyes and sucked in the spring sun. It felt delicious. Black wasn't a great color for the summer time, being so near to the south, but the air conditioning relieved her of the heat. She slid into the seat and started the car. With the door still wide open she immediately opened the sunroof. Time to release life's pressure out the roof.

Laura pulled out of the driveway and headed down the snake-like river road, thinking a good country drive would settle her mind.

The lieutenant felt it was important she knew he was there. Moving up, he gave her a little bump.

Laura looked up in her rearview mirror and recognized Snedicker's face—his grin. Again he drove up until he was just behind her bumper, but this time he didn't touch it. He could sense her fear. Then he bumped her again.

"What is that crazy asshole doing?" Laura said. Her Altima was low to the ground, like a sports car, but it was also light. And she wasn't a skilled driver. When she was a teen, it took her three times to pass the driving test. But she had learned over the years that all you had to do was to avoid the other vehicle. That skill was about to be tested.

She went faster around the curves in the road. The faster she went, the faster the lieutenant went, bumping her again and again.

Laura grabbed onto the steering wheel with both hands.

He backed off as he went around a big curve. The lieutenant loved death, the finality. His mind wandered as he allowed Laura to think she was free of him. He remembered his father killing his mother and then handing him the gun. One, two, three shots rang out as they filtered through his body.

Laura took a deep breath. The lieutenant wasn't in sight. Maybe he went off the road, or decided he'd had enough fun.

"That son of a bitch is crazy."

Laura grabbed a Kleenex and wiped her face. Looking up in the rearview mirror, she saw him coming again. Faster.

The lieutenant's adrenaline was at full peak. He smashed into her car hard.

Laura screamed as her car flew into the ravine.

Before Lt. Snedicker climbed down the hill, he reached under the seat and retrieved an ice pick. Laura was leaned against the steering wheel, her head bleeding. He checked her pulse. She was still alive and still buckled. He walked to the other side and searched for the severance records. Finding the papers he moved to the back of the car, and proceeded to puncture the gas tank with the ice pick. Quickly he withdrew a long piece of candlewick from his pocket, stuck it in the gas hole, lit it, scrambled up the hill, and drove down the road, watching the explosion in his rearview mirror.

Chapter Six

Two Years Later

Austin had been Willowdale's lap dog. He fought his way out of the streets of Austin, Texas, and worked his ass off through college as a cook, laborer and finally an intern on a political campaign. One stint in politics and he was hooked. As an intern, he found out you had to do things in politics whether or not you liked it. And right now, he had to be the referee between Vice President Warren Willowdale and his wife, Ann. It was not a fun time, but he knew in the end it would lead to the White House.

"You asked to see me?" Austin said as he walked into the VP's office.

"Yes. Austin, I need you to do me a favor. This is a big favor," Warren said.

"I'll take care of it," Austin said.

"Ann is beginning to look a bit haggard. I think she needs a short vacation."

"You want me to find someone to take care of her while she's gone?" Austin asked.

"Not exactly. I want you to take her. Let her rest, and make sure she doesn't go blabber to the press about something."

"Mr. Vice President, she's got all kinds of people she can call on. You don't need me to babysit her, do you? I'm sorry—I don't want it to sound ... but come on. We can find someone better for the job, right?"

"Listen, it's only for four days, and I think you could use a little break. We've got a long, hot summer coming up, and it's going to be a bear between now and the convention and the drive to the election. You look like you could use it, too. Besides, Mrs. Willowdale asked if she could use you as her bodyguard. It'll do her some good, and maybe you'll warm up to her a little. We don't want any animosity showing up in the campaign."

Warren stood up from his desk and looked at Austin. "Truth be told, the two of us have been going at it lately. I just want her out of my hair for a few days," Warren said.

"I understand, but you know I'd prefer not to. As I've said before, I only work for you."

"Then consider this part of the run to the presidency," Warren said. "Now go see my secretary. She'll show you the itinerary."

"That's it? It's a done deal?" Austin said as he took a breath to hold his temper back.

"You'll be taking a private jet. I've made arrangements with one of Churchill's fleet.

"You already set it up before you even talked to me?" Austin said.

"Thanks, Austin. Now go," Warren said. "See you at the end of the week."

Austin walked out of the room and slammed the door.

* * *

"You know I didn't want to do this, Mrs. Willowdale," Austin said.

"Then why are you here?"

"I'm an obedient employee," he said.

"Call me Ann. Please, Austin, you could have gotten yourself out of it if you wanted to. There are lots of people who would love to have taken this job. Besides, I can take care of myself."

"Let's just cut the cat and mouse game here. Warren said you requested me."

"So I did," Ann said, giving him a mischievous smirk.

"I'm surprised. We don't always see eye to eye. I know you're starting to get on his nerves, so he was quick to do as you asked. He just wanted me here and not some other schmuck."

"Can you make sure I don't see the Secret Service people? Have them hide out of my sight. I may decide to do a little nude bathing," Ann said.

"I'll make sure I'm out of sight, too," Austin said.

"That's not necessary," Ann said.

* * *

It was a quick trip to a private estate in Grand Cayman. Warren told Austin they were going to use one of Churchill's jets. He surmised it was Churchill's estate, too. *Too bad I couldn't take a withdrawal from his bank account,* Austin thought, as he made arrangements with the secret service.

"I've taken care of the Secret Service, Mrs. Willowdale," Austin said. "I think I'm going to make a few calls. You know, campaign stuff. Then maybe I might grab my Kindle."

"Austin, I said you may call me Ann. This is a vacation, so let's keep things informal."

Ann walked into the bedroom and she called him ten minutes later. "Austin, could you help me?" she called from the bathroom.

What the hell does she need now?

The door was partially open. Austin gave a knock and cautiously entered. Ann wasn't in sight. As he came around the corner, Ann stepped from the bathroom naked.

"Mrs. Willowdale, I'm sorry," Austin said and turned to the door.

"No, no, Austin. Don't run away. I told you I needed help." Ann grabbed Austin by the shoulder, reached around, and slid her hand down to his crotch.

"I don't think this is a smart move."

"Austin, turn around. You'll like what you see."

Austin turned slowly and took a good look.

"Yep, I like what I see. Definitely."

He allowed Ann to unbutton his shirt and then his slacks. Dropping his boxers, he grabbed Ann and kissed her. Ann pulled Austin to a king size bed. It was covered with light pink silk sheets. The sliding door was open to a patio, but the sheer white curtains were pulled across. The soft breeze dragged the curtains in and out. Exactly what Austin had in mind.

* * *

It had been a grueling campaign, and he just made it tougher by bedding the Vice President's wife. She must have planned it.

Austin sat out on the patio in the shaded area near the pool, thinking what a dumb move he made, when Ann walked out. He had gotten out of bed after several rounds, and Ann fell asleep.

She lit a cigarette and sat down facing Austin. She positioned her chair close enough so her foot was on the space just in front of his crotch.

"You know this is the dumbest thing I have ever done," Austin said.

"Don't be so dramatic. It's just sex."

"That's it? Just a casual screw?" Austin said.

"That's it. A screw never hurt anyone. In fact, I feel so much better. Let's have another," Ann said. It was just a tease—unless he agreed.

"No, I think we've done enough. Let's pretend this never happened. Better yet, let's make sure this doesn't happen again."

Ann laughed, and then said in a sultry tone, "We'll see."

Chapter Seven

Neil O'Connor tipped the flask back until it was empty, ignoring the droplets of whiskey that trickled down the corner of his mouth. Tears followed the creases of his face until they found their way onto his soiled raincoat.

"I'm sorry," he said. His voice was garbled, barely coherent. He pulled each arm across his face to wipe the tears and hide his eternal shame. "I'm just sorry it wasn't me. I would have done anything to change things." His words were slurred, though he didn't notice.

More than twenty years ago, the city was paving Neil's street and a large dump truck ran over his son in front of his house. Neil had gone into the house for a second. He told everyone it was to go to the bathroom, when in fact he was going to get a beer. His son's tricycle rolled down the driveway in front of the truck. Neil had dragged himself through life numbly ever since.

The death had taken the dauntless Pulitzer-winning reporter, father and family man down a dark road he couldn't leave. The what-ifs played in his head—day after day. He had maintained a semblance of himself, but not to the point that other reporters thought much of him.

He had a tough time getting through the election during the past year and a half. Now only six weeks away, he had been contemplating calling an end to his career. He was finding it impossible to be a reporter, something he no longer enjoyed with so much hanging over his head.

Neil shoved the flask back into his jacket, got out of his car, and pulled his outdated whiskey and mud-stained raincoat tightly around him. He tossed his hat onto his head and headed to Second Chance Bar to refill his flask.

Chapter Eight

Neil took a sip from his glass and then pulled his flask from his jacket. "Joe, can you fill this for me?" he asked the bartender.

"You know I'm not supposed to do that."

"Just fill the damn thing."

"You don't have to talk to me like that." Joseph grabbed the flask and a bottle of Jameson and walked into the back room.

Neil was already in his mid-morning stupor. Halfway down the long bar sat Todd Hebron.

"Hey, old man, do you have to act like an asshole all the time?" Todd said.

"Why don't you mind your own business, Pretty Boy," Neil said. He chuckled to himself as looked toward Todd.

Todd pushed his stool away from the bar and started to walk toward Neil.

"Yeah, come on, Chickie. Why don't you come over here so I can knock the shit out of you? You're not worth my effort to get off this stool," Neil said.

As Todd approached Neil, the bar's side door opened, and in walked Rori.

"Come on, asshole," Neil said.

Todd saw Rori and stopped. Rori had been working with Neil as part of as an assignment to learn the ropes. She would go off on her own, but Neil was her mentor. Neil, Todd and Rori were all reporters with *The Washington Independent Review Online*, a small online reporting service, typical of the migration of newsprint to the internet.

"What's the matter, Pretty Boy?" Neil said.

Todd stood about ten feet away as Rori walked up behind Neil and grabbed him by the shoulder.

Neil was startled and turned to see who grabbed him.

"Rori, pull up a seat. I was just about to kick Todd's ass. You saved him."

"Causing trouble so early in the day at this fine establishment? You buying or crying?"

"Joe will be back in a minute. He's on a personal task for me," Neil said.

Rori looked over toward Todd. "Morning, Todd."

"Morning, Rori."

Todd went down the bar and grabbed his beer, then moved back closer to Rori. "Would you like to have dinner sometime?" he asked.

"Go on back to your cave," Neil said.

"Who's asking you, old man?" Todd said.

"You guys are such kids," Rori said. "No, I don't think so, Todd."

"You sure? You name the place," Todd said.

"I'll pass."

Neil chuckled out loud. "Even Rori knows an asshole when she sees one."

"I'm not addressing you," Todd said.

"I'm not addressing you. Boo hoo hoo," Neil said.

Todd flipped him the bird and went back where he was sitting before. His face turned red. He wasn't used to being turned down. He took a final sip of beer and walked out the front door onto Fifth Street.

Joseph came out from the back room and walked up to Neil. "Ask like a gentleman next time or I'm not even going to serve you," he said as he returned the full flask.

Neil smiled and said, "I may have been a little rough."

"I think you should apologize to Joseph for causing trouble in his bar," Rori said.

Neil looked over his glasses at Rori. "You *tink* so?"

"Yes, I *tink* so," Rori said, repeating Neil's slur.

"Joseph, I didn't mean to be such a jerk. I know I get a little carried away."

Joe stood listening as he dried a glass. "That's fine, but I don't know what's going on in that head of yours. What have we known each other, twenty-five years?"

"Something like that," Neil said.

"You use to be such a nice guy. The older you get, the crankier you get. Now you're picking fights with my customers. Jeez, Neil, you can't be doing that. I won't have anyone left if you keep chasing them away. You're starting to become a number one jerk."

"Wait a minute, Joe. Todd is an asshole and a troublemaker," Rori said.

"I'm not talking to you, Rori. I'm talking to Neil."

"You know what, Joseph?" Rori said.

"What's that?"

"Neil was right. You are an asshole. Neil, pay the man. We're getting out of here."

Neil tossed forty bucks on the bar. "Keep the change."

Joseph stood at the end of the bar, fuming. Neil drained his glass.

"Joey, boy, we'll have to decide if we're coming back," Neil said as they headed to the door, his arm around Rori's shoulder.

"Don't come on my account."

Chapter Nine

Vice President Warren Willowdale smiled to himself as he looked out the window, admiring the October colors. Air Force Two circled the small New England villages of East Granby, Windsor Locks and Suffield, Connecticut, and descended and landed at Bradley International Airport. The plane pulled across from the main terminal, half a mile away, and stopped near the Connecticut National Guard landing zone.

It was two weeks before the election and Willowdale felt the presidency was wrapped up. Believing that, he tried to keep his campaign close to D.C. The outskirts of Hartford, Connecticut, were the ticket for an easy commute.

The short hop was nothing like a long, wasted flight to the West Coast—and putting up with air traffic and road traffic. And doling out imitation smiles and fake waves, as though he was glad to be there, wherever the hell there was.

Willowdale's wife, Ann, was not with him. She stayed back in Georgetown to go over the campaign's schedule with Austin, the VP's press secretary, advisor and confidante of twelve years. While the Vice President descended, Ann was ascending to her second great climax of the morning. When the wheels rolled down the runway, Austin was rolling in the sheets and giving a final thrust to an enthusiastic Ann.

At the edge of the tarmac, a fence separated Air Force Two from the Vice President's supporters. An old woman with a walker cart with a basket, stuffed with unknown belongings, pushed herself up to the front of the fence. Her salt and pepper hair looked too much like a wig, setting a Secret Service agent, one of the Vice President's advance team, on edge. A man standing on a picnic table leaning on a crutch caught the eye of a second agent. That agent passed on a coded message before he moved toward the man.

The door to the plane swung open. After a ten-minute wait, the Vice President stepped through and lifted both hands in the air to the crowd at Bradley International.

Secret Service agents preceded Willowdale and stood behind him. They scanned the crowds, rooftops, drainage ditches and grassy areas along the runways, searching for anything out of place.

One Secret Service agent pulled the man off the picnic table as another approached the old lady with the walker. The agent showed his ID and turned the lady away, to the back of the crowd. The all clear was passed to the agents on the plane. The Vice President, smiling broadly, stepped three quarters of the way down the stairs, stopped and waved once more.

The first bullet hit the agent behind Willowdale in the shoulder. As he reached for the VP, he was hit with another bullet to the temple. The impact spun the agent around, and he plunged over the rolling stairs and onto the ground, landing on his head and shoulder. His blood spattered as his skull crashed against the tarmac.

Another agent, already waiting at the bottom of the stairs, reached up and pulled Willowdale down the rest of the stairs. The team's support vehicles had been directed out of the way, enabling Willowdale to walk up to the fence and meet his constituents. Now, it left the VP and his crew without protection or escape. The agent exercised his only option—he covered the Vice President with his own body, which twitched as the sniper's armor piercing bullets riddled him from a half-mile away. Blood poured from him and onto Willowdale as though it was water running through a colander.

A Suburban raced into the area in front of the plane, and two agents tossed the body of the dead agent aside to grab the Vice President and drag him into the SUV. Everyone was in a panic. No one could remember protocol. As they screeched away, they left both dead agents out in the open, to the horror of screaming onlookers.

* * *

Churchill Brewer took the papers from Terrance, his longtime bodyguard, and stared at the headlines.

"Wilted Willowdale"

"No Guts, No Glory Willowdale"

"Willowdale Scared Witless"

For Churchill, the photos said it all. One showed the frightened Vice President staring down in fear at a Secret Service agent, his mouth hanging open. Another showed one of the agents lying on top of him, and a final photo depicted the vice president's legs hanging out of the SUV. *The LA Times*, *The New York Times* and *The Washington Post* showed similar pictures from different angles.

After so many times when the Vice President would say the wrong thing, at the wrong time, Churchill felt the VP's wife, Ann, was right. They needed an event to make Warren look heroic. When Ann brought up the idea of a fake assassination attempt, Churchill thought it would be a good way to go for a sympathetic vote to push Warren over the top. This was about who would control world power. If a couple of agents had to be sacrificed, so be it. It was worth the risk. Looking back, he knew he should have let Warren in on it.

"I guess I shouldn't have tried this," Churchill said to Terrance, not bothering to read the articles. "Not good." He shook his head.

Terrance was not only Churchill's long-time bodyguard, but their relationship had developed into a friendship. Churchill brought him on board after he left the Navy SEALs. Terrance had nowhere to go. Churchill was at a summer outing in the Italian Alps with world business leaders and Terrance was on site as part of the summit's bodyguard protection, when extremists broke in. Terrance happened to be near the area when two of them came at Churchill with knives and clubs. Terrance killed both intruders using their own weapons, finishing one with the club and slitting the throat of the other—after Churchill nodded to him to finish the job. Churchill did further checking on Terrance and hired him to be his personal bodyguard. No one ever got near Churchill again. Their friendship developed over the next twenty years.

Churchill was a hard man who did his utmost to direct the future. Fear and money garnered more wins than losses. He was the type of man who made people jump at the sound of his voice and cower out of the room if they were not on his side. He was a cigar-smoking control freak in both business and politics. His was the final word.

Churchill was a longtime friend of Vice President Warren Willowdale. Despite Warren's gaffes, Churchill was using all his influence and spending large sums to get the Vice President into the Oval Office, something few had ever done. Unfortunately, the VP didn't always cooperate.

"Well, Terrance," Churchill said in his gravelly voice, "I guess this was a mistake. I don't think I'm going to be sleeping in the Lincoln bed in January."

Chapter Ten

On Election night, Warren Willowdale stood at the podium. The sad, blank faces of the waiting crowd told the full story. Still they chanted, "Willowdale! Willowdale! Willowdale!" The outcome of the election was obvious, but they didn't want to hear the truth. He knew it would be hard to admit and a lie would make everyone feel better, but eventually they would have to face reality. Willowdale was willing to share little reality. He needed to continue with his dubious rhetoric.

He looked around the crowd, waved to them, turning from side to side, looked toward his wife and at Austin Garcia, as well as others from his campaign. He held up his hand to calm the crowd and started to speak. "It has been my honor to be a soldier for the American people," he said, trying not to fall back on his sometimes strong Southern accent.

The crowd roared and yelled out his name.

Holding up both hands this time, he continued. "No, no. It has been a courageous fight, but we have come up short," he said. As he said those words, his mind and body began to revolt. He grabbed onto the podium to steady himself, trying to hold a smile at the same time. He felt as though he was going to fall into the crowd. The room began to move. He started to hear voices. His ears rang.

His grip tightened around the podium as he tried to regain his composure. "What the American people—" Willowdale couldn't remember what he was supposed to say. He reached down, grabbed a glass of water and drank. His teeth chattered and the water dripped down his chin. Those in the crowd turned to each other then back to the Vice President, watching in astonishment.

Austin appeared at his side, held his hand over the microphone. "What's going on? Are you okay?"

"Just a bit overwhelmed by the crowd. Austin, I don't know what I was saying."

Neil O'Connor stood to the far side, away from Austin, and thought the Vice President was acting strange. He tried to read Austin and Willowdale's lips. He appeared to say *remember.* Neil put it into his memory bank along with what he had seen on the campaign trail the past few weeks. The VP was agitated with crowds, at one time yelling at a fan who was trying to touch him. Neil may have been tipping his flask most of the day, but he was pretty much coherent. As he watched, he felt something was going on, maybe ever since the assassination attempt.

Austin pointed to a spot further down in the speech and said. "Keep it brief and let's get out of here."

Austin stepped away and Willowdale gathered himself, wiping his brow. "It is defeat we face now as this battle ends, but there will be future battles to fight and we will win this war—this war for the American people."

As he tried to continue, the voices in his head quieted. The room stood still for the time being. The crowd went crazy.

Willowdale waved again, turned and kissed his wife, and then shook hands with Austin, steadying himself. "Get me the hell out of here," he said.

Austin took the Vice President's right hand and held it up as if they just won the election, and they worked their way off stage.

As they exited, Ann asked, "What's going on, Warren?"

"I'm—I'm just a little exhausted and disappointed."

Ann could barely understand his trembling voice.

Feeling the vibration from his phone, Warren reached into his jacket pocket. When he saw who it was, he turned to those around him and asked for privacy.

* * *

Before Warren spoke he took in a deep breath and then cleared his throat. "Churchill, thanks for calling. I really appreciate everything you've done for me," Warren said. His voice was still shaky but he told Churchill he had just come off stage and was trying to gather himself.

Churchill Brewer met Warren at Bridgton Academy in western Maine when the two were young men. He became his lifelong friend and political mentor. Brewer was a billionaire and seeded his money wisely.

"It's one of those things," Churchill said. "There's always the next time and another battle down the road."

Warren took in a big gulp of air. "Thanks, Churchill. I've always been appreciative that you have… Well, you know, you have always stuck by me."

"That's what friends are for, and that's what money's for. What good is money if you can't use it for your own good?" Churchill gave out one of his signature laughs, his belly shaking as he puffed on a cigar. "I'm just sorry the little thing I tried in Hartford didn't put us into the White House."

Warren's mind couldn't comprehend what Churchill just said. It was an empty echo. He just thanked him and pocketed his phone. He leaned against a wall with sweat pouring off him.

Waving Ann over, he said, "I need to get to my room. I—I need a drink."

"I'll join you."

Chapter Eleven

Rori Cahill already filed several quick articles on the election. With everyone at the hotels partying or crying in their beer, it was much easier. *God, I love technology,* she thought.

She'd come a long way in thirteen years. A long way since Aunt Charley rescued her. She'd finished high school, graduated from Syracuse University, done a stint in the Marines and finally landed a journalist job she wanted.

Having completed a long day, it was time to turn into a party girl. Each hotel had celebrations for the election of Joshua Clement as president. Most people attending didn't care about the election and were looking for nothing more than a reason to party and maybe get lucky.

Rori left President-elect Clement after filing her coverage on her tablet and went to another hotel. She wanted to see if any of her friends were around and get some reaction, along with a drink. (Maybe she'd get lucky, too).

When she arrived on the tenth floor, parties were going on in the hallway and most of the rooms, too. She stuck her head in and out of open doorways as she traversed, getting waves from acquaintances, but she saw none of her friends. As she got to the end of the hallway, she decided she'd take the stairs down to the ninth floor. Halfway down, she ran into Todd "Pretty Boy" Hebron.

He wasn't a friend, and he was drunk. He tried, on numerous occasions to date her, but he wasn't her type. Despite turning him down, he persisted.

"Hey Rori, how you doing? You having a good time with that old man you work with? Why don't you let me talk to our boss and you come work with me instead of that drunk?"

"You mean under you?" Rori said. "No thanks, Pretty Boy."

"Under would be nice," he said, slurring.

"I don't think so. Anything you could teach me, I learned when I was thirteen."

"Why you have to be so defensive? I—I just want to be friends."

Rori turned to continue down the stairs, but Todd grabbed her and spun her around, pressing her against the wall. "You have to learn to be a little nicer." His hands rubbed her over her body like probing tentacles. When one hand touched her breast, the hair on the back of her neck stood up.

Rori knocked his hand away. "You mean all I have to do is put out and you'll be my friend?"

"Now you got it," Todd said, sliding his mouth down the side of her neck.

Rori reached under her jacket, pulled out her Ruger 9 mm, and pushed it directly into Todd's groin. "You like the feel of a gun on your balls? This could be your worse day of your life."

Todd first felt the push, then looked down and saw the gun. He bolted upright, almost falling backward. "You don't have to be pulling that out. I was just joking."

"This is my friend, Jack. He's got a mind of his own. You'd better be on your best behavior—because Jack doesn't like assholes."

Rori slid away from the wall. Once she was repositioned, she shoved Todd into the corner with the gun poking him.

He glanced at the gun, and the effect made the liquor wear off. His words no longer were slurred and his mind cleared, to a point. He straightened himself up. His nerves had taken over, and he felt as though she was going to pull the trigger at any moment.

"Don't you think you should put that away before it goes off?"

"Jack only goes off when I tell him to go off—most of the time. But you're right, Jack could let go any minute if he's pushed. Are you going to push him?"

"No, na, na, no. I won't push him."

"Good. Jack's very peaceful and forgiving…unless you give him a reason not to be. Now, I'm going to tell you a little story you can file in your memory bank.

"A long time ago, someone just like you did something similar to what you were trying to do, only they got a lot further than you're ever going to get. Of course, that was before I knew Jack and decided to carry him around with me all the time."

"I'm really sorry. You know it's just the alcohol."

"No, it's not—it's your arrogance. The alcohol just tells you that you can do whatever you want, Pretty Boy."

"Don't call me that. I don't like it."

"Shut the fuck up. I'm telling the story." Rori pushed the gun against the top of his head until he was sitting on the floor of the stairwell landing. Then she traced the barrel of the gun down the side of his face.

"Let's just forget this ever happened," Todd said. His voice was trembling.

"So, as I was saying. This guy got his way, but I got back at him. You know what I did?" Rori said.

Todd said nothing.

"I said do you know what I did?" Rori yelled.

"No—no what?"

"I told him I liked it. I told him to meet me out at this special spot. We met up, and I buried him naked after I shot his balls off."

The fear that Rori was trying to instill was working. Todd wet his pants. Trying to pull himself up, Rori slapped Jack hard across his temple. Blood gushed from his face. She figured this wasn't the first time Pretty Boy had pulled this on someone. She wanted to get the message across that he better change his ways. She only wanted to instill fear, but she hated guys like this. She had no intention of shooting him. She hadn't even taken the safety off.

"Oh my God, I'm bleeding."

"It beats being dead," Rori said. "Don't go blubbering on my boots. You listen to me. If you even look at me—if you ever look at me, if you ever think about looking at me again, I'll take you out into the Maryland hills and bury your ass. You'll just disappear. No one would ever suspect a little girl like me could do anything to a big guy like you. Besides, I don't think you'll be telling your friends I kicked your ass."

Rori couldn't let it go. She was having too much fun. She thought a minute all the while pointing Jack at Pretty Boy. "Take your pants off."

She nudged the gun into his neck.

"Stop it."

"I said take your pants off."

"What? I'm not going to," Todd said, the piss pooling under him.

Rori pulled the hammer back, making sure Todd heard the click of the gun.

"Okay, okay. I'll—I'll do it," he shrieked.

Rori grabbed his pants, trying not to touch the wet area, and hung them over the stairs, then let them go. They bounced around on railings until they came to rest about four flights down. She could hear the change and whatever else in his pockets clinking as it fell down the stairwell.

"Now get the fuck out of here and remember what I said." Rori stepped into the ninth floor hallway and disappeared into the noisy crowd.

Chapter Twelve

Alone in the room, Warren Willowdale downed several Beefeater martinis. He loved a good dirty martini, but not now. Now he was not looking for taste. He wanted to be numb.

He waltzed around the large room from one side to the other with his dog, Lady, following him. He stopped and looked into the mirror next to a glass coffee table. The voices were back. He started to talk to them. "I'm here, I'm here," he said, raising his voice. "I know it's my fault, but I'll get back. I'll get even."

Warren swayed and then toasted his reflection in the mirror. "You're a loser who lost to an idiot." He put one hand up against the wall to support himself. At first he thought the feeling he was having was from the alcohol. Then his arm collapsed, and his shoulder hit the mirror and broke it. Shards slid down the wall as though magnetized against the sheetrock and crashed to the floor. His drink slipped from his hand and shattered when it hit the table.

Warren bent over and put both hands on his knees to steady himself. He pushed his back up against the wall until he was almost standing straight. But when he pushed himself away from the wall to find a chair, he lost control. He tried to ease himself to the floor, but instead fell onto his back, breaking the glass table. He was sweating profusely—no longer the Vice President, but another pathetic human statistic in the annals of historical failure.

* * *

Willowdale had been VP for the last four years. Only four sitting Vice Presidents had ever been elected president. Nixon had done it but was not a sitting VP. According to the so-called experts, he would be the fifth.

He grew up in Virginia and married his college sweetheart—and her money. He learned the value of favors, which helped his ascent in the party. He was a man of self-interest, nothing more. He was six feet, two inches and weighed in at two hundred and seventy-five pounds. His hair was thinning—almost gone. He used a comb-over to cover his head. His stomach bulged from under his chest and protruded down like a ski slope, dropping off just before it reached his penis. His only attractive aspect was he could speak like a Sunday preacher. His rhetoric sounded right for the common man (not that he actually cared for such people).

Every time he slipped, Churchill Brewer bailed him out. The latest was at the Bradley International Airport. The plan was supposed to bring in a sympathetic vote and to make him look tough. But Warren Willowdale was not tough.

If it weren't for Brewer, he never would have made it this far. Brewer was his confidant. He liked Warren because he was manageable, and they both understood where power came from, and power produced wealth. To Warren and Churchill, it was simple mathematics.

Warren was a pussy. When the front page showed pictures of him being pulled down the aircraft stairs and an agent lying on top of him, Warren was pale and his eyes bulged as he shook with fear. It was enough to show he was no leader.

Chapter Thirteen

Ann sat resting in the sitting room of the luxurious suite. Her husband was in the other room with his dog. A wet bar and closets separated the suite's two living rooms. She listened to Warren whine when they first got back to the suite. After a drink, she decided she'd heard enough and went into the second living area for some peace.

The high-back chair added the comfort she was looking for as she viewed a luminous D.C. A noise in the other room startled her. At first she thought Warren was talking to Lady. She listened for a few seconds and then called out his name, but got no answer.

When she walked into the room, she found him lying on the floor covered with glass, potato chips and crackers with goat cheese. There was a cut on the side of his head. "Warren? Warren?" she shouted, getting down on the floor beside him. "Warren, can you hear me?" Lady lay beside him.

Warren stared blankly and said nothing . . . Ann was afraid he had a heart attack. He wasn't unconscious, but unresponsive. She composed herself and called Austin Garcia.

"Where are you?" Ann asked. "I need to see you."

"Do you think that's wise with your husband around?"

"No, not that. I need you here right away. It's Warren—I think—I don't know what's wrong. He's on the floor," she said.

* * *

Austin was in Grant's Bar when Ann called. He fought his way through the crowd without showing emotion.

"Hey, can we sit down for an interview in the next day or two?" a reporter asked as their bodies brushed each other.

"Yeah, we can do that, but give me a couple of days to catch my breath," Austin said over the noise of the bar.

The place was unusually large for a hotel. Three bars and spacious eating areas were all spaced far apart. This was D.C., and they wanted to give the patrons (mostly politicians) plenty of room to discuss their trade.

On the way up to the room, Austin made a phone call. "Good evening, Dr. Moskowitz. This is Austin Garcia."

"What can I do for you, Mr. Garcia?"

"The willow tree has lost a branch," Austin said.

Austin put his plan in motion. If he got to the room and the Vice President couldn't wait, he would call 911. Until then, he would assume it was not a major concern. His thoughts would only be to get him out of the public's eyes.

Dr. Moskowitz went to his tablet and checked his list. He knew who it was but checked to be sure. The words that popped up on his screen got him excited: codename, tree, VP rank, 1, $$$$. "We'll be there within the hour. Where's the location?"

"Kirkwood Hotel," Austin said.

"Make sure someone meets us at the back entrance," Dr. Moskowitz said. "I'm going to make a call to a doctor friend of mine. He'll come and check on the patient to make sure he's stable. Can you tell me what's going on?"

"I'm on my way up to the room. All I know is my friend has fallen," Austin said. "Doctor, use our broken-leg plan and we can go from there."

Dr. Moskowitz knew the area well. He'd made this trip at other times for both political hacks and coked-up CEOs or their wives. In other cases, patients were flown in on special charters. Some would just drag themselves to his door. How they arrived made no difference as long as they could pay and had other information he could sell. "Very well. I'll get him there immediately."

As soon as Dr. Moskowitz hung up, he made two calls. First to have a doctor check in on Willowdale and then to his accomplice.

"Vitaly, I'm going to need a much bigger deposit. The vice president has broken his leg, and we better discuss just compensation."

"I'll give you a call in the morning," Vitaly said.

Austin had made arrangements to have Moskowitz on call but he knew nothing about the doctor's other plans. Had he known, he would have found a different doctor—or asked for a share. He also had an attorney on call in case they need special advice. Dr. Moskowitz was the same doctor that treated Warren for his broken leg when he was skiing. It was never leaked that he was drunk at the time.

"It's best you not stop by until the air has cleared a bit," Moskowitz said. "Take a day or two and see what's out there for bids. He may have something interesting for your old comrades. See what they'd like to know and we'll take it from there."

"There are a few things I'd like to know," Vitaly said.

"Let's get whatever we can, and maybe this will be a good time to finalize our partnership."

Vitaly listened to the doctor's tone. "Sure we'll see. Let's not make any rash decisions."

Chapter Fourteen

Before Willowdale had given his concession speech, Austin had made arrangements with the Secret Service agents. They were moved to the main lobby, and away from the Vice President. He had hired his own private agents, all of whom were ex-SEALs. The agents didn't like it and complained all the way up to the president. The president told them to keep an eye on things, and besides, Willowdale was only the Vice President for a couple more months.

Austin barely noticed the guards as they waved him through. He was focusing on trying to find a spin. Always looking for some bullshit spin with Willowdale. Always trying to find a way of covering his ass. Always looking for a side door when there was only the front.

"I don't know what's wrong with him," Ann said as she met Austin at the door. Lady, an Irish setter, barked until she recognized Austin, then followed him into the suite. Austin looked over at Willowdale sprawled on the floor. Lady had moved to lay beside him with her nose resting on his chest. Austin rushed to the Vice President's side and felt his forehead. It was warm but not excessively warm. His shirt was soaked.

"The last time I saw someone like this…it was a friend of mine. He had had a nervous breakdown."

"Should I call and see if they have a house doctor?" Ann asked.

"No . . . not with all the reporters around. It'd be on the internet in thirty seconds. Someone will be up here shortly."

"Could it be a heart attack?" Ann asked.

"I don't think so. Did he complain about pain down his arm?"

"No. I don't know. I was in the other room, and he was talking to himself or the dog . . . You saw him on the stage."

"I didn't say anything before, but he told me he didn't even know what he was saying when I approached him on stage. I thought something was wrong, but he just said he was tired. His breathing is rapid," Austin said.

Austin turned to say something to Ann when there was a knock on the door. He opened it to a guard, who said a doctor was waiting at the elevator. Austin looked and waved the man in.

"Dr. Moskowitz has sent me," the doctor said.

Austin nodded and took him to the Vice President. Lady barked several times until Austin got her to lie down. The doctor talked to the dog a few minutes until she seemed comfortable.

"Would you like me to take her into the other room?" Austin asked.

"No. She wants to stay near her owner." He looked at Willowdale and got down on his knees beside him. "Could you give me a little privacy?" the doctor said.

"Of course," Austin said. He took Ann by the arm and walked into the other room. Ann put her hand to her mouth and began to shiver. "I feel like my whole world is falling apart."

"Get yourself a drink and it'll be taken care of in no time," Austin said.

Ann made herself a martini. "Do you think it's his nerves?"

"My best guess," Austin said. "The doctor will let us know. If it were a heart attack, I think he'd be gone by now." Austin was calm. Besides thinking about how to spin it for the media, he was deciding what he would do if Willowdale died.

The doctor came out and Ann turned quickly to him.

"I'm Dr. Skinner."

"Doctor, this is Mrs. Willowdale, the Vice President's wife," Austin said.

"I've checked on the Vice President and he's resting," Skinner said. "I've given him something to keep his system stable. His pulse is rather rapid, but that could be from a number of things . . . heart attack, nerves, PTSD. They all have similar symptoms: sweatiness, memory loss, being on edge. How has he been?"

"You know about the attempt on his life?" Austin said.

"Yes. Did he seem different after that event?"

"Not right away," Ann said. "But he was having trouble sleeping lately."

Austin looked to her. This was the first time he was hearing this.

"He didn't go back out on the campaign trail for several days. When he did, he was snapping at everyone. I'm not so sure he wanted to be there any longer," Austin said. "There was tonight, too."

"What happened tonight?" the doctor asked.

"He didn't know what he was saying in his concession speech," Austin said.

"Although you don't normally pass out with these symptoms, I think it's the accumulation," Skinner said. "Everyone is affected differently. The election, the assassination attempt and then the election loss. We'll know more after we do some tests at the hospital."

"Was it a heart attack?" Ann asked.

"I don't believe so," the doctor said. "It does seem to be more about his nerves. I've never had anyone shoot at me, but I can only imagine how it'd affect me. I mentioned PTSD because of the assassination attempt. Did he say anything about voices?" the doctor said.

"Not to me, she said and looked to Austin.

"Other than his irritability and the way he acted on stage, I couldn't tell you," Austin said. "An assassination attempt might be enough for me to drop out."

"Very well," the doctor said. "I think he'll be fine. I'm going to call Dr. Moskowitz and let him know my findings. He should be here soon and I'll stay nearby until he is."

"I'll get him a blanket and pillow," Ann said.

"That would be good," the doctor said. "It's best to leave him where he is in case he's broken something. When the doctor gets here, they'll put on a neck brace and make sure he doesn't do further damage."

Austin could have just as easily picked Willowdale up and moved him to his bed. He was six-two and massive in the chest. His suits had to be made special to fit his bulk. He was proud of it, and wore it as a badge to gain presence.

Austin walked back in with the doctor and Ann. He began running scenarios through his head. That was his job. He scoured the room for clues. The shattered mirror, the table, the martini glass, all over the floor where the Vice President lay. While his eyes took in the room, he searched his memory for similar political scenarios, desperate to see if he or anyone else ever faced this kind of situation before.

"Think, think." He paced around the damaged room. He noticed the pretzels and other snacks knocked onto the floor. Lady was drooling pretzel bits.

"Pretzels," he said.

"I'm going to step out in the hall and call Dr. Moskowitz," the doctor said.

Ann looked at Austin. "What are we going to do? He'll be the butt of all the jokes. He'll never live this down or become a viable candidate for anything ever again."

Troublesome scenarios were racing through her mind. She thought little of her husband at this point, but she was terrified of the shame his condition would bring on her. It hadn't always been that way. It seemed the further up the political ladder he climbed, the further down the ladder their love life slipped. It had become a marriage of convenience and security.

Austin put his hand up and keeping his voice low, in case Willowdale woke up. "Stop. I don't need to hear you whine."

Ann was taken aback and raised her hand to slap him.

Austin caught her arm, brushing her breast. He held her arm, and with his other hand, pointed a finger at her. "Don't pull that shit on me. I know you too well. You are only thinking of one thing—yourself."

"Are you any different?" she said.

"No. But then again, I'm not his wife. You, on the other hand, are here for the ride. You—like most politicians—are in it for one thing, and it's not the country.

"And you are in it for the good of the nation?"

"I'm in it for me. The only difference is I admit it. Me first, everybody else can go to hell. I learned to think of me first on the streets in Texas. And if I hadn't learned it on the streets, I sure as hell would have picked up the truth just by living here in D.C." Austin gave Ann a gentle push.

She fell back into a chair. "How can you speak to me like that?"

"Listen, Ann. I don't work for you. I work for the man in there on the floor. I made that clear to him a long time ago. Long before—well, you know, before we got…involved."

Ann's expression was blank. She took a sip of her martini. "Tell me, Mr. Campaign Guy, what are *you* going to do?"

"Here's what we're going to say and do. You just saw the doctor here. That's how fast this is going to go. I have an ambulance coming."

"Who's this Dr. Moskowitz—is that his name?" Ann asked.

"He's my backup plan. It's someone I setup a long time ago. When I need a doctor, it means I need him now. I have other people on call if other things happen. As I was saying, an ambulance will be here shortly. This doctor is on call and he'll take Warren to a special hospital. I'll say the Vice President was eating some pretzels and they got stuck in his throat. As he started to cough, Lady came over, almost as a rescue. He turned and tripped over the dog. He grabbed the mirror to steady himself but pulled it off the wall, and then fell onto the table. We think he may have broken his leg."

"But people will speculate," Ann said.

"Who cares?" Austin said. "Hell, it worked for Bush some years ago and was quickly forgotten. I'm paid to do what needs to be done and say the right things. I've never failed him yet, and I'm not about to now."

He went over to the door and waved over one of the private security men. Austin whispered in his ear. The man turned and pointed to another guard and told him to follow him, as they walked to the elevator. From there, they proceeded to the basement to wait for the ambulance at the service elevator.

"I don't know if I can do this," Ann said.

"You *will* do this," Austin said, louder. "You will handle this just like any of the other lies that you, me and all the other politicians spread every day. You'll tell the lies just as you would have if you'd won the election. Got it?"

Ann looked as though she was about to cry. He hadn't meant to be so harsh, but he couldn't stand her whining. He sat down next to her, pulled her close and kissed her cheek.

"How'd you know what to do? How could you be prepared for something like this to happen?" Ann asked, looking up at Austin.

Austin pushed himself away and stood. He wandered around behind her, then circled back to face her. "If it wasn't this, it'd be something else. I'm paid to be prepared. You have to be aware of the people around you. It's pretty easy to figure out who you can trust and who you can't. Money is the equalizer that makes people trustworthy. Besides, Warren's always had friends who can influence people with a little arm-twisting, if they ever decided to reveal themselves to be untrustworthy."

"You mean like Churchill Brewer?" Ann asked.

"For one. He's the worst."

"He scares me," Ann said.

"He should scare you. He scares me, and he should scare Warren, but he doesn't see it. Churchill gets more out of Warren than Warren's ever gotten out of Churchill."

"You know, he's saved him many a time," Ann said.

"Yeah, but he's gotten a lot of valuable information out of your husband, and that has only made him richer," Austin said. "If Warren ever missteps, lies or refuses him, he'd think nothing of throwing him to the lions."

Chapter Fifteen

"Let me know the moment they appear," Austin said to one of the security guards at the rear entrance. Replacing the receiver on the phone, he picked it up again and called the front desk.

"This is Austin Garcia. On behalf of the Vice President, please make an announcement for the reporters in an hour. A press conference will be held in the second floor conference room. Please go into the bar and repeat the announcement," Austin said.

Austin knew it was going to be a tough night, but not in his wildest dreams would he have thought it was going to be this bad.

I know Willowdale can be an asshole, but I have a job to do, and I will do it any way I can and to the best of my ability.

* * *

Ann was impressed with her husband's press secretary and campaign manager and showed her approval with a pleasant smile.

Austin explained how the doctor would put a cast on Willowdale's leg. "We'll take some pictures and pass them along. We'll wait until after he is drugged up. The doctor knows what to do, and I'll take care of the rest of the bullshit," Austin said as he pulled Ann to him. "I'll make everything disappear, okay?" He kissed her hard, like he hadn't seen her in a long time. They both pressed up to each other, and he wanted to take her right there, but he knew time was short. He gave a hard grab to her ass.

Austin was not only an egotistical maniac, but a hot-blooded young Mexican who loved to have sex anytime, anywhere. This was just a warm up for later.

His phone rang, "Bring them up the service elevator," Austin said to the security guard on the other end of the line. A moan came from the other room.

Ann jumped and then panicked. Straightening herself up, she went back into the other room. When Ann got there, however, her husband was motionless.

Austin went into the bathroom, washed his face and tucked in his shirt. He could do little about his erection, but it would take care of itself.

Chapter Sixteen

Dr. Moskowitz nodded to Ann but said nothing as he entered the hotel room. He walked over to Willowdale. Ann had already put Lady into one of the bedrooms. She barked just the same as the doctor came in.

After checking on him, Moskowitz waved to the ambulance attendants to take Willowdale.

He took Ann's arm and walked her into the other room. "I'm Dr. Madison Moskowitz," he said. "Dr. Skinner has informed me what he believes is going on. I will take care of everything here, and you're not to worry. We know what to do, and everything will go through Mr. Garcia, from me. No one involved with his care will speak of any of this. You have my word."

Austin walked into the room after freshening himself up and tucking himself back into his shorts. He already knew the doctor's procedure. It was his idea and no one knew Willowdale like Austin. "Here's how this is going to work," he said. "The doctor already knows what to do, but I want everything to go off without a hitch. I'll hold a press conference to distract the reporters. While I'm at the conference, Warren will be transferred to the hospital. I believe all of the reporters will be with me, and out of the way."

"Do you think that's safe?" Ann asked.

"We'll make sure the guards have all the areas covered. We don't want someone to come down the alley or out the back way," Dr. Moskowtiz said. "It's late, so we should be okay. You see, I've done this sort of thing before."

"By the time I announce to the press we believe the Vice President has broken his leg, the good doctor will be heading down the highway.

Mrs. Willowdale, you'll decline all statements. Make no discussions as to how it happened or anything else, understood?"

"Yes, I understand," she said.

It's amazing how Austin turns it on and off so quickly, she thought. *One moment, I'm in his arms or we're making love, and the next, he's all business. He's a real man. Not like Warren, who looks like a bookstore owner from P-town with that comb-over.*

"Mrs. Willowdale, are you okay?" Austin asked. "Do you need to be checked out?"

"I'm fine. I was just…lost in thought for a moment," Ann said. "I understand. There'll be no problem with me."

* * *

"He'll be out for a while," Dr. Moskowitz said. "When we get to the hospital we'll give him a full workup. Once we understand where we are, we'll make some decisions for his treatment. Just the same, I think I have a good handle on what's going on. If need be, I'll give him another shot. The last thing I want is for him to wake up with the press around him."

Austin dialed the doctor's number, and then quickly hung up. "When I get down to the second floor, I'll hit the send button to call your phone, Doctor. The ring will be your signal to leave. Ann, you go with the ambulance and I'll pick you up later. Where will he be, Doc?"

"He'll be in the back villa, V7."

Austin stepped into the hallway and walked to the elevator. The security guard stepped aside as he approached. He pressed the button for the second floor, where the press would be waiting. *It'll be a scriptless moment,* he thought. He was quick on his feet. He had to be quick working for Willowdale. He knew how to lie, to make people believe his words and ask for more.

Chapter Seventeen

Austin Garcia stepped into the conference room. Some reporters were sitting while others stood in the back. They yelled questions as he walked across the room.

"Can we talk to the Vice President?"

"What does the future hold for the Vice President?"

"Will he run for president again?"

"Can you explain how you had a solid lead just a few weeks ago and were the favorite that you came up short?"

Austin ignored them and offered no response. He smiled and walked to the front of the room while sizing up the press.

At the podium, he tried to buy time for the ambulance to get Willowdale out of there. "Everyone, please take your seat." He pressed the send button on his phone, waited until he heard the doctor speak, then hung up. He stood looking out into the crowd with his hands up in the air, waiting for the reporters to settle down.

"I heard one question," Austin said. "You asked what the Vice President's future looks like? Tonight, it doesn't appear to be all that great. But trust me when I say you haven't seen the last of Vice President Willowdale."

One of the reporters looked at the fellow journalist sitting next to him and whispered, "That's too bad. He's such a dickhead."

The reporters all laughed.

Austin looked toward the group where he heard the comments. He'd stalled long enough. He hoped the doctor, Ann, and Willowdale were on their way.

"What I'm about to say is a bit embarrassing, but I want to be honest with you and the American people. I know Vice President

Willowdale would want nothing less, as he has always spoken with truth and transparency. Last night—I mean tonight. These things tend to wear you down when you've been up all night," Austin said laughing. Other reporters laughed along with him.

"Tonight, the Vice President was obviously upset about his loss and, to be honest, he was angry. He personally felt he offered the country and the world the best hope for the future. He felt this and still feels this, but the American electorate has spoken."

He took a pregnant pause.

"As I said, the vice president was upset. He was talking with Mrs. Willowdale about what had gone wrong in the campaign, and as he talked, he became a bit agitated. He was drinking water and eating pretzels, and he started choking."

A murmur rippled through the crowd of reporters.

Austin continued. "Everything happened so fast. As he choked, his dog, Lady, came over in what Mrs. Willowdale believes was a protective gesture. The Vice President turned, and tripped over Lady and a glass table. He fell and broke his leg."

The reporters started yelling more questions.

"Is this some sort of fabrication?"

Austin held up his hand to calm them. "Let me continue. The Vice President is okay, but the doctor is pretty confident his leg is broken. X-rays will provide confirmation." Austin took a deep breath. "Now, let's have some questions."

"Were you in the room when this happened?"

"No, I was in the bar here in the hotel."

"Is he going to the hospital?"

"Yes, in fact he's already left."

"Which hospital is he going to?"

"He's been taken to the Maryland Life Rehabilitation Center," Austin said.

"Isn't that a drug rehab hospital?"

"It's a private facility that does have a drug rehabilitation facility, but it's also a rehabilitation center for all of life's problems. It has one of the best private surgical groups in the area, as well as some general practice groups. As you know, the Vice President has been there before when he broke his leg skiing. I'm not sure, but it may be the same leg," Austin said, laying a foundation for the facility.

As Austin answered questions, he looked over the crowd of reporters and made note of Rori Cahill entering the room.

She was a petite, attractive reporter in her mid-twenties. She had an infectious smile that made her almond-shaped eyes glow. Her high-cheekbones were dotted with freckles. When she was angry or disgusted, those same eyes shot bullets at the intended target. Her black shoulder length hair moved softly as she strolled across the room. Her shapely figure and ample breast captured most eyes when she entered a room.

Despite her good looks, most of her fellow workers were standoffish. She had an edge to her personality, and the fact she carried a 9 mm made most of them feel a bit intimidated.

Rori was a loner most of the time. As an only child, she learned to be independent and kept to herself. After Rori's parents died in a car accident, she went to live with her Aunt Charley, a spunky spinster who opened the world for Rori. She taught her how to shoot, how to live, how to be independent.

Before Rori was thirteen, Aunt Charley enrolled her in the NRA shooting course. She was a marksman at fourteen. Rori become the daughter Aunt Charley never had. Aunt Charley became the mother Rori wished she had, teaching her how to give and get respect. If people didn't understand the concept, Aunt Charley taught her not to care.

Rori walked toward a small group of reporters milling about in the back. Spotting her mentor, Neil O'Connor, she approached.

Once Neil saw Rori, his droopy expression turned to a smile.

"What's going on?" Rori asked as she moved up to him.

Neil couldn't resist using a line from an old television commercial. "The Vice President has fallen and he can't get up."

Rori looked at him, raising her eyebrow and shook her head, not understanding the joke.

Rori wasn't even alive when that commercial was made. "He has broken his leg. Maybe he's shook up what few brains he has," Neil said as she moved closer to him. His smile grew wider.

Neil was a good friend. He was someone Rori trusted. He was well over twice her age and Rori looked at him as a father figure.

Unfortunately, although he could be sweet and gentle, his anger would occasionally turn to an alcoholic's anger. Rori could handle it just the same.

When he bent over to speak, she smelled the booze. She knew he drank liberally and accepted him as he was. She felt there was more to his drinking habit than he ever wanted to discuss.

Rori was told to use Neil as a quasi-boss, and he could help her with the ropes. Having done so, she was looking for a big break. To date, it had eluded her. Neil, on the other hand, was looking forward to when he could say goodbye to the D.C. crowd. He wanted to settle down on his little farm near Gettysburg, where he could write his historical novel, enjoy life and drink his whiskey whenever he wanted to—as if he didn't already.

"Where have you been?" Neil asked.

"I covered the winner, if you can call him that," she said. "I'm sure it wasn't as much fun as the one you're covering."

"This looks like it's going to lead me to retirement," Neil whispered. Neil's instincts were kicking in. He had watched the Vice President in recent days since the assassination attempt. He felt there was more going on here. He just had to stay on the story and not allow his drinking to get in the way.

Rori didn't understand why Neil thought this was a big story, but then Neil always preached to her about "developing instinct." Rori's only instinct came on late nights with hot guys—and the occasional hot girl.

It had not been much of a campaign. Neither candidate had been able to cultivate a large number of supporters. Instead, the voters decided to choose the lesser of two evils. The public was so disinterested in the two candidates, the voter turnout was only forty-two percent, a record low.

"Austin just announced the Vice President was choking on pretzels and then tripped over his dog and broke his leg," Neil said.

Rori was laughing so hard, she thought she was about to pee her pants. Neil, somewhat unsteady, leaned over to her and asked, "Do you want a pretzel?"

She gathered herself and straightened up.

"Neil, I saw an ambulance, but there wasn't a name on the side. Was that the Vice President's?" Rori asked.

"It must have been. You should have waved them down and asked for an interview and a ride," Neil said.

"If I'd gotten here a little earlier, I might have stopped them." Rori gave Neil a strange look. "I had a minor altercation with Pretty Boy."

Neil looked at her and raised his eyebrows.

"Where's he being taken?" she asked.

"The Maryland Life Rehabilitation Center," Neil said. "It's out in the middle of nowhere, past Poolesville."

"Where the hell is that?" Rori said.

"It's like thirty, forty miles or so northwest of here. Out in bum-fuck," Neil said.

Rori whispered in Neil's ear. "Let's get our asses out of here and see if we can find this place. I don't like just standing around listening to someone else's story. Why don't we check out your instinct and see if we can find our own?"

Neil looked at her and then turned back to Austin, as he thought for a minute. He knew she was right, but didn't know if tonight he was up to detective work in his old age. His life had changed in so many ways over the years. He was no longer Neil O'Connor, Pulitzer Prize winner. He was no longer the reporter who uncovered the congressional money scam. He was no longer a father.

Neil gawked at Rori as she tried to entice him to follow. He listened to Austin at the same time, as he spun his web. Rori shook her hips, looked up at him with a smile and fluttered her lashes.

"What the hell? What've we got to lose?" He stumbled behind Rori heading out the door.

Chapter Eighteen

Austin stepped outside the conference room after the press conference and dialed Dr. Moskowitz's cell phone.

"Dr. Moskowitz, this is Austin Garcia. Make sure you take him into x-ray, and surgery. We don't want our motives questioned. God forbid, the records ever get out."

"You don't have to tell me how to do my job. And the records never get out from the hospital. I'm not one of your politicians in that slush pot of whores."

Austin was taken aback by the doctor's reaction. He was supposed to be part of the Willowdale team.

"Take it easy, doc. I'm just trying to make sure there are no slipups. I'm used to dealing with Washington people. If the Vice President is to survive this, nothing can be left to chance, that's all I'm saying."

Though, he is right. Most politicians would surely screw this up, and it'd be on the front page tomorrow. At least it would bump the president-elect from the front page.

The doctor's voice settled some after Austin explained. "I understand, and everything here will be fine. We will run the plan. You must understand—this is not my first time. I've taken care of people from all over the world. Nothing has ever gotten out."

He didn't care anything about the politicians or any of the other rich snobs in his facility for that matter. The group of investors he put together understood the ten-year tax benefit and how the government would continue to pour money into the system just to look good at election time.

The patients were pampered drug addicts or crybaby politicians who got themselves into situations they couldn't handle. The MLRC covered their tracks. In the end, it was all about the money. When the

61

vice president left this facility, Moskowitz would have enough money to buy a house on Nantucket. Then again, he already had one of those.

The selling of confidential information was far more lucrative than the care of patients. It was paying off many times more than that of the government subsidies. In a few years, he would be selling off his interest in the hospital.

"Tell Ann I'll pick her up, and she doesn't need the limousine," Austin said.

"Very well, Mr. Garcia," Dr. Moskowitz said.

* * *

Austin went up to Warren's empty hotel suite. Looking around at the broken mirror and table, he shook his head then walked over to the wet bar and poured some tequila. It tasted good, but it would have tasted so much better if they had won.

He walked into the center living room, shut off the lights and climbed into the chair Ann sat in earlier, and stared out at the Capitol Dome. Tipping his head back, he thought how far he had come. He was tired of feeling like he used a lot of energy and didn't get where he wanted. He liked politics—no loved it, but so much of it was twisting of the truth. He had donated his share of half-truths—shit. Say one thing and do something different. His weary mind took him back to a time where it all began.

He had survived getting beat up by a local gang. He was just a skinny twelve year old, almost thirteen. He promised to himself he would never let that happen again.

Over the next four years, he worked out, lifting rocks, building himself up until he was a bulk of a young man. He and his friend Juan returned to the place the gang beat him and beat up the leader and a couple members. The revenge built his confidence and put him on the road to claiming his territory.

Maybe it's just a power trip. Of course it's a power trip, and it's all about me. I've eaten my share of shit.

He gulped the remainder of his drink, locked up the room without turning on the lights and went to the parking garage. He had to pick up Ann.

Chapter Nineteen

Despite little chance they would be able to get in to see the Vice President, but maybe they could get some nurse, anyone, to give them some information, Neil and Rori headed to the MLRC facility and got lost on their way. Traveling back and forth on the same road several times, Rori lost her patience with Neil, who was drunk. She made him pull over so she could drive.

By the time they reached the Maryland facility, it was nearly midnight—way past Neil's bedtime. But it was Rori's time to howl.

"I guess I should have turned right when you told me to," Neil said.

"What you should have done is let me drive from the beginning. Haven't you learned after all these years of marriage, it's best to listen to the woman?"

"Just because you got lucky once doesn't mean I'm going to listen to you every time," Neil said, tipping his flask.

"If I drank from a flask, I'd be bombed all the time." She tried not to judge, but she was around Neil enough to know it was best to be honest.

Neil ignored her as she finally pulled into the hospital grounds.

They went directly into the main building, where there was a desk with a guard.

"May I help you?"

"I'd—we'd like to make an inquiry. We're reporters," Neil said.

The guard buzzed them into the lobby.

"We'd like to talk to someone about Warren Willowdale," Neil said.

"Let me check the computer. It doesn't look like we have anyone by that name."

"Don't you know who Warren Willowdale is?" Rori asked.

Scratching his head, the guard said, "The name does sound familiar, but I can't seem to recall."

"He's the Vice President…of the United States," Rori said, nearly shouting.

"Oh, *that's* why it sounds familiar," he said, chuckling.

Rori looked at Neil, rolled her eyes, and mumbled under her breath. "This country's going to hell."

"I don't see the name in the computer. I guess we don't have him."

"Is this the only way you would know? I mean on the computer?" Neil asked.

"If he were here in this building, he'd be on the computer. Though this doesn't include the villas," the guard said.

"What're the villas?" Rori asked.

"The other facilities down the hill, but I don't have access to that program."

"How can we get there?" Rori asked.

"You can't. You have to be a family member or have a family member sign you in. All of that has to be pre-approved prior to coming here."

"So that's it?" Rori said.

"Is there someone in charge we can talk to?" Neil asked.

"Not at this hour. You'll have to come back during regular business hours. If that's all, I'm going to ask you to leave."

"What's your name again?" Rori asked.

"Don't pull that on me. I'll get in trouble if I let you in. I've seen a lot of bullshit from people and reporters."

"In case you haven't noticed, reporters are people too," Rori said.

The guard didn't respond.

"Thanks just the same," Rori said.

"Yes, thank you," Neil said.

They both turned and walked out of the building, followed by the guard. Once outside, the guard checked the door to make sure it was locked.

"That was a waste of time," Rori said as they stepped into the cool air.

"Nothing ventured, nothing gained," Neil said. Looking toward the driveway, he took another sip from his flask. "I bet that driveway there could lead us down to a story."

Chapter Twenty

When Austin arrived, he went right to the villa. Had it been rush hour, it would have taken at least double the amount of time to get there, but not this late. The driveway appeared to be open, but further down, out of view from the main hospital, was a gated entrance to the villas. Each villa had a separate front desk with a guard outside the door. There were two nurses per unit, sometimes three depending on the client. Being the Vice President and knowing that he would be demanding, Willowdale would have three.

Austin walked into the villa after the security guard checked him over. Once inside, his ID was checked again against a visitors' list, approved by Dr. Moskowitz.

"One moment please," the nurse said. She picked up the phone. "There's a Mr. Garcia here."

"Yes, I'll be right out," Ann said. She hung up the phone and walked into the hallway. Its opulence matched the Vice President's room. Money always trumped everything for the Willowdales.

Austin gave Ann a hug. The nurse stared but said nothing.

Austin motioned Ann down the hallway. "How's he doing?"

"He's resting and will be out for the night. The doctor is checking on him," Ann said.

"Let's go in," Austin said. The doctor was entering information on a chart. Another chart hung on the end of the bed with Willowdale's medical information, the treatments completed and his medications. All of it was fake. It was a medical record of lies the doctor and Austin would spin tomorrow.

The doctor had already prepared the false records with the head nurse. Everyone was in on it. No one spoke outside the hospital, because the pay was thousands more than any other similar job. It was just too good to be true, and loose lips meant lost jobs.

In the doctor's hands were the real records. The information that showed the Vice President was on Medifinne. If anyone with medical experience were to see this, they would come to one conclusion: Willowdale had a nervous breakdown.

Medifinne was a miracle drug, discovered by accident. It was an offshoot of a drug being developed for repairing nerves for people who had Amyotrophic Lateral Sclerosis, also known as Lou Gehrig's disease. Although it never worked for its original intent, it had been used with success for psychiatric patients.

At MLRC, patients left the hospital with all of their records. There were supposed to be no other copies, but Dr. Moskowitz made his own rules.

* * *

The doctor finished making notes in the real record, then turned to Ann and Austin. "He's resting, and I think I'm going to keep him out until about two this afternoon, at which time I'll bring him around. You can come by around four. Is that okay with you?"

"That'll be fine," Austin said.

"I think you should be able to talk to him at that time. I've given him a new treatment. It will aid him in his recovery. He will be in a deep, restful sleep, which is what we are doing to aid him. This treatment is new and it may seem a bit harsh, but it's better than electric shock."

The thought of using electric shock on Willowdale scared Austin, but then maybe that's exactly what he needed.

"Are there any side effects?" Ann asked.

"Not now. At one time there were problems, but those have been ironed out," Moskowitz said. "This is going to help him recover faster."

They all looked toward the Vice President. No one would know anything was wrong.

"I'm not going to put a cast on his leg until sometime next week. It depends on when the media will see him or when he's being released. His records show he had surgery tonight and has had a temporary cast put on his leg."

"The miracle of modern medicine," Austin said. "Can I touch base with you by mid-morning, so I can at least have a news conference?"

"Let's make it more like late morning, say 11:30. You can have your news conference, or at least give an update. I'll tell you what you can say," Dr. Moskowitz said.

Abruptly, the doctor walked into the other room and over to a built-in bookcase. He slid his hand along the bottom side, where he pulled part of the molding out that was hinged. Then he pressed a button and hidden drawer opened at the far end of the bookcase. He put the records in and returned to the button. In a movement, the drawer disappeared and the molding was back into place.

Dr. Moskowitz went back into Warren's room. "Mrs. Willowdale, Mr. Garcia, I believe it's time to leave. Don't worry about a thing. In a few weeks, the Vice President will be back on top of his game."

Chapter Twenty-One

Austin looked at his watch. It was 1:30 a.m. Once he looked at his watch, his body started to react, and the exhaustion began to set in.

The doctor left the room, and the two of them stood there looking at Willowdale.

"You know, we almost made it," Ann said as she walked around the bed and sat down. "We almost grabbed the gold ring. It was in our grasp, and we would have had it, had he not been such a coward."

Austin said nothing at first. "If only the assassination attempt hadn't happened, we would have won."

"Maybe I shouldn't have talked to Churchill," Ann said.

Austin turned to her. "What?"

"I knew what he was like. I knew at any given moment he'd do or say something stupid. I—I just mentioned to Churchill..."

"You mentioned *what* to Churchill? What did you say to that—that animal?" Austin walked off into the sitting area to calm his temper.

Austin's tone startled Ann, but she waved her hand at him. Then she got up and followed. "I just mentioned perhaps we needed a special moment."

"I don't want to hear this. Don't tell me anymore. I'm sorry I asked."

"Whether you know it or not, it's exactly what you signed up for. You're just as much a part of this as he is or I am. You just haven't figured that out yet. You love having sex with the Vice President's wife because it gives you a high. You want the power, just like anyone else in D.C. It's all part of the package"

"You're right—I love the power, but I'm learning I'll never get it while I'm with him. And I'm using you for the thrill. And you know what? It's not going to last forever. That's something you better get into your head." Austin turned to leave.

"Take me home, please," Ann said.

Austin knew he was being manipulated. It was all about sex. He wasn't sure if he wanted to touch her any longer, but it had been a long time since he thought with the right head. He looked around for a moment, trying to find a way out of this situation. They just insulted each other, but still there was the sex.

Ann looked at him, and then put her hand on his shoulder. "Look at me. I just wanted to shake things up a bit. I'm sorry. I know I shouldn't have, but I guess I wasn't thinking. Haven't you done things you later regretted?"

"Oh yeah. I'm thinking I'm about to now."

"What do you mean?" Ann asked.

"I think I should just walk away and end this whole charade right now."

"Oh, please don't," Ann said. "I need you more than ever. I need to be by your side. Take me home."

Austin was uneasy. He was trying to listen to his conscience. He knew he had to make a change. He held out his hand, biting his lower lip, and Ann took it. After checking on the Vice President once more, they headed to the door.

As they got there, Austin stopped for a second to listen. He thought he heard a sound coming from Willowdale's bed. He walked back and took a quick glance. Willowdale was rolling over but it was quiet in the room. No—no, he was just hearing things. Besides, the doctor said the Vice President would be out for hours. Austin stared at Willowdale and thought a few moments. His mind was in turmoil. The shit with politics, lying, cheating and now sneaking around with the Vice President's wife. His conscience was trying to talk to him. He just hadn't understood what it was saying.

* * *

He knew he was living dangerously, and he liked it that way. Bedding the Vice President's wife gave him a high. He couldn't stop himself. It was like being in bed with your high school teacher. Knowing it's wrong, knowing trouble is headed your way—but it's so good while it lasts.

Ann was wrapped around his finger, although she may have felt different, but she'd do anything to and for him just to keep him coming back. He knew it was only a matter of time before word of their affair got out.

He had come a long way from his hard times as a kid. So many of his family members had traversed the desert just to be in the country.

He tried not to think about the situation. Willowdale had a lot of powerful friends who would think nothing about executing a fair and just punishment, if the Vice President so desired.

Once Austin and Ann returned to the main lobby, they resumed their facade.

"You can turn the cameras back on, Nurse Boothroyd," Austin said. "Can I see the emergency contact numbers you have?"

The nurse recited Ann's number, but Austin stopped her before she got far.

He added a new number. "Please use that as the primary number. Mrs. Willowdale's number is the backup."

The nurse looked to Mrs. Willowdale to get approval.

"That will be fine," she said. "Mr. Garcia will know how to get in touch with me." *He'll probably be in my bed.*

Nurse Boothroyd entered the information into the computer then flipped the camera switches on for each of the rooms. The red lights flashed next to each screen, and the Vice President came into view. He wasn't moving, but all vital signs were normal.

"Goodnight, Miss Boothroyd," Austin said as he walked Mrs. Willowdale to the front door.

Ann said nothing.

Austin always tried to make everyone feel good and important. By acknowledging the nurse, he had created a relationship. That was his way to deal with a world of back-stabbers in D.C. and he had refined it to an art.

Make them feel like they have his undivided attention, even if he wasn't listening to a word.

Ann, on the other hand, often treated others as though they didn't exist. Perhaps it rubbed off from her husband. Perhaps it was the money—but then, she had always had money. It was what attracted Warren to her.

Austin opened the door for Ann, then walked around the car and turned back to look at the hospital toward the window of Willowdale's room. He jumped into the SUV and followed the winding driveway through the villa gate and out past the main entrance.

Chapter Twenty-Two

Austin and Ann drove past the main hospital, but they didn't notice Rori and Neil leaving the main building.

"Wasn't that Austin Garcia?" Rori asked, as Neil reached for his flask.

"I believe it was. It looked like Mrs. Willowdale in the front seat, too," Neil said. He smacked his lips after downing a big sip.

"I wonder why she's not in the limo?"

"Maybe she's getting a better ride with him."

"You think he's banging her, huh?" Rori said.

"That's a little rough, don't you think?" Neil said.

"Is he banging her or not?" Rori said, laughing. "Call it what you want, but he's banging the second lady."

"I'd say so," Neil said.

"What's a good-looking hunk like Austin doing banging and old buzzard like that?" Rori asked.

"Will you stop with the banging stuff?" Neil said.

"I could say it another way…."

Neil looked at her over his glasses. "That would be nice."

"So she's hanging on Austin's pole, is that what you're saying?" Rori couldn't help herself. Neil could be a little stodgy at times, and she just had to crank him every once in a while.

"You're despicable," Neil said. "And you don't understand what it's all about. When you've been here as long as I have, you'll get it. D.C. is all about power and money. You can't get one without the other."

"I think D.C. stands for Dick City," Rori said.

"Close," Neil said. "What you have to do is cultivate the city. People need to get to know you. You can't go around calling them all assholes. If you do, you'll be all alone."

"Are you working on it?" Rori said.

"Yes—no—kind of," Neil said. "As I was saying, you've got to cultivate the city. As you do, you start to develop an instinct. You can tell when people are telling the truth and when they're lying."

"So, as we were saying before about this banging thing—how come you haven't written about it?"

Neil took another sip. "I'm working on it."

"Let me work on it with you."

"I've got quite a bit on my own."

"Is it documented?" Rori asked.

"Pretty much. Let's see where *this* story goes, and then we'll top it off with the bangers," Neil said.

"Where is it? Where are you keeping your work?"

"Why you looking at me like that?" Neil said.

"You could have a heart attack tomorrow, and I won't know where the story is."

"You're just a bitch, aren't you?" Neil said.

"I think you've had too much to drink, Neil. You just called me a bitch. I thought you loved Rori."

"You want my story. I thought you loved Neil."

"You know I love you and Maggie. But you're right, I am a bitch, and I want the damn story. Where's it at?"

"I'll let you know some time," Neil said.

"How'd you figure it out?"

Neil took another sip. "Instinct."

Rori looked down the winding driveway and then to Neil. "Do you think we can get down to the villas to look around?"

Rori had parked at the far end of the parking lot where there were far fewer lights. "Let's give it a try," he said. "I'm not an old goat yet."

At the beginning of the night, Neil was reluctant to even join Rori. Now here he was enjoying every minute. Part of it was because he liked being around Rori, but he was also enjoying their mission. He felt a spark he hadn't felt from his work in a long time. It was much better than following a couple of philanderers.

"Walk to the car and open the door. When you get there, bend down as if you're getting into the car, but I want you to slide back to the rear. We'll wait and see if they picked us up on camera. If we get caught, we get caught. No harm, no foul. Do it quickly," Neil said.

They got low and slid back like a couple of cat burglars.

"Keep down for a few minutes to see if we're observed. If they saw us, they'll be here soon," Neil said.

Neil reached into his right coat pocket and to retrieve his electronic key. He came up empty. "Where's my key?"

"I've got it, here," Rori said. She tossed the key to Neil and was surprised he caught it.

If they were spotted, he could open the trunk and pretend to be looking for something. Who cares if they knew it was a lie. He set the key onto the bumper so he could sip from his flask.

Rori looked over at Neil as they squatted down behind the car. "You're something else, Neil O'Connor. It looks like you're enjoying this."

"I used to like this kind of thing. I guess I've gotten too comfortable. Got my head looking toward retirement and haven't been focusing enough on the here and now. People do that when they get close to retirement," he said, his mind roaming his past. "It can be tough to slow down and do a good job when you know you're nearing the end. But still, you need to pay attention to your life and not what it was or will be. What it is."

Rori smiled. "Did you do this sort of thing a lot when you were younger?"

Neil thought for a few seconds. "I suppose I did." He was in whiskey heaven, just spitting out words. "I forget—it's been so long, so many whiskeys ago, but after Sterling, I guess . . ." Neil's words drifted off.

Rori looked at Neil in the partial darkness. She didn't know who Sterling was and was afraid to ask. It wasn't the first time she'd heard the name. It was always after a lot of whiskey. She was hesitant to ask when he was sober, thinking he might get mad. She was afraid to ask when he was drunk, thinking he'd tell her the whole story. In the little light shining on his face, she could surmise his pain.

"You were saying?" Rori asked.

Neil was startled at her voice, as if he were miles away. "Yeah,

yeah, I'm sorry. I was just saying, after a while you wonder why you bother beating your head against the wall." Neil's went silent again for a moment as his thoughts drifted. Then he started rambling.

Rori leaned against the bumper, letting her butt slide down to the ground as she imagined Neil's pain. Her mind took her back to the day she was rescued. To the time her parents were killed. Whatever Neil's pain, she could relate.

"You ready to go?" Neil asked.

"What?" Rori said.

"I said are you ready to go, or have you chickened out?"

"Me? Chicken out? I don't think so. I'd already be down there if I didn't have to drag your drunken ass around."

"I may have had a few, but I can still kick your ass," Neil said.

They moved into the bushes that paralleled both sides of the driveway and lawn. It gave them adequate cover. They slithered in and around the bushes beyond the lower guardhouse, now far away from the parking lot and several hundred yards from the gated entrance to the villas. There was no turning back.

They had circumvented the guardhouse by following the bushes away from it. To their surprise, the fencing only went part of the way around the facility. Thick bushes grew where the fence ended. It made it hard, but not impossible, to break in.

Neil and Rori zigzagged their way around the property, using the trees and hemlock bushes for cover. When they were certain they were out of sight of the gatehouse, they tried to work their way back toward the villas. As they slithered, they could see lights lining the driveway, and occasionally people moving around inside the villas. They began to maneuver themselves around the bushes.

It was both exciting and scary, but Rori was no chicken. She had always been a tomboy and was usually up for anything. Though she was apprehensive about sneaking around where the Vice President was staying. *What if he has guards or secret service guys with guns? They might mistake us for assassins.* Unable to speak to Neil, her thoughts were now running wild in the darkness.

She lost sight of Neil for a second. Working her way to get closer to him, a branch snapped back and hit her in the face. Unable to see

Neil, she grabbed into the dark to find him. She caught his shoulder and bent over, her eyes watering. The sting was almost more than she could stand. She held her breath, holding her scream inside.

"What's wrong?" Neil whispered.

Rori said nothing at first, but then Neil saw her bent over.

"What are you doing?"

"That last branch slapped me square on the nose. Son of a bitch hurt," she whispered.

"Keep your voice down," he said.

As they made a turn to get around the bushes and closer to the villas, a guard walked by with a flashlight. He stopped directly in front of them, then turned and headed toward them. Neil grabbed Rori and pulled her back, putting a hand over her mouth. Holding her from behind, he whispered in her ear. "Guard."

Rori could smell the Jameson.

The guard took a couple more steps toward them, off of the paved driveway and searched with his light.

Neil continued to keep his arms wrapped around Rori, her hair in his face.

The guard aimed his flashlight around the bushes and, seeing nothing, returned to the paved driveway to continue his routine.

As the guard moved out of sight, Neil released her.

"Boy, that was pretty close," Neil whispered. "Sorry I grabbed you."

"It wasn't all bad," Rori said. "You just took my breath away."

"I'll take your breath away," Neil mumbled.

The guard moved down the driveway and was out of sight except for an occasional glow of his flashlight.

Neil took Rori's hand and pulled her across the driveway and the yard leading up to the villas. There, they clung to the wall of the building, hidden by more bushes, and peered through the window. Inside, two nurses sat talking and viewing monitors. *There must be a camera somewhere. Hope it's not on us,* Neil thought. They saw another nurse walking down a hallway.

In the first building, they saw a female patient neither of them recognized. Moving on, they approached each building with the same caution.

"These must be the villas," Neil whispered.

"Aren't you the bright bulb?"

"Don't be such a wise guy or I'll kick your ass—again," Neil said.

"I must have missed the first time. Just keep going, old man."

Neil moved further down the row of villas, one by one. After finishing most of the buildings, Rori grabbed Neil's jacket to get his attention.

"Maybe the guard wasn't lying. Maybe he's not here," she said.

"Let's keep going. Why would Austin lie? We saw him here."

"Maybe he lied because it's politics," Rori said, as Neil walked out of earshot.

They continued until they came to the last building and peered into a room with a light on. Neil moved up and looked through the window. Rori followed his lead. They looked at each other and then back into the room.

The Vice President was walking back and forth aimlessly. He looked unsteady and grabbed on to furniture as he paced.

They couldn't believe what they were seeing. No cast, no bandages—nothing.

After gathering themselves and taking a deep breath, they looked back into the room. This time, two nurses came in and grabbed the Vice President. Willowdale's hands and arms were waving in the air as though he were swatting flies. He appeared to be unsteady.

Each nurse grabbed an arm and put their considerable weight into pushing him back to the edge of the bed. While one of the nurses went to the phone to make a call, the other put a little pressure on each shoulder and got Willowdale to lie down again.

When the other nurse returned, she prepared a needle, rolled the Vice President over on his side, and gave him a shot in the ass. Warren tried to pull away but he was exhausted and showed little fight. After administering the shot, they covered him up and waited a few seconds until Willowdale was asleep.

"That'll keep him out," one of the nurses said. The other glanced toward the window. Neil and Rori ducked.

Hearing no alarms, they returned to the window. Rori saw one nurses go into another room. She followed along the building to the next window and watched the nurse go over to a bookcase and fiddle with something. After a moment, a drawer opened at the other end of the bookcase, and the nurse retrieved some paperwork, wrote something down and replaced it. She then went back and fiddled with something again, and the drawer disappeared back into the bookcase.

Looking to the window, the nurse knew something was out of place. "Who pulled those shades up?"

Rori ducked down, as the nurse walked toward the window and dropped the blind down.

Scurrying back to Neil, she got him to get down as the same nurse came to his window and dropped the shade.

"We better talk to the cleaning people to make sure they put the shades down after they dust and clean," the nurse said. "Can't anybody do their job?"

Still trying to keep to a whisper, Neil said, "I don't think they're going to let us interview the Vice President."

"Let's get out of here."

They were on the opposite side of the parking lot from their car. No matter how they returned, they were taking a chance. They knew their luck would last for only so long.

"I've seen enough," Neil whispered. He pointed in the direction of the main building and started to move quickly. They weaved their way around more trees and bushes. It was a repeat of what they did to get down to the villas, albeit shorter, and with a lot less cover. When they reached the main building, they took a quick look to see if anyone was around, then dashed off across the parking lot in a quick walk.

As they got halfway across the lot, a guard stepped out of the building. "You two, stop." His belly bouncing over his gun belt, he hurriedly came down the steps. Neither Neil nor Rori stopped—or even thought about stopping.

"Get your key out, Neil baby," Rori said. "I'll drive."

He was searching for it at the moment, and was starting to panic. Fear was sobering Neil. He fished around in his usual pocket, but it wasn't there.

"What are you doing? Where's your key? Come on, Neil," Rori said again. "Let's get to it. He's coming fast."

"I'm looking, I'm looking." He remembered he had his keys out when they were at the back of the car crouched down. He left them on the bumper. He was ahead of Rori and went straight to the back of the car where the key was thankfully still there. Frantically Rori yelled one more time. "Neil, you got the key?"

Neil held it up in the air and pressed the button to unlock the doors. The guard was just coming across the parking lot. Neil had no intention of stopping. He was happy Rori had backed into the parking space.

Rori ran around the car and jumped into the driver's seat. Neil was barely in the car when she floored the pedal. The guard was only about thirty feet away as she flashed her high beams into his eyes.

The guard held his hand up for them to stop. Neil waved and then covered his face as they drove by.

Neither of them said anything until they drove a couple of miles, then they both started to speak at the same time.

"What the hell was that all about?"

"What was the Vice President doing in that room?" Rori said. "What was that shot for? And what about the secret drawer?"

"What secret drawer?" Neil asked.

"I forgot—you weren't with me."

"Calm down, tiger. Talk slowly."

"Just shut the fuck up," Rori said. "The nurse went into the other room and was messing around with something."

"Is 'something' a new journalistic term?" Neil said, as he sipped at his flask. "And has anyone ever told you that you swear too much?"

"Sure."

"That's it . . . *sure?* What'd you tell them?"

"I told them to shut the fuck up."

"Think about it."

"I'll think about it, now shut up and listen. She was doing something under the counter, and then at the other end a hidden drawer popped out. The nurse went down and pulled out records, wrote something down and went back to the other end…and the drawer closed."

"The drawer disappeared?" Neil said.

"Yeah, just like you're going to one of these days when I bury your ass," Rori said.

Neil chuckled. "I'll have to tell my wife how you treat me. If I disappear, you're to blame."

"What are you talking about? Maggie will be in on it."

"What we saw tonight is serious shit," Neil said. "They've got some sort of cover-up going on here, and I don't know what it is. I'll have to let my gut work a little. I've got an inkling, but let's see what tomorrow brings. The Vice President was supposed to have a broken leg, but I didn't see a cast. Did you?"

"Nope. He was walking around—or was he dancing by himself?" Rori said. She paused a moment, then put her hand over her mouth. "Oh my god, this is so exciting. Neil, what do we do?"

"Not sure, but whatever we do we have to be careful. Politicians get angry if you show them up or take their money. It's obvious there's more to this than what we were told."

Chapter Twenty-Three

The guard from the parking lot called down to the gatehouse. "Have you seen anyone down there, or denied anyone entrance tonight?"

"No," the guard at the gatehouse said.

"Lt. Snedicker and I will be right down. Let everyone know." After hanging up, he went into the main building and spoke with Snedicker. Under normal circumstances, the lieutenant wouldn't be at the hospital at this hour, but with the VP being admitted, he immediately returned. After explaining what happened in the parking lot, they both headed to the gatehouse, where they stopped and talked to the guard.

"Who did the last rounds tonight?" the lieutenant asked.

"I did," the gatehouse guard said.

"Did you observe anything unusual?"

"No sir. Except I thought I heard something in the bushes, but when I investigated, I didn't see anything. I think it was just the wind or a raccoon."

"Lock the door and the gate down and then get into the car," the lieutenant said.

They drove down to the area where the guard heard the noise. Snedicker and the two guards got out of the car, and the guard pointed toward the direction where he walked into the bushes.

"I put my light all over there and there, but I didn't see a thing," he said.

"Give me your flashlight," the lieutenant said. He walked over to the bushes almost exactly as the guard had done. The rain that had plagued Election Day subsided hours ago. The lieutenant went in further than the guard had and spotted a matted down area. He noticed what appeared to be footprints, but he couldn't tell how many. He moved the light all around, and noticed something on the ground. He bent over and picked up a gold shamrock earring. The lieutenant slipped it into his pocket.

The two guards stood out at the edge of the driveway, waiting for the lieutenant to return.

"Stay here. I'll be right back," Snedicker said.

He walked toward the villas, almost in the exact same path Neil and Rori had taken. He could see tracks through the grass. He continued to walk up to the window by the nurses' station and he could see someone had been there, too. He continued around the buildings until he walked up to the Vice President's window. There, he saw two separate sets of footprints. The lieutenant was visibly shaking with anger. His jaw tightened and his fists clenched. He took his foot and erased any evidence of footprints. When he returned to the nurse's window, he did the same, and then went back to the two guards.

"Get in the car," the lieutenant said. They did as they were told, and waited until the lieutenant got in the passenger's seat. Turning to the backseat and pointing to the guard from the gatehouse, he said, "You know, I ought to fire you right now."

The guard said nothing.

"And you," he said, pointing to the other guard. "You should have pulled your gun out to stop the car. What we have here is a breach of security. I ought to kick both of you out onto the street."

"Boss, I looked into the bushes," the gate guard said.

"Shut up," the lieutenant said. "I don't want to hear either of you mention this ever again. I'm going to have to get this cleaned up, and if I can't, you could both lose more than your pensions."

Chapter Twenty-Four

"Rori, a good journalist must develop sources and be willing to follow their instinct," Neil said, as they drove back to D.C. "That instinct may thread a fine needle, but you do what you have to do in order to get the story."

"Yeah, yeah. I've heard the instinct shit before."

"Are you mocking me?" Neil asked.

"I guess I am. What are we going to do?" Rori asked.

"I'm not sure. I'm mulling it over."

"Is that like moseying with your mind?"

"Never thought about it that way, but it sounds about right. I've always had this feeling in my gut. I don't know about others, but I get this intuitive sense. I don't know how to explain it, but it comes over me."

"Like what happened to me the moment I met Todd," Rori said.

"What do you mean?"

"He tried to corner me in the stairwell a couple of hours ago. He was drunk."

"Did you put him in his place?"

"What do you think? We had a discussion. He won't bother asking me out again."

"Must have been a pretty good discussion. Glad to see you kids are playing nicely."

"I introduced him to Jack," Rori said.

"Who's Jack?" Neil said.

"Jack's my friend," Rori said and patted herself under her left breast.

"Oh, so it's true? No wonder you don't get many dates. Do me a favor and keep Jack where he belongs," Neil said.

"I will unless you misbehave." Rori laughed.

"Okay, so what are your thoughts? I mean how do you think we should handle this?"

"Why not just put it out there? Why don't we just call them on it and say they're all lying bastards. When they deny it, we can tell them we know better."

"No, no, not yet," Neil said. "I think we better see what they say tomorrow. We need to do a little more detective work."

"What I'm really ready for is a little shut-eye, but other than that I'm damn ready to see what we can dig up. You know, Neil, I like being around you. I've always liked being around older people."

"I do fit into that category of being older, don't I? I like being around younger people. I like to share my knowledge and my experiences . . . I guess. Hopefully it will keep others from making the same mistakes. I never had anyone help me out until I already made a few. Or perhaps there was someone and I just wouldn't listen. I can be a hard-nosed shithead from time to time. Irishmen have been known to be little a bit of know-it-alls."

Rori sat listening as Neil talked and sipped, while she chauffeured him back to D.C.

"Listen, we need to approach this whole thing in a different manner. This is not like an ordinary story. I don't know what's going on with the Vice President, but something is happening. I think you and I should just keep this to ourselves, agreed?"

"I'll follow your lead," Rori said.

"If Willowdale got a little drunk and fell, that could be the whole deal. They seem to be going through a lot of trouble just to cover up a little booze, though. Tomorrow we may find he's okay and he just bruised his leg in the fall. Hell, I've fallen a lot, but then again I'm not the Vice President.

"Should we load something online?"

"Nah, it's not worth the grief we'd get. The Secret Service would be knocking on our doors by the time we hit the bed. It's best to think like an attorney. Know the answers before you ask the questions, and don't put all your cards on the table until we know a little more."

Rori didn't like Neil's strategy. She was unaccustomed to biting her tongue and waiting. *Somebody's going to pick up the scent and beat us.*

"Stop right there," Neil said.

"What do you mean? I didn't say a thing."

"I know what you're thinking. You're thinking you'd like to start the ball rolling. File a report on what you think we know, or you'd like to go to your editor and let him know what we saw. If you do that, the editor would put you with someone else—someone other than me. He'd definitely put you with someone with more experience than you have. He'd probably think I'd fuck it up. You know my habit and all. But he knows I have a lot shit in my head I can teach you and it'll be no time before you're on your own. Besides, I'll probably be out of here in another year.

"I could be wrong. But if they assign you to someone else, trust me, that guy wouldn't share a thing with you. Both of us will end up with shit. May as well put our names in the obituary section. You have to listen to me or we're done right now. You can go your way, and I'll go mine."

Rori's face turned a bit red, thinking Neil was picking up what she was thinking. *What else could he pick up with this instinct thing?* She could feel the blush, but it was dark in the car, and Neil couldn't see her face.

"I think you should put that flask away. You have to drive yourself home from my place, so cool it, old man. I'm just trying to blaze my own trail. I understand you do have this instinct thing going for you, but let me make a name for myself."

Neil let Rori jabber on, hoping she'd run out of steam and cool herself down. She pulled up to the curb and started to get out, but Neil grabbed her right shoulder and pulled her back. His tone had softened some, but was still compelling.

"Listen, we'll get some sleep and then I'll give you a call. We'll see what Austin has to say, just don't go running to our editor. I meant what I said. Let's say I pick you up around noon? I doubt if anything will happen before then."

"You okay to drive? If you're not, leave your car here and I'll get you a taxi."

"I'm fine," Neil said. He got out of the passenger seat and walked around to the driver's side. "I'll call you later."

Chapter Twenty-Five

Neil was a creature of habit, and despite being up until 3:30 in the morning, he was out of bed by 7:30. Taking his time with his coffee and waiting for the effects of last night's booze to wear off, he had a talk with his wife.

"I think I'm getting a little old for this late-night stuff," Neil said. He gave Maggie a big hug. Of course, he couldn't resist grabbing her ass.

"You're the same pig I married thirty years ago," Maggie said, and then grabbed his ass.

"And who's the pig now?"

"Takes one to know one."

Despite having remnants of Jameson flowing through his blood, Neil was out the door at 8:30. It was no different than any other day.

Neil headed to the B&B Bar. It was a sleazy joint he sometimes visited early in the morning. The locals, when they had too much to drink, called it the Bucket of Blood. There'd be no reporters, and that's what he liked. It was only a short drive, but it wasn't always open this early.

Neil pulled his old boat, an early 90s Oldsmobile, into an alley. He banged it into a dumpster. Another dent.

"Who's there?" John asked hearing the banging on the back door. "We're still closed."

"Come on, John. It's me, Neil."

Neil listened to John unlocking the back door, throwing back four deadbolts and removing a metal bar.

When the door opened, Neil smelled sour beer and dirty mop water. He did his best to ignore it, but covered his nose. Then he looked at John.

"What happened to you?"

John was sporting a black eye and cuts on both sides of his face. There were other wounds, one of which made him limp.

"I guess I'm not as tough as I thought," he said. "There was a time when nobody could kick my ass."

"How's the other guy?"

"Can't tell you."

"Why's that?"

"He was gone by the time I woke up."

"I suppose that's a good thing," Neil said.

"Damn right it is. If he were still here, I'd probably be in the hospital," John said, and then burst out into a deep cigarette laugh.

"I would have brought you flowers and a drink."

Neil maneuvered through the back room, skirting bags of garbage and empty liquor boxes. A sink off to the side had grease creeping up the side and was filled with day-old mop water. He forged his way into the bar with his hand covering his mouth and nose. The smell there wasn't much better.

"I'll take care of myself," Neil said. "You can finish up what you're doing."

Neil was one of the few John would allow to go behind the bar.

"Can I buy you an eye-opener?" Neil asked.

"Yeah. Just pour me what you're having and leave it at the end of the bar. I'll sip it as I finish up."

Neil grabbed two water glasses off the back of the bar. Ignoring the film on the glasses, he filled them halfway with Jameson. He placed one at the end of the bar for John and the other where he could get it on the other side. Grabbing the TV remote, he moved to a stool on the other side.

"Okay if I put all the stools down for you?"

"Sure, I've already cleaned around there."

Neil took a look down the outside and could see it had been swept but not much more. It had last century's grime lingering on the floor, encased in yesterday's booze and spit. Neil pulled the stools down one by one.

This early in the month, the locals' pockets were still lined with cash. Having paid back their IOUs, they were eager to show their faces at the bar again, at least until the end of the month.

Neil pulled himself up to the bar and leaned his head solemnly in his hands. Mumbling to himself, some prayer-like words, and then reached over and wrapped his fingers around his glass.

"Here's to you," he said and drank a mouthful.

"What'd you say?" John asked.

"Oh, checking on a memory," Neil said. "And here's to you, John."

John stopped by and toasted Neil back. "And to you, old friend." John took a couple of mouthfuls.

"Careful with that stuff. Before long, you'll be thinking you can kick someone's ass again," Neil said laughing.

Neil looked to the glass doors where three locals were peering through the window. The café curtains blocked them from seeing Neil and John, but they could see shadows moving about.

"I guess the natives are getting restless," John said.

"Turn on some lights so I can see what I'm drinking."

"As if that ever stopped you." John turned on the rest of the lights and proceeded to unlock the doors. "Take it easy, boys. There's plenty for all."

"Bobby, how you doing?" Neil asked one of the patrons, an old man whose face was ruddy with gin blossoms.

"Oh, I've seen better days. But who gives a flying fuck? And you know what?"

"What?" Neil asked.

"I don't give a fuck either." He turned to John. "Let's get the magic juice flowing here." His voice was garbled, and he started laughing to himself, as if he'd made the funniest joke in history.

Neil glanced up to the TV. WETA was having a morning discussion about the election. This was Arlington's PBS station and had been a go-to for Neil for many years. "Did you vote, Bobby?" Neil asked.

"No. I wouldn't waste my time with those two. Together they wouldn't make a whole brain." Bobby again laughed at his own humor. His toothless smile made him look older than he was.

"Good one, Bobby," one of his fellow drinkers said.

"You have a point," Neil said.

A gay couple who were regulars settled at the short end of the bar. "The usual, boys?" John asked.

"Unless some friend came along and left us some drinking money."

"That didn't happen," John said. He poured three drafts and then grabbed some cheap rye whiskey called Five Joes and poured three shots.

Neil squirmed with chills at the thought of the cheap booze. He turned his interest to the news on the TV then switched to the national news.

"We have breaking news. Vice President Warren Willowdale fell last night, and we're just getting pictures in of him with a broken leg."

"Holy shit," Neil said.

He got up and moved over to a booth to give Rori a call on his cell phone.

Her phone rang and rang. "Come on, Rori," he said. "Get your ass up." While he waited for her to answer, he walked back to the bar and got his drink. Bobby was already eyeing it. Finally Rori picked up.

"Hello," she said in a grumpy, barely audible tone. It was a tone Neil had never heard before from his partner.

"Get up, Rori. Get your TV on," he said.

Rori was so tired she had forgotten to turn her cell phone off. She felt like she hadn't even slept. She flipped the TV on and then said, "I don't see anything."

"It's off now, but they just showed the Vice President in a cast lying in bed," Neil said. "They said he was put into a cast around 12:30 a.m. We were there way after that and he was walking around without a cast. Do you know what this means, Rori?" Neil said.

"Well kind of..." she said, yawning.

"I'll tell you what it means. It means we've got a story. Get yourself ready and I'll be over in an hour," he said as he hung up the phone.

Neil put a twenty on the bar and said, "Keep the change. Here, Bobby, try this." He handed him the rest of his drink.

Neil walked out the door as Bobby took a sip. His eyes lit up, and soon both members of the gay couple were asking for a sip, too.

"No, I don't want to ruin your taste buds," Bobby said and smiled as he finished it off.

* * *

Neil pulled up to the curb where Rori was waiting, in the same spot where she had passed the vehicle back to Neil just a few hours ago.

"Don't you ever sleep?" Rori asked as she dropped into the passenger seat.

"Plenty of time to do that after I'm dead," he said.

"Where we going?"

Neil's thoughts bounced around as he tried to make a decision.

"TV said a news conference was going to be held in two hours. I've been to a ton and they never start on time. We could go there and see what they have to say, or we could go back out to the hospital to see if we could shake the tree. Maybe some good things will fall down to us," Neil said.

"As long as it doesn't fall on us." Rori wasn't used to this kind of work. She was doing things never taught at Syracuse. When she graduated, she wasn't sure she wanted to be in a boring job, so she joined the Marines. It was a short stint—she was kicked out near the end of boot camp. She denied starting the fight, said it was the lieutenant who accosted her, prompting her to deck him and kick him in the face. The Marines didn't believe her.

After leaving the Marines, she couldn't find a job in the bad economy so she joined the Staples management training program. That lasted a year and a half. It was the same old story. A supervisor putting his hands on her and promising promotion. It didn't end well when Rori showed up at the man's house and asked the guy's wife if she could fuck her husband again. By the time she got to work, the fireworks had already started. When the supervisor pulled Rori into the office, she gave him a quick knee to the groin and then an elbow to the side of his neck. Any further harassment and she would file a lawsuit. She stayed until she had secured a job as a reporter at the *Washington Independent Review Online.*

Rori was a diamond in the rough. She had finished ninety-eight percent of boot camp in the Marines and had taught her to be tough and to stand her ground. Staples taught her some management, and that freaks were everywhere, which brought in her Marine training. She was hoping Neil would teach her how to be a good reporter.

Rori had something on her mind. The fact that she had to kick Neil out of the driver's seat last night bothered her. She dreamt Neil had driven them off the road and into a tree. She wasn't sure if it was her right to speak about it. It was about follow-through and having a partner that wasn't going to get her killed. It was about working with a troubled soul.

"I have to ask you something," Rori said.

"Shoot."

Rori took a deep breath. "Are you going to stick with me on this whole story, or are you just going through the motions until you get tired of it and retreat to Clancy's or that other place you go off to? Or are you going to get me killed while you're half-drunk?"

Neil pulled over so quickly the car almost went up over the curb.

"Why, you little bitch. What gives you the right to speak to me like that? I was out here tracking stories long before you were ever brought into this world. Don't go talking about me finishing a job." Neil's shouts volleyed inside the vehicle.

Rori wasn't about to take anyone's shit. Aunt Charley taught her not to.

"Don't you come off to me like you're the king of reporting and I don't know anything," Rori said. "My life hasn't been all sugar and spice. I've earned everything I've fuckin' got. If it upsets you that I bring up a well-known fact, then bite me, old man. I don't need your 'holier than thou' attitude. I'm not one of those blonde bimbos. I just—"

"Get out of my car," he said.

Rori didn't budge. She turned toward him with a look of defiance. "I'm not going any place, got it?" she said, pointing at Neil.

"You'll get out of here or I'll drag your ass out," he said.

"You won't drag my ass out of anywhere. I'll shoot you."

Rori was steaming. She looked Neil in the eye and actually put her hand on Jack.

Neil started laughing. "'I'll shoot you'," Neil said mocking Rori. "Boy, I got you." Neil couldn't stop laughing. "God, wait till I tell my friends at the B&B."

"You don't have any friends," Rori said.

Neil continued laughing. "I've gotta' take a piss."

"I was just going to tell you I felt I could trust you," Rori said. "You're such an asshole."

Neil was angry, but this was Rori, and despite him being pissed off she brought up his drinking, he knew she was right. The more he argued with her, the more he realized something had to change. It just wasn't all that easy. He started to say more but stopped when Rori's words reached his brain and he heard the word *trust*.

"What do you mean 'trust'?" he said.

"Forget what I said. I don't trust you at all."

"I had you when I said I was going to drag your ass out of the car. If you could have seen your face…"

"Now I know Maggie's going to help me make you disappear—especially if you're like this at home."

"If you say so," Neil said.

"I need to be serious," Rori said.

"Okay, serious talk," Neil said, chuckling.

"You have a reputation of starting out like a reporter but ending up at the bar. I've got my whole life ahead of me. I need to know I can trust you to help me through all of this. I can do it myself or get others to work with me, but if I do it myself I'm likely to miss something."

The car was silent for a few seconds, but to Neil it felt like hours. He looked over at her sheepishly.

"So you trust me, huh? He took another sip from his flask then offered it to Rori.

She grabbed it, and took a long sip.

"Hold on there. I didn't say drink it all." Neil took the flask back, thinking about another swig, but resisted and put it back into his jacket pocket. He then placed his hand on her shoulder and said, "You're now hereby under the training and care of Neil O'Connor Trust Reporting School. I'll not let a little Jameson come between us."

Rori touched his hand and said, "Drive on, you old man."

"Which do we do? News conference or hospital?" Neil asked.

"Both," she said.

"The girl wants to live dangerously."

Neil pulled the car back into traffic. "Get your tablet out—no get your paper and pencil out and make some notes for questions."

"Shit, you rushed me so much I left it on my kitchen table. Go back and I'll get it."

"No, just take mine from my briefcase. You can't just rely on technology. Sometimes you have to rely on old-fashioned footwork, and that starts with pad and pencil. Pencil's don't freeze up or run batteries down."

Rori reached back and pulled out a hardcover notebook from his briefcase.

"Can I use this?"

"No. Put it back," Neil said.

"Why? What's in this?"

"Put it back," Neil said.

Rori held the notebook up and said, "These are your notes on the Austin and Ann—the *bangers*—aren't they? Can I look?"

"They are, and no you cannot. They're for my eyes only."

"I thought we were partners"

"Not yet, put it back. There's another pad and pencil in there."

Rori reluctantly dropped the notebook back into his briefcase and pulled out a pad of paper.

"Okay, non-partner, what do you want me to put down?"

"Make a list of what we know. Others will ask similar questions, but they don't know what we know. We'll get our questions on the record. When we get there, I want you to go ahead and ask the first questions, and I'll follow up. You go to the left side of the room, and I'll go to the right. No one will think anything of the questions. No one will give me a second thought."

"What do you suggest?" Rori asked.

"Let's not be cute about this. What do we know? The Vice President fell, he may have broken his leg, he was supposed to have surgery, his leg was supposed to be in a cast, but wasn't," Neil said. "Stick with his broken leg and let's see if he had to have the surgery. I'll ask if there were any other injuries. That's something we don't know, but it will be a reasonable question. If he says no, I'll follow up to see if he's able to walk around. We know the answers to two of those questions. We can take it from there." Neil glanced at the sheet of paper she was scribbling on. "Slow down, honey. I need to be able to read it."

Rori smiled.

* * *

The news conference was at the same hotel as the night before. Neil let Rori out at the street corner and went to the garage to park. When Rori walked into the hotel, she didn't notice the man in the MRLC uniform standing off to the side.

Lt. Snedicker recognized her from the security camera footage. He recognized the car she got out of, too.

He entered the hotel and ran up to the mezzanine level, knowing an entrance there led to the parking garage. He reached the top of the stairs just as Neil came through the doors.

Neil walked right by him, oblivious, but the man noticed him.

Neil and Rori took their positions, away from each other, but within eyesight. The room was smaller than the ballroom they were in the night before. Once in position, they looked over at each other. Rori gave Neil a wink, along with her patented smile.

Neil's eye caught a man in the back corner of the room. He looked a bit out of place. His uniform was similar to that of a policeman—perhaps hotel security. Neil couldn't make out what it said on the front pocket.

Never mind, he thought, as his eyes glanced off the man and back to Rori.

The room went quiet as Austin Garcia walked up to the podium.

"Good afternoon," Austin said. "I'm sure after the long night it feels like we never went to bed."

Banger, Rori thought and then smiled.

"Come on, tell your lies. Enough of the bullshit opening statements," Neil mumbled. Other reporters nearby looked over toward him and smirked.

Austin read a statement reiterating what he said the night before about how the Vice President had fallen. He told reporters it was confirmed Willowdale had broken the same leg he broke skiing four years ago, and then asked for questions. Several reporters asked general questions before Rori got a chance to ask hers.

"You said the Vice President broke his leg and had to have surgery, is that correct?" Rori asked.

"Yes, that's correct. He had to have surgery to install some pins. He's in a temporary cast. Once things heal in a week or so, he'll be put into a walking cast. That's what his doctors say," Austin said.

Round one was right on cue, and he even added some more incriminating information, Rori thought.

Neil noticed Rori smile at the answers, and then he too smiled. He raised his hand a couple of times, but Austin seemed to purposely ignore him. Neil cleared his throat and got louder, as Austin was calling on another reporter.

"Were there any other injuries?" Neil yelled to Austin. The reporters in the room went silent.

"And Austin," Neil said, "is the Vice President up and walking around?"

Austin's face turned red. "There's no need to yell," he said.

Neil shouted back. "I wouldn't be yelling if you weren't trying to ignore me. Were there any other injuries and is he up and walking around?"

Austin's face was beet-red. He took a deep breath and a slow sip of water.

"No, there were no other injuries, and no, he's not going to be walking around until sometime later today. I spoke to the doctor this morning, and he said it may be at least until tomorrow before he can move around."

"You're saying he hasn't been able to get out of bed?" Neil said again.

"Correct," Austin said.

The door in the back of the room opened and closed. Neil turned at the sound of the door closing and saw the man in the uniform was gone.

The news conference was short. Austin thanked everyone and stepped down from the podium.

Neil motioned to Rori with his head, letting her know it was time to leave. Rori walked to the back room and headed to the garage.

Neil walked toward Austin.

Austin saw Neil coming. He turned to his right, away from the lingering press and walked quickly to get away from him. He was tired and wasn't up for the usual brawl. But it was too late.

"Sorry about that," Neil said. "Just trying to file a story today."

"Forget about it," Austin said. "I did pass you up. I'm sorry. It was unprofessional on my part."

Austin shocked even grumpy Neil with his admittance. That was exactly what Austin wanted to do—defuse the situation and pretend to take the blame. Austin knew he made it hard for people to dislike him because he would either come at them with his cleverness or his so-called honesty.

Neil smiled and began to walk away, but Austin called him back.

"You know, Neil, you ought to get your problem under control."

Neil's fedora was tipped high in the front. It always got higher the more he drank.

"What the hell business is it of yours?"

Austin puffed up his chest, like he was about to do battle, but said nothing.

Neil's eyes were burning a hole into Austin. "I didn't say anything to you about *your* problem."

"And what problem is that?"

"Lying," Neil said and walked away.

Austin stood there, steaming, when a bellhop walked over and handed him a message in a small envelope. Austin read the note.

Please come up to the hotel suite after the news conference.
–Mrs. Warren Willowdale.

Austin shook his head. *I didn't know she came back to the hotel.*

Rori was waiting for Neil when he reached the garage.

"What took so long?" she asked.

"I had to apologize to Austin. I can't afford to be on his bad side. The son of bitch kept ignoring me and I can't stand that," Neil said. "He was okay until he made a comment."

"What did he say?" Rori asked.

"Doesn't matter."

"Did you say anything back?" Rori asked, knowing Neil's often-combative demeanor.

"I told him he shouldn't lie."

"You know life would be so much better if you got rid of that flask. I think guys like Austin would feel a bit different if you only had a pen or computer in your hand."

Neil looked across the tops of the car as they prepared to get in, pulled the flask out, and took a swig.

"You know what?"

"What?" Rori said.

"You talk too much, and Austin thinks too much of himself."

Chapter Twenty-Six

Neil drove out of the garage and turned right, taking no notice of the Ram pickup behind him pulling away from the curb.

"Do you remember the way to the hospital?" Rori asked.

"Kind of," Neil said. "But if I don't, I'm sure you'll correct me."

"Bet your ass I will."

Neil smiled and reached into his jacket, grabbed his flask and offered it to Rori.

"No thanks. Once was enough for me. You ought to watch yourself," she said. "Do you want me to drive?"

Neil chuckled. "I've been driving like this for some time. When I take a swig it helps settle my thoughts. I think my system has adjusted over time. It's like exercising. When you start, you're slow and you ache the first few times. After a week or two, the aches are gone and you can go forever."

"Strange way to look at it, but I don't think your liver feels that way."

"Well, you can't live forever, and I'm not sure I want to." Neil smiled as he pulled onto the exit ramp.

He put his flask away and they took a left toward the hospital. As they came around the curve on their approach to the facility, a non-descript beige Dodge Ram pickup, five hundred yards ahead of them, turned into the driveway and drove around toward the back. The cold, rainy weather of the day before was gone and Rori was enjoying the sun. Its rays were caressing her face and blanketed her body as she thought about Aunt Charley.

Almost a decade ago, Aunt Charley and Rori sat on the front porch viewing the ski area of Song Mountain just south of Syracuse. Rori was a senior in high school.

"You know, you're seventeen and will be going off to college in a year or so. Have you given any thought of what you'll study?" Aunt Charley said.

Aunt Charley was an uncommon mother. Never having raised children before, she treated Rori as though she was a friend. It was different than when her parents were alive.

"I think I'd like to go into journalism."

"Think that's wise? Most newspapers are defunct."

"Aunt Charley, you have to keep up with the latest. Newspapers are mostly online. They're making more money in advertising online than they ever did in print. They still need good journalists, and tablets make it easy to stay independent."

"Good. Stay independent and don't let anyone use you as a doormat."

"Can I shoot them if they do?" Rori said.

"Yep," Aunt Charley said.

* * *

A guard stepped out of the hospital just as Rori and Neil were walking in. Neil stopped and looked at him. "Howard? Howard Shapleigh, is that you?" The man was older and much bigger, but Neil recognized his big grin and held out his hand. "I haven't seen you in years, since you moved out west. How are you doing?"

"Neil O'Connor, you old goat," Howard said with his big hand held out. "Haven't seen you—I can't even remember the last time we saw each other. What are you doing here? No one's sick, I hope."

"Just trying to check up on the Vice President's condition," Neil said.

"I wouldn't know anything about that. I only work here part-time. I just cover the desk for breaks, walk the floor, check locked doors, make copies—easy things like that, just for beer money."

Neil's instinct's kicked in. "Do you think we could have a beer sometime?" he asked.

"Well, why not? But I'm just on my way out," Howard said.

"Come on, I haven't seen you in years, and now you're going to disappear just like that?"

Howard putting his hand to the side of his face. "I don't know…"

then he looked over at Rori. "Well, okay. There's a bar a few miles down the road. Take a right out of the driveway and then you'll see it on the left. It's The Black Sow. Turn onto Catnip Road, can't miss it. I usually stop for a quick one on my way home."

"We just have to stop in here for a few minutes then we'll be right there." Neil shook hands with Howard and went inside the hospital.

Daytime in the hospital was a lot busier. Once they were buzzed inside, they approached the desk where an armed guard stood.

Neil introduced himself and Rori to the guard.

"I'd—we'd like to get a pass to see the Vice President," Neil said.

Rori said nothing, just observed Neil and the people working near the desk area. The guard said nothing. He turned and walked away. Halfway down the hall, he entered an office.

"You have such a way with people," Rori said. "Why don't we just threaten these bastards?" Her temper was starting to rise.

"Stay calm," Neil said. "You can't just come in and shoot the place up. Didn't your aunt teach you any patience?"

"What you're seeing is what she taught me."

A man came out of the office, and walked toward them with the original guard in tow. There was a familiarity about the man at a distance, but Neil couldn't pull his face from his memory. He had a lot of medals hanging on his uniform. *Another wannabe.*

The guard got closer and the familiarity grew, but Neil still couldn't put it together. It was gnawing at him and seemed to be just under the surface. His whiskey-saturated brain couldn't recall.

The man stepped to the front desk and introduced himself as Lieutenant Snedicker. Neil re-introduced himself and Rori.

Rori couldn't hold her tongue any longer. "We'd like to see the Vice President."

Lieutenant Snedicker gave a wry smile. "I'm sorry, I'm under strict orders. Unless you are approved by the office of the Vice President, I cannot oblige you."

Rori stared at him. "Listen, you Barney Fife wannabe, if you can't give us permission, get on the phone and find someone who can."

The lieutenant wasn't amused. "It'll do you no good to throw idle threats."

"Who's making idle threats?" Rori said, looking to the phone. She wanted to reach over the counter and smack the receiver against his head.

"Take it easy, Rori. The lieutenant has a job to do."

Rori looked to Neil and wanted to smack him, too.

Neil turned back to the lieutenant and apologized. "I'm sorry. These young people are so impatient."

The lieutenant relaxed a bit. "The best I can do for you is ask the doctor to come and talk to you."

"That's a good start," Neil said and gave Rori a wink, as the lieutenant called the doctor.

After a brief conversation, the lieutenant hung up the phone. "The doctor is just finishing some rounds and will be here in a couple of minutes. Please take a seat over there."

Neil sat while Rori paced the sterile entryway. The lieutenant stared at Rori. After several minutes, a man in a long, white coat came through a pair of double doors, carrying a bag of microwave popcorn. He was a little over six feet and balding. He stopped at the front desk, where he talked to Lieutenant Snedicker. He then walked over to Neil and Rori with a big smile on his face.

"How do you do? I'm Dr. Moskowitz. Care for some popcorn?"

"No thanks," Neil said.

Rori ignored the offer and just stared at the doctor.

"How may I help you?"

Neil introduced himself and then started to introduce Rori, but she interrupted and introduced herself.

"We're reporters from the *Washington Independent Review Online* and would like to see the Vice President."

"You're not the only ones inquiring, but I'll tell you the same as I've told the others. The Vice President has requested no one be let in, and I have to adhere to his wishes," Dr. Moskowitz said.

"Can you tell us of the Vice President's condition?" Neil asked.

The doctor hesitated, but then said, "I can only tell you he is doing well and will be out of here in no time."

The lieutenant, who was now standing a few feet away at the desk, looked toward Neil and their eyes locked onto each other. Neil realized he had seen the lieutenant at the news conference. He was the man in the back, guarding the door.

But he hadn't been guarding the door—he was looking for someone. He was trying to see our faces. The lieutenant knew who we were.

His stare was contemptible.

"If I may be discreet and off the record," Dr. Moskowitz said.

"Of course you can. We're not vultures. We're trying to get a story."

Dr. Moskowitz smiled. "Of course you are." He continued in a lower tone. "From what I gather, the Vice President is a little embarrassed about the situation. You know, losing the election and then breaking his leg. I think he feels a big cloud has been cast over him. Do you see what I mean?"

Neil nodded. "I know exactly what you mean. It does feel a bit like a cloud, doesn't it? Boy, a few weeks ago he was a shoe-in to be president and today he's in hiding at a private facility. Sure does seem like he's making the cloud bigger by the day."

The doctor's smile washed away, and his eyes became cold. "Well, I'm sorry I couldn't be of more help." He turned and walked away.

As the doctor left, the lieutenant approached Rori.

"I found this on the steps last night." The lieutenant held up a gold shamrock earring. "You were here, weren't you?"

Rori answered before she had time to think. "Yes I was and I did lose one."

He handed it to Rori and excused himself.

"I'll be seeing you," Neil said to the lieutenant as he was walking away.

The lieutenant stopped and turned back toward them. "I'm sure you will."

* * *

"Keep an eye on those two, if you know what I mean," the doctor said to the lieutenant.

"I have already been checking them out. He's a washed up drunk and she's just a pup," the lieutenant said, staring out the window to make sure they left.

Pulling out of the driveway, Neil explained what he surmised. "The lieutenant was at the hotel, standing in the back corner. It didn't connect before I just saw him. He was looking for someone—you and me."

Rori felt a little scared and a little pissed about being tracked. She patted Jack with her hand and said, "I think I need a drink."

Chapter Twenty-Seven

The Black Sow was in its own lot next to a small diner.

Neil pulled in and Rori immediately piped up. "How convenient, you get drunk at the bar and go next door for coffee and breakfast."

"I'm sure you've done that a few times," Neil said.

Rori smiled and said. "More than a few."

Walking into the bar, they spotted Howard sitting in a booth next to a row of windows at the far end of the room.

The Black Sow was a hangout for the locals as well as hospital workers. It was mostly empty during the day except for some regulars. As the shifts changed at the hospital, the nurses and any other crew workers stopped by for one or two for the road, which usually led to three or four.

On payday the place was packed. Still, it was an old bar. The sour smell of beer hit you as soon as you passed through the doors. Rori had an instant memory of a place her Aunt Charley had taken her, called The Scythe Tree Inn. The bar itself was sticky and grimy. Locals didn't care. It was *their* spot, like every other local spot across the country. This spot . . . was one that hadn't been eaten up by the Washington overflow, although it was getting closer by the year.

Wooden barstools against a mahogany bar greeted visitors. The lights were kept dim, making it feel more mysterious and dangerous. The windows all had café curtains, which gave the booths more privacy. In the back of the bar was a pool table and shuffleboard. It wasn't a place you'd take a first date, unless said date wore cutoffs and was adorned with tattoos.

"Howard, you must forgive me, I never introduced you to my associate. I must be getting old. This is Rori Cahill. She works with me at the *Washington Independent Review Online,"* Neil said.

Howard looked her over, put his beer down and extended his hand. "Pleased to meet you." He immediately started talking as though someone wound him up with a key sticking out of his back. "It's like I told you. I'm just making beer money, and I didn't even know the Vice President was at the hospital until this morning. I'm not even allowed to go down into those—what do they call 'em…villas? Don't want to get mixed up in politics. Had to deal with that shit all my life."

"How's that going?" Rori asked. Rori looked Howard over as he pondered her question. His hair was still thick. His skin was dried out and hung loosely around his jowls like an old carpetbag.

"Not bad, but my wife died two days after I retired. I had to get out of the house. That's why I found this job. Things are getting better. It's amazing how you plan all your life and then bam, all your plans go up in smoke in a wink."

Howard took a big gulp of beer, as tears gathered in the corner of his eyes. Putting his glass down, and looked at Rori. "It's much better since I started here. There are a lot of nice people at the hospital. I'm even seeing one of the nurses." He perked up when he mentioned the nurse.

"This nurse treats you pretty good? Kind of gives the heart a jump-start?" Neil said jokingly.

"Oh yeah, she gives me a jump-start all the time," Howard said. His smile grew as he talked about her

"Does she work down at the villas?" Rori asked.

"No, no. She works up at the main area with all the druggies. I mean—sometimes she does some overnight stuff just before they admit someone into the villas."

Rori smiled. She watched and listened as Neil started tugging at Howard's threads of info.

"Had she ever been down there?" Rori asked.

"No. She told me it was easier working with druggies than the prima donnas they get down there. All money people, and you can't take a piss without someone knowing it. No, she never wanted to go work there."

Neil and Rori looked at Howard as he spewed the information.

"Let me order a round of beers to toast old times," Neil said.

Howard needed little prodding, for beer or more information.

"So, Howard, you were talking about your nurse friend," Neil said.

"She said she was thinking about going down to work at the villas a while back, because the pay was so good, but then that accident happened. After that, she wanted no part of it."

"What accident?" Neil said. "Here, have another beer."

"A friend of hers, a nurse. I can't remember her name."

"What about the accident, Howard?" Rori said.

Neil looked across the table at her and held his hand up.

She got the message: *Don't be so pushy*. Rori stood. "I'll be right back. I need a snack."

"Can you fill this too?" Neil asked, handing her his flask.

"I'll think about it."

Neil tipped the flask up to his lips, making sure it was empty.

"You know, after you left the neighborhood, it was never the same. The parties got dull without you and me keeping them going. Those were some good times," Neil said.

Howard smiled at those words. "So how's your son? He must be all grown up and married with kids by now?" Howard asked.

Neil hesitated for a moment. "He died. He got hit by a car a couple of years after you moved out west."

"I'm sorry," Howard said.

"Yeah, me too." Then reached for his flask, but found an empty pocket. He reached over and finished Rori's beer in one gulp.

The silence was deafening. Neil looked toward the bar and was glad to see Rori coming back to the table.

"So, Howard, tell us about this accident," Rori said with a big, impatient smile. She reached over and put her hand on top of Howard's.

Howard blushed a bit and continued. "I'm not sure about all the details. I only know secondhand from my nurse friend. You see, her friend kept telling her about how great the pay was. My friend, Maureen—that's her name, Maureen—was going to apply for a job down there, and then the accident happened."

Howard pulled his hand away and took a sip from his beer.

"Maureen's friend, the one who wanted her to come down there to work, got caught with a cell phone and was fired. Cell phones aren't allowed at work. She stopped for a drink at this bar. Bert over there served her. After she left, she went off the road not far from here. She got killed right there at the scene. DOA. The police said she was drunk, but not according to Bert. Of course, no one asked him."

The table went silent. For the first time in a ten-minute span, Howard stopped talking.

"Do you think we could talk to Maureen?" Neil asked. Before Howard could answer, he said, "Tell you what, why don't you and Maureen come for dinner on Saturday night? Maggie would love to see you, and you can introduce Maureen to us all."

"Got a cell phone on you?" Howard asked. "I'm not allowed to carry mine on the grounds, so I leave it at home."

Rori handed him her cell. Howard looked confused on how to use the phone.

"Let me dial. What's the number?" She punched the number in, and then passed it back. When Howard started to talk to Maureen, Rori got up and walked over to talk to Bert, her glass in tow. She flashed her long eyelashes, showing off her green eyes.

"Can you get me two more?" she said sliding her glass toward him. "I'll take the same glass. It's seasoned already."

"Girl after my own heart," Bert said. "Have a seat."

Rori started to get onto a barstool, but felt its stickiness. "I think I'll stand."

Rori smiled at Bert. He looked in his mid-forties, but guessed he was younger by the way he moved behind the bar. His hair was messed up, and sported a two-day-old beard.

Bert smiled back.

Rori took the opportunity to start asking him questions. She was learning things from her old companion, but Rori knew how to shake her ass and flaunt her tits with a smile (in that order) long before she met Neil. Still, she was starting to understand his "instinct."

"What's your name?" Rori asked.

"Bert. Bert's good," he said.

"So is it Bert—Bert Good or just plain Bert?" She gave him a big smile.

"Really it's Bertrand," he said. "Seems my parents thought if they gave me a distinguished name I'd make something of myself. Kind of dumb. As you can see, it didn't work out too well."

"Don't put yourself down. You've got a lot of life left." Rori, still her impatient self, thought, *Enough of this tits and ass bull, let's get down to the real shit.* She handed Bert the money for the beer with an extra ten-dollar tip. "Keep the change."

Bert was all smiles.

"Hey, Bert. My friends and I were just talking about some lady who got killed in an accident a while back, not far from here. Was she in here that day?"

Bert acted a little goofy, and then said in a low voice, "She only had one beer. She said she was just fired, and needed to wash the crap away. I bought it for her. I asked her if she was having more than the one and she said no. I know because I bought it for her. She got up and said goodbyes and walked out the door."

"Was she drunk?" Rori asked.

"No. She was a bigger woman, and I can usually tell if people can't handle their booze."

"Did the police come in and question you?"

"Never did."

"Did you call anyone about it?"

"I was going to, but then I heard stories about that place where she worked. Scared the shit out of me. I decided to keep quiet."

"What kind of stories?"

"Things like people dying for no reason. I mean, the nurses tell me things they shouldn't. The booze opens them up. They say people seem to disappear, too. I think it's just a spooky place.

"Does sound strange. I'd be careful myself," Rori said. "So you were saying something about why you didn't talk to the police."

"Yep, I was going to talk to them, but one day, this lady came in out of the blue. She said she heard the nurse had been in here before she died. She asked me to stay out of it. Said she was working on something and it would be better if I stayed clear of the whole thing."

Rori made some mental notes. "How long after the accident was she in here?"

"I guess it was six to eight weeks later. It was the same time it came out in the news that she was drunk. I know one thing."

"What's that?" Rori said.

"She wasn't drunk when she left here. And the accident happened within fifteen minutes after she walked out the door."

Bert moved closer over the bar toward Rori and lowered his voice even more. "I don't think it was an accident. That's why I stayed out of it."

To Rori, he seemed a little nervous, like someone was listening. "This person who came in here, did you know her? Was anyone with her?"

"Hadn't seen her before. She was sitting at the bar with a man, but he didn't talk, just listened. She asked me off to the side. We walked back by the pool table. After talking to me there, she handed me an envelope."

"An envelope? What the hell for?"

"You're not a cop or something are you?" Bert asked.

"No," Rori said quickly.

"In the envelope was five thousand dollars. She said it was to help me keep quiet about the whole ordeal."

"She just gave you the money and that was it? Interesting. I better get back to the table before the beer gets warm, although I think my buddies would drink it anyway."

Rori reached over the bar on her toes and gave Bert a peck on the check. "I'll be back sometime." Rori let her ass swing as she walked back to the table.

Bert stood there watching.

* * *

When Rori got back to the table, Neil said, "We're all set for Saturday night."

Rori gave one of the beers to Howard but didn't touch hers.

Howard drank his beer down then asked Rori if she was going to finish hers.

Rori pushed it over to Howard.

Neil laughed. "You haven't changed a bit, Howard. Doesn't take much to get your pump primed."

They all had a good laugh, and then Neil excused himself to go to the bathroom.

"You don't like to sip, do you?" Rori said.

"I do for the first one, but by the time I get to the second one, the valve opens up. I've always been a gulper," Howard said. "Neil and I use to have a good time in the old neighborhood. I kinda of hated moving away, but I got an offer out west, and my job here was drying up. It's too bad about Neil's son. He was a cute little one."

Rori looked at him with a blank expression.

"Oh…you don't—I probably shouldn't have said anything. He just told me when you went up to the bar."

"What happened?" Rori asked.

"All he said was he got hit by a car then changed the subject."

Just then, Neil came out of the bathroom. Rori and Howard were quiet as Neil sat down. Rori's was finding it hard to hold herself together. The experience of losing a child would be enough to drive anyone off the deep end. Her thoughts slipped back to her parents' deaths.

"You two are looking at me like I pissed on myself. See you Saturday night? Say about six, for cocktails?" Neil said. "What's Maureen drink?"

Howard held up his beer. "Beer, mostly. Just like me. That's why we get along so well."

Rori remained quiet and then excused herself for the bathroom. She didn't have to pee, but better try before they left to go back home.

She sat on the toilet, thinking of what Howard just told her. She thought about when her parents died and how she felt. *What if it had been the other way around? What would my parents have felt? Would they have turned to alcohol, like Neil?*

It was one of the few times since she was a kid that she thought about her parents. The pain she hid from everyone with a gruff exterior seemed minuscule compared to what Neil had to endure. Neil knew little of her background, and until now she knew little of his. Neither of them realized they had an emotional link.

It was all too overwhelming. Feeling vulnerable sitting on the toilet, it was about to break her shell. She had to get out of there. Grabbing her underwear and jeans she quickly pulled them up, washed her hands and got back out to the bar with a hide-the-pain smile plastered on her face.

Neil stood up. "So we'll see you on Saturday," he said to Howard. He reached over, and the two men shook hands.

He looked out the bar window over the café curtains and spotted a silver sedan across the street with a man inside. He seemed to be paying a lot of attention to the bar, but made no motion to come in. Unable to make out who it was, Neil sat back down.

"Are you working again before Saturday?"

"Yes. Tomorrow," Howard said.

Neil pointed his finger at Howard. "When you get to work, go right in and tell the lieutenant you ran into me. Tell him we're dear friends. Tell him I asked about the Vice President and you didn't answer any questions. You couldn't because you don't know anything. If he thanks you and asks you to keep him informed, tell him you will and you're having dinner with me over the weekend. If I'm right, he'll ask you to come in and tell him about it afterward. Agree to it, and I'll tell you what to say over dinner. Are we clear on this?" Neil asked.

"Okay…but I can't see why."

"Howard, look through that curtain. There's a car over there. If I'm right, someone is watching us. For some reason, they don't want us to know anything about the Vice President's visit at the hospital. Please, Howard, do as I say. If they're watching us, it means they're watching you, too."

"Okay," Howard said.

Neil shook his hand again and got up from the table. He and Rori headed for the door while Howard finished his beer. Rori waved her fingers to Bert as she passed the bar.

"Is it someone from the hospital?" Rori asked.

"I can't tell. My eyes are so bad. When we get out there, see if you can recognize them. If my suspicions are right, it's the lieutenant."

Rori hurried out the door and looked quickly at the car, which was making a quick U-turn. The sun was lowering in the west, making it difficult for her to see. The car sped away before she could get a good look.

"Can't tell who it was," Rori said. "But I'll tell you one thing: he's headed in the direction of the hospital. Let's follow him."

They both jumped into the car and started to pull out when Lt.

Snedicker pulled right along Neil's door and dropped down the window of his black SUV.

"Nice day for a drive and a beer," he said, through the open window. "Can I buy you both a drink?"

"We'd love to, but how about a rain check?" Neil said.

They waved goodbye and headed to the highway instead of the hospital.

"It's too late to follow them now," Neil said.

"Was that planned or just coincidental?" Rori asked.

"Not sure," Neil said. "If it wasn't the lieutenant in the first car, who else could it be? I think we better be careful from here on in. Too many people are keeping tabs on us."

"Maybe on Saturday we can get more information from Maureen," Rori said.

Chapter Twenty-Eight

The lieutenant returned to the hospital and walked directly into Dr. Moskowitz's office.

"Come in, Lieutenant," Dr. Moskowitz said. "Vitaly and I were just having a discussion about our encounter with these reporters."

"I saw them at The Black Sow. They may have met with someone, or at least talked to the bartender," the lieutenant said.

"I know, Vitaly was there, too."

Vitaly looked across the room in disgust at Lt. Snedicker. "I told you before you should have taken care of him. You leave too many loose ends."

"Don't tell me what I should do, you fucking commie."

"You always wait until there's an incident before you act. That's your problem," Vitaly said.

The lieutenant's adrenaline kicked in. "My problem is you, not some drunken reporter."

"Maybe you need some lessons on how to take care of problems— without pushing them into a ravine." Vitaly curled his lip and gave the lieutenant a smirk. "You lack imagination."

Lt. Snedicker moved toward the Russian. Dr. Moskowitz jumped up and moved around the desk.

"You two, you're fighting like a couple of drug dealers. Stay civil."

"Everything you do is too emotional," Vitaly said.

Vitaly remained cool and spoke calmly, but took a step to meet the lieutenant, all the while ignoring the doctor's protests. "There are a number of ways you could poison that bartender. Or you could just rob him and shoot him. Like I said, you have no imagination, and that's what will get you in the end."

"Are you threatening me?" the lieutenant said.

"Just saying what I believe are your weaknesses."

Lt. Snedicker was seething and wanted to strangle Vitaly. His chest puffed up and his heart was pumping heavily. He squeezed both hands into fists and was ready to unleash his rage on Vitaly when the doctor stepped in again.

"Enough," Dr. Moskowitz said. "Lieutenant, just keep an eye on those two reporters."

"I'll do my job. You don't have to worry about me. Just keep your commie friend out of my business."

Lt. Snedicker turned and walked out the door, slamming it behind him.

Dr. Moskowitz looked at Vitaly. "You know you'll have to deal with him at some point."

"You want it done today?" Vitaly smiled.

"Wait until we get our information from the Vice President. If he manages to do something about those reporters, too, then after would be a good time."

"I can do it anytime. I've take care of maniacs before. It would be my pleasure."

"Just make sure you don't turn your attention toward me. You know I have safeguards in place if something happens to me."

"I know, I know. You've told me before. I would never think of such a thing."

Chapter Twenty-Nine

Maggie glanced at the clock. It was long past six. Howard and Maureen had missed cocktail hour. Maggie fed Rori wine and mini crab cakes as she finished up the meal. Everyone's appetites had been stirred by the smell of roast beef, mushroom risotto and squash with a spoonful of pumpkin pie spice. It was enough to feed an army, but right now it looked as though it would be dinner for three instead of five. Maggie was worried. Howard had always been a punctual man. He hated to have someone else drink his beer.

Neil sat in the backyard, drinking his Jameson and staring at the stars. His thoughts were always in the same place, his son. What his son might be like today. But more than anything, how he shouldn't have gone into the house to get a beer. He told everyone he went in to go to the bathroom.

Rori looked out the window and watched Neil. She put her hand over her mouth, feeling once again flooded with emotion. This was all more than she wanted to deal with. She took a deep breath and turned her back to Neil. What she wanted to do was go out and kick Neil in the ass and tell him enough is enough. Life sucks sometimes. Sometimes we make mistakes but the longer we hang on to those mistakes—the more mistakes we make.

"Is he always like this?" she said to Maggie.

"Not always, but as the holidays draw closer it starts to get worse. It just tears him up inside." Maggie peeked into the oven to check the meat.

"May I impose and ask what happened? Howard mentioned an accident."

"I'm sorry, I thought you knew since you work so closely," Maggie

115

said. "Oh dear, I'm sorry. As I remember, we were out of something. I ran to the store and Neil was watching our son, Sterling in the front yard. "Somehow, he let Sterling out of his sight. Maybe the phone rang or he went to the bathroom, whatever. It doesn't matter anymore."

Maggie's eyes glistened as she spoke. "Sterling's tricycle went down the driveway and was hit by a work truck. That may be why they were in the front yard—workers were on the street, and Sterling wanted to see the big trucks and equipment. He loved to play with his trucks."

Maggie's mind drifted as she recalled the painful moment.

"You don't have to say more," Rori said.

"Nonsense. It's good to let it out once in a while. By the time I got back, the police, fire trucks and ambulances were all over the place. They said it happened so fast. That he—that Sterling never suffered. I wish I could say the same for his father. Neil never forgave himself. His whole personality changed. He started drinking and swearing, things he never did before. It's like he was swearing at himself all these years. But you know, he's never been harsh to me or treated me in anything but a loving way. He knows I don't hold a grudge. It was an accident. The problem is he's never forgiven himself."

Maggie wiped her eyes and stood, watching Neil. "It's like watching him die, day by day."

Rori was leaning against the counter with her arms folded. "I shouldn't have asked."

"Don't worry about it. Your mind plays tricks on you, and the pain starts sneaking into your soul, until you've built up this pressure. A little cry or sometimes just a discussion eases it away. If nothing else, at least it lets the pressure out. He was a lovely boy," Maggie said.

Maggie had enough. Her pressure had been released. "Let's have dinner. Just because Howard's not here doesn't mean we can't eat."

Just then the doorbell rang and in walked Howard, covered in dirt, with grease on his hands and face. "Is there any beer in the house?" he yelled from the hallway.

Maggie heard the loud, familiar voice. Neil heard Howard from the backyard and came in.

Rori looked Maureen over as she walked in. She was somewhere in her early fifties, ten or fifteen years younger than Howard. Her straight black, short hair was stylish and made her look even younger. In fact, she was the complete opposite of Howard—youthful, energetic, elegant. *I hope I look that good when I'm older.*

Howard, who headed to the bathroom to wash up, came out and held his hand out for a beer.

Neil obliged.

Howard took a quick gulp. "We had a flat tire on the way. Shit, I haven't had a flat tire in twenty-five years. There I was changing the tire, and this car comes up out of nowhere. It swerved to the left, then to the right—I jumped over the hood of the vehicle to avoid becoming road kill. Hence the dirt. The guy was acting like he was aiming for me."

Rori and Neil looked at each other, acknowledging the possibility someone tried to kill Howard.

Maggie put her arm around Maureen and left for the kitchen.

"Would you like a glass of wine?" Maggie asked.

"That would be great."

"Howard's such a wonderful man. Full of himself—and his beer, but a wonderful man just the same," Maggie said.

"With Howard, I feel like a kid again. He can make me melt in his arms."

"I'll take one of them," Rori said.

"You'll have a few bad ones before you find a good one," Maureen said.

Maggie laughed. "That's for sure…"

"All right, let's get everyone to the table. Dinner is just about ready to come out of the oven."

"It smells delicious. I haven't had a good homemade meal in a while," Maureen said.

"Could you see everyone has drinks and water at their place? Ask Rori to assist you."

By the time the drinks were poured and extra beer was supplied for Howard, they sat down to enjoy their meal.

"I'm not use to drinking beer out of a glass," Howard said.

"Behave yourself," Maureen said. "I think I'll have a beer myself."

"Well, well. I guess we know who wears the pants in *this* relationship," Neil said.

"I only let her think that on occasions like this," Howard said.

"Next thing I'll have to do is cut your food rations to trim that belly," Maureen said, laughing.

"Ooh," everyone said at once.

"Sounds like the whip is cracking," Rori said, and then she raised her glass. "To good friends, new and old."

"Hear, hear," Neil said, and all the glasses clinked together.

Howard took an extra sip.

"So, Howard, was there anything you could see wrong with the tire?" Rori asked.

"It looked like a gash in the sidewall, but that could have happened when it went flat. I wasn't concerned about the tire—but that silver Mercedes came at me…"

"It's a good thing I yelled to him when I did," Maureen said. "Such crazy drivers these days."

"You sure it was a silver Mercedes?" Neil asked.

"I'm pretty sure," Maureen said. "I see quite a few come and go at the hospital."

"Well, the important thing is you're safe and in good hands," Neil said.

Rori's eyes lit up thinking the car Maureen described sounded like the car at The Black Sow. She didn't know models, but it was silver.

The conversation was pleasant throughout dinner. As they exchanged war stories of the old neighborhood, Rori grew anxious. Neil told Rori it would be better if he started the discussion about the hospital, but of course Rori wanted to dive right in.

Neil explained to get information, you had to do it delicately. He talked about newsgathering as though it was a war, emphasizing tact and planning. Rori agreed to his terms, but her thoughts were different on how to fight. She liked to drop a bomb and ask questions afterward. She felt the dinner was unnecessary and wanted to meet Maureen at The Black Sow. In her mind, too much dancing was going on.

Rori's mouth was half-opened when Neil started the conversation.

"Maureen, Howard told us you had a friend who worked in the villas—that she died in an accident," Neil said.

Maureen was curt when she answered. "No, I had a friend who was killed, and the police did nothing about it."

Rori jumped in. "We don't mean to pry, but we're working on a story, and we thought maybe you could just tell us about your friend and the hospital."

The expression on Maureen's face said it all. "Is that what this dinner is all about? Not to catch up with old friends but pry?" Maureen reached for her beer and gulped it.

Neil and Rori looked toward each other, then to Howard. Howard took the hint.

"Maureen, they didn't mean anything," he said.

Maureen was no longer in the mood for social chitchat. She turned to Howard. "Shut up, Howard. I don't like people prying into my private life."

"Who do you think you are, telling me to shut up? You think I'm one of those druggies at your hospital? I don't need to take shit from anyone. You think you can talk to me like that just because I'm a security guard?"

Howard stood up to leave. "You coming or not?"

Maggie stood up. "Sit, Howard."

He looked at her and fell back into his chair.

Maggie reached over and touched Maureen's hand. "Maureen, these two are always after a story. It's their nature. If you knew Neil as I do, then you'd know he's the nicest man you'll ever know—next to Howard, of course. If Neil saw a guy bend down to tie his shoe, he'd look for an angle to turn it into a headline. It's what he does, and I suspect Rori's the same."

The table was silent for few seconds, which felt like hours. Maureen gazed down, then picked her head up and asked, "May I smoke?"

"Of course you can," Maggie said. She wasn't fond of smoking in her home but was willing to make an exception to defuse the moment.

Maureen stood up, went into the kitchen, and grabbed another beer. Then she walked into the hall entrance to retrieve her purse. She returned to the table, sat and opened her purse for a blunt cigar and a lighter.

Neil's eyes followed the puffs of smoke curled up to the ceiling. He knew there was a paint job in the future, but this story was more important. Watching Maureen turn the cigar for an even light made Neil's stomach churn.

"I used to smoke cigarettes, but I stopped. Once in a while I still have one, but I don't inhale these," Maureen said. She took a couple of puffs. "Howard would you give us a few minutes?"

Howard looked indignant, but he got up to leave the table.

Neil spoke up. "Why don't we just go into my office?"

Maureen carried her beer in one hand and her cigar in the other. The pungent odor followed her through the hallway and into the office. Neil carried an empty glass. Rori grabbed it and poured three fingers of Jameson into it, then a glass for herself. Neil raised his eyebrows as he saw her take a sip.

Maureen puffed away as she took a seat in a leather chair. Neil dumped a pewter paper clip tray onto the desk. "Here, Maureen, use this for an ashtray," he said, as he placed it on a small table next to her.

She took another puff, and then put her cigar down in the makeshift ashtray. She exhaled and took another gulp of beer. What little of the wine and beer she drank was affecting her. Reaching over with her right hand she picked up the cigar again, and then put her left foot up on a footstool. "Where do you want to start?"

Rori stood holding her glass of whiskey. She was anxious, but didn't want to upset Maureen again.

"Tell us about the nurse. What was her name? Was there anything unusual about her? We don't know what we're looking for. Anything you say may lead us to something."

Rori took a pad off Neil's desk.

"Her name was Laura Gorham," Maureen said. "She was maybe ten years younger than me, a bit overweight but a beautiful person. I remember when I first saw her long red hair. I thought she had the most beautiful features I'd ever seen. We became friends and used to stop at The Black Sow together. It's a bar a few miles down the road from the hospital."

"We know the place," Rori said.

"Did Laura work there long?" Neil asked.

"About twelve or thirteen years."

Neil recognized something in the way she was talking about Laura. He found it odd that she asked Howard to give her privacy.

"Did you love her? Were you in love with her?" Neil said. He tried to be gentle—it was a tough question for Neil, and he wasn't sure he asked in the right manner. Rori hadn't picked up on it, but waited for her to respond.

Maureen took a puff on her cigar and a sip of beer. "Yes, I was very much in love with her, and she with me. It was the first time I was in love with a woman, and probably the last. Now I'm with Howard."

Rori had her own side affairs, and hated it when people cast unwanted stares. Being of the temperament, she was always willing to put them in their place.

Neil took a gulp. His instincts were right. She spoke in a manner that reminded him of old movies from eighty years ago. It was dramatic, but real and touching, and someone was in love. Maureen was probably right about how Laura died, she was murdered.

Rori held her glass up. "Here's to Laura."

"Hear, hear," Neil said.

Maureen took a sip and then set down her cigar and drink. Holding her face in her hands, she began to cry. It was a loud, deep cry. "I'm sorry," she said through muffled tears. "I haven't cried in a long time."

Rori looked at Neil and said, "Take a walk old man. I'll call you back when Maureen feels better."

Neil added some whiskey to his glass and walked out the door.

Rori walked around behind Maureen waiting for the crying to stop. She gritted her teeth then came around and faced Maureen with one hand on her hip. "Are you okay?"

"Yes, I'm fine. But it does feel good to let it out. I don't have anyone who I can talk to about Laura, or the way I felt about her. Talking about her brought it all back."

"There's no need to apologize about anything. I've been there, and it hurts. People make jokes about your feelings. It's not a joke when you lose someone you love. And it doesn't make any difference whether they're male or female. Your heart doesn't know, or for that matter, doesn't care."

Rori moved over behind Neil's desk looking for tissues, and saw them tucked into an open drawer. She grabbed a handful and gave them to Maureen, who mopped up her tears and blew her nose. Then Rori handed her the box, along with the wastebasket.

"Are you going to be okay?"

"Oh, yeah, I'm fine."

Rori went to the door to call Neil.

"Is she through with the crying stuff?" Neil asked Rori once she emerged into the hallway. "My glass is empty, and all the good stuff is in there."

"I know what you mean. I think she's done," Rori said. "Her lover was murdered, and she allowed it to build up inside."

"I know that feeling," Neil said.

"I don't know if she can tell us anything, but I think we need to know if Laura had any family," Rori said. They both went back into Neil's office.

Rori walked over to a chair and sat looking over at Maureen. Neil leaned against the desk with his arms folded.

Maureen, cigar in hand, held her empty beer glass up. "Do you think I could have a little of what you guys are drinking?"

Neil took her glass and filled her request from the wet bar.

"My, my… What's the world coming to with you two women drinking a man's drink? There won't be any left for me."

"I'll buy a bottle," Rori said. "Pour some for me, too."

"Nice taste," Maureen said, "I shouldn't be drinking this. It'll make me horny."

Neil choked on his drink.

Rori cleared her throat. "Maureen do you… can you think of why anyone would want to kill your friend, Laura?"

"Not really. I wasn't working that day, but she called from her car. I thought it was funny, because a lot of us just stopped carrying our cell phones to work. They weren't allowed inside the buildings or on the grounds. Though a lot of people did leave their cell phones in their cars. Everyone became paranoid. They thought someday they'd forget and carry their phone into the facility. Anyway, I didn't recognize the number Laura called from. She said it was her son's phone and she had just been fired for bringing it into the building."

"Her son?" Neil asked.

"Yes, he lived with her. He's in his twenties."

"Did she have any other children?" Rori asked.

"No, no," she said, and then hesitated for a moment.

"What aren't you saying Maureen?" Rori asked.

"I don't know if I should. It's not my place."

"Come on, Maureen. We want to help you and we might be able to find something to help us find out who killed Laura," Neil said.

Rori gave Maureen a sympathetic smile. "We can only help if you tell us what you're thinking."

"I don't see how it could possibly help, it…was personal to Laura," Maureen said.

Neil didn't let up. "What difference would it make? Laura's dead, and whoever killed her is out there walking free. Whether or not you tell us what happened is not going to make a bit of difference to Laura now," Neil said.

Maureen bit down on the cigar, then tossed it around in her mouth, not using her hand.

Rori stood up and folded her arms across. "Well, what's the story?"

"No one else knows about this—not even her work. When she was young, she gave birth. It was at some convent out in California, where she stayed during the entire pregnancy. No one knew except her parents and the convent—not even her son. She gave the child up for adoption. Did I say it was a girl?"

Neil and Rori said nothing, just stood there and let Maureen talk.

"She never knew what happened." Maureen took a deep breath, sipped some whiskey, and took a couple of puffs on the cigar. "—that is until she received a letter from her daughter. The rules have changed so much in the past fifty years. It's so much easier for adopted kids to find their parents. Laura and the girl corresponded, and they were just about to meet around the time Laura was killed. I went over to cleanup her personal affects and found the letters she received."

"Maureen, do you know who she is—the daughter?" Neil asked.

"I don't remember her name, but I bet I could find it amongst some of her things. I took all the letters—I didn't even tell her son. I just stuffed them in a drawer and didn't bother reading them. I figured I'd get to it eventually." Maureen gulped some whiskey.

"Could you—would you allow us to look at them?" Neil asked.

"You're reporters. I'm supposed to trust you?" Maureen said.

"Do you trust Howard's judgment?" Neil asked.

"I guess so."

"Ask Howard if I'm trustworthy. He and I go back a long way," Neil said. "If you believe him, I'll vouch for Rori."

"I guess in the long run you have to just believe we'll honor what you ask of us," Rori said.

"I'll talk to Howard later," Maureen said. "If he backs you, then you can see the letters. If you don't hear from me, you can come over tomorrow and go through them.

"We'll be discreet," Rori said. "Maureen, I want to ask you something. Did you ever go to The Black Sow and talk to Bert?"

"Not about Laura. I know Bert. He'd seen us in there often."

Neil let Rori handle most of the questions with her new friend, but felt it was time to put an end to the evening. "I think we've upset you enough for one evening. Howard and Maggie are out in the family room. He's probably finished all of my beer. You better let Howard drive. And if he can't drive, I'll take you guys home."

"I just need to freshen up a little," Maureen said. "Howard shouldn't see me like this."

"There's a bathroom attached to the office," Neil said. "I'm going to find Maggie and rescue my beer from Howard."

Rori sat behind Neil's desk thinking about what the coming days were going to bring. She knew they had a story but really wasn't sure how one thing was going to lead to another. She was happy she had Neil to depend on.

"I'll text my address if Howard gives a green light. What's your number?"

Rori grabbed a piece of note paper from the desk and jotted her number down. "Here you go."

Maureen put the paper in her purse.

She washed her face and reapplied her makeup, then straightened her hair. Rori grabbed the ashtray with the cigar, and flushed it down the toilet.

"You ready?" Rori said.

"I think so, Maureen said.

"Good, let's find Neil.

Chapter Thirty

Warren lay in bed trying to read the papers. He tried not to think of how bitter the week had been. He was supposed to be resting. The doctor didn't want outside information to get him upset. It made little difference, because he couldn't focus on the words. It was like looking at something through coke-bottle glasses with perfect vision. He threw the newspapers into a pile and let his head fall back. Staring up at the ceiling his eyes came in and out of focus.

I'm weak like the rest of the world. I lost the election, and I know some people are genuinely concerned for my health. I lost the election, but not by enough I should have to hang my head.

"Mr. Vice President? Mr. Vice President," Austin said. "I'm sorry I don't want to interrupt."

The Vice President heard something, but the voice was dream-like and far away.

Austin touched Willowdale's arm. "Mr. Vice President."

Willowdale came back to reality, realizing he was not dreaming.

"Yes? Austin? Is that you? It's good to see you. I didn't hear you come in. I think I was in a fog. I—I don't know what's happening to me."

"Mr. Vice President—"

"I told you before, when we're alone you may call me Warren."

"I know Mr. Vice—Warren, but I speak and think of you in utmost respect." He did respect the Vice President, but only to a point that it benefited him.

"I know you want to show respect, but you and I have been together for a long time and not many people know or care about me as you do. You have been with me through thick and thin, and right now is the thinnest of times."

"I must give the Vice President his medicine," the nurse said, as she entered the room.

"Does it have to be right this moment? We're having a discussion," Austin said.

The nurse hesitated. "I'm under strict orders to make sure he gets his medicine at the proper time. I must call the doctor if you interfere with the timetable." The nurse looked to the phone and realized it had not been turned on. The doctor didn't like outside contact until the patient started to show improvement. Most of the time it was a coordination between the doctor and clients.

Austin, sensing her need, reached into his jacket pocket and withdrew his cell. "Here, use mine."

The nurse dialed the doctor and explained the situation. "He wishes to speak to you, Mr. Garcia," the nurse said.

Austin took the phone. "I'll be finished within a half-hour," he said to Dr. Moskowitz.

"Austin, you're the media guy. I'm the doctor," Moskowitz said into the phone. "You have your rules and we have ours. If you want the Vice President to get better, you have to listen to me."

The doctor had been through this many times with other clients at the hospital. Someone always wanted to step in, as if they knew better. Most of the time he could reason with the clients, although it was the rich ones who were the worst. If they didn't get it, he'd put them in their place.

"If the Vice President gets off of his medicine routine, his treatment won't work the way it's meant to. We don't want him sneaking out and doing something crazy, do we? Let the nurse do her job. Understood?"

Austin said nothing at first. "Understood."

"It's easy to know when the medication begins to take effect. He'll start closing his eyes while he's talking to you. I suggest you get the important things taken care of first. He'll never be able to finish a full conversation after it hits his bloodstream. We don't want to put too much on him at once, just remember that. In a few days he'll be much better, and then you can bring him out in public."

Austin hung up on the doctor. Putting his phone back in his pocket, he turned to the nurse. "Go ahead and do your job."

The nurse injected Warren with Medifinne. It worked quicker than any other medicines on the market. Dr. Moskowitz had used it for a year with great success. One patient committed suicide, but Moskowitz figured that was coincidental. It was possible (though never proven) the patient was given too much for his body weight. New procedures were put into place to correct overdosing from happening again, if that was indeed what happened. In any event, Medifinne would make the Vice President better in a much shorter span of time.

Austin looked at Warren. "You know you've had a nervous breakdown. You fell in the hotel and we had to sneak you out from the vultures after your speech."

"I already surmised all that," Warren said. "I guess I'm not the man I thought I was. I tried to hide it, even from you. I think the assassination attempt had a greater effect on my nerves than I thought."

"It was a tremendous campaign. It was a courageous fight, and Warren this is not over yet. There will be other campaigns, and we'll make sure you win."

Warren's voice began to fade. "I know, Austin. I'll get them . . ."

Chapter Thirty-One

The smell of bleach and ammonia often associated with hospitals wasn't at the Maryland Life Rehabilitation Center, at least not in the villas. All cleaning was done with acidic fruit cleaners. The facility was designed to make patients feel as though they were at a resort.

A married couple that moved from California cleaned and maintained the villas. Rosemary and Gerald–Gerry–Waterford thought about moving east for a long time. Rosemary was the cleaning person, while Gerry was in charge of maintenance and repair. The couple had been fully vetted by the hospital before given access to the villas. Their last employer was an attorney who had been in an accident. He no longer had a need for their services, but gave them excellent references.

The hospital was more than satisfied with their performance. For the first six months, they kept to themselves, doing their job and exceeding expectations.

The plan had been hatched by Gerry. He knew Rosemary wanted to go see her mother before she died. He decided, after her unexpected death in a car crash, they would do their own investigation. After what Bert had told them at The Black Sow, they didn't believe the police report that said she was drunk.

Pretending to be cleaning and maintenance people was a small price in order to find out the truth. Rosemary's father had been in an accident and needed a full-time nurse. That was something Rosemary had arranged but didn't feel she could do it. He also had money and friends, both of which helped the two create a past, so they would have a background in place when applying for jobs at the hospital. Both had worked similar jobs while in college. It also didn't hurt that Rosemary's father had a large sum of money in a company that in turn invested in the hospital.

Motive brought them east, but motives are a personal thing. Having defined themselves as ethical workers, they were viewed by management to be everything their references said and more.

Chapter Thirty-Two

Rori leisurely drove her pickup to Maureen's the next day. She had slept late. Pulling up to the condo, she began to recount the events of the previous evening. Maureen was an impressive woman. She and Howard were a strange match. The fact that she had been with another woman didn't bother Rori, but it was clear Maureen kept her options open.

Stepping up to the door, she rang the bell. Maureen came quickly.

"Good morning," Maureen said, arriving at the door in a bathrobe, a towel around her head. "I see you got my text. Howard couldn't say enough good things about Neil. Did you have any problem finding my place?"

"Piece of cake," Rori said.

"I guess it's not morning, is it? I slept late. After I got home from Howard's, I went back to bed and fell into a deep sleep."

"No worries," Rori said as she walked through the doorway.

"Coffee?"

"That would be fabulous. I slept late myself."

"You don't have to rush away?" Maureen asked. "Would you like breakfast?"

"No. I don't have to rush, but I have a lot on my mind. I'll take some coffee and maybe a slice of toast. If that's okay?

"Whole wheat?"

"Fine," Rori said. She didn't feel chatty this morning, but she also didn't want to cut Maureen too short or she wouldn't get the letters.

Maureen reached down in a cabinet and pulled out some bread. "One or two slices?"

"One's good," Rori said.

Maureen popped the toast in and poured Rori a cup of coffee. "Just grab it when it pops up. I'm going to dry my hair."

When Rori was younger she enjoyed playing around in the kitchen with Aunt Charley. Waiting for the toast, her thoughts drifted. She'd learned a lot from her Aunt Charley, including how to seek her own path.

There was a moment when she and Aunt Charley sat on the front porch, as they often did, just before she left for college. Aunt Charley explained her primary life philosophy.

Roads present themselves to us throughout our lives, and we don't know where they will lead. We just go about our lives trying to make it through the day, the week, the years. We meet people, we lose track of people, we divorce people and we ignore people. These are all paths that we take, and although we may not be aware at the time, they are choices that will define our life.

Most people never stop to think about why they chose a particular path, why we choose one option over another, and I think that's a good thing. Life is about living, not analyzing every little step.

Rori was trying to choose her own path and what Maureen had in those letters might take her. The toast popped up and she got up, spread the butter and refreshed her coffee. It was good and strong. The way she liked it. By the time she put her coffee and toast on the table, Maureen came out to join her.

"Here, you can look at these." Maureen said, and slid a packet of letters across the table.

Rori picked the packet up and stared at them. She wanted to jump right into them. But thinking about what Neil would do, she pushed them aside instead and decided to finish her toast first.

"Good coffee," she said. This was going to be tough. She kept eyeing the letters.

"I like it strong so I always buy a dark roast or an espresso bean."

"Are you okay after last night?" Rori asked.

"Oh, yeah. I hide a lot. As we talked, it just kind of brought it all back. And then you fed me whiskey. I think Howard had to take a heart pill after," she said laughing.

Rori wanted to get personal and make a comment on how good she looked to her, but thought better. "Let me use your bathroom?" Rori said.

"Just down the hall on the right."

Rori came back from the bathroom and had her hand on the letters before she landed in the chair.

The first letter talked about who she was, without a name. It explained a stamped envelope was enclosed, addressed to a P.O. Box. The letter was short and asked if Laura was interested in meeting with her in the future. If she wished to continue to correspond for now, she could send information about herself. It was signed R. Occupant.

"Nothing in here," Rori said. "Did you read any of these?" she asked.

"No," Maureen said. "I never opened the letters. We talked about her daughter, so I saw no need to peer through them. I thought sometime I would, but it wasn't on my priority list. I had visions of meeting her daughter and telling her about us. The longer I thought about it, the worse the idea sounded."

"No one gives a shit about who you love." Rori said. "And if they do, fuck them." She grabbed another letter.

Dear Laura,

I was so glad to see you returned my letter. I know you were young when you gave me up. It must have been a difficult decision. Even though you weren't able to keep me, you chose to have your baby, and for this I thank you.

The letter went on to explain her life and how she thought about contacting Laura but worried she would be rejected. It continued on about her adopted parents treating her as their own.

Hoping to meet you soon, but I don't want to push you,
—R. Occupant

So she wasn't sure her mother wanted to meet her, Rori thought.

Maureen sat looking at Rori as she read the letters. When Rori opened the third envelope, a picture slipped out and fell to the floor.

"I'll get it," Maureen said. On all fours, she retrieved the picture from under the table.

Rori took it from Maureen's hand before she was back in her chair. She had goose bumps. It showed a young woman posed along the ocean leaning on rocks.

Staring at the image, she mumbled. "So this is what you look like, R. Occupant. Is this what Laura looked like, too?" She wasn't knockout beautiful, but attractive just the same. She turned the picture to Maureen. "Do you see Laura in her daughter?"

"I see a lot of Laura. It's the eyes and smile."

"She wanted to take her time to feel confident her mother would accept her," Rori said. "She wouldn't even give her name, instead using a formal advertising delivery address."

Having been raised by someone other than her mother, Rori felt she understood the reluctance to open up completely. Rori put the image on the table so she could view it as she read the letter.

> *I'm enclosing a photo so you can see what I look like. You can let me know if I have your features and who I look like. I'd like to have one of you, if you feel comfortable. I live in California with my husband and near my (adopted) parents. I am a doctor, and something tells me I got my brains from you. My specialties are pediatrics. I enjoy helping children mend. It's a satisfying and rewarding life. When and if you feel we could meet, I'll make arrangements to come east.*
>
> *— R. Occupant*

Maureen turned the picture toward her so that she could get another look.

"Have you ever seen her before?" Rori asked.

"She looks familiar. I think she was at Laura's funeral. She was away from everyone. But I've seen her someplace else, too. I—I just can't place where."

Rori got excited. "Come on, Maureen. Think, think where it was. This could be important. Think hard. I've got to call Neil."

Rori grabbed her cell from her purse.

"Hello?"

"Are you home?"

"Yes, I'm working on a write-up of the election. Where are you?" Neil said.

"I'm at Maureen's and I've been going through some of the letters from Laura's daughter. I found a picture in one of them. Maureen said she saw her at the funeral and somewhere else, but she hasn't figured out where yet."

"Do you want me to come over to Maureen's to help out?" Neil asked.

"No, no. Why don't I come over to your house and we can go through the rest together?" Rori said. She could hardly hold her excitement in.

"That's okay with me. I should be done shortly."

"I'll see you in a while," Rori said. "I've got to go, Maureen. Neil's going to help me go through the rest of the letters and we can make notes together. I hate to just run. I enjoy your company."

"Maybe we can get together sometime," Maureen said.

"That would be nice. Maureen, you don't have a problem with me taking these, do you? I'll make sure they get back to you."

"No, go ahead."

Chapter Thirty-Three

Rori headed for the expressway in her 1954 black Chevrolet five-window, step-side pickup. The truck belonged to Aunt Charley's father. Aunt Charley had driven it off and on, but she never went far. She told Rori she had traded it off and bought a new car and then surprised her with it for her high school graduation present. Of course, she'd given it a complete makeover. It now had a 350 engine, PS, PB and AC. Aunt Charley knew enough about Rori not to have it painted pink or some other girly color. Black was a stronger color, and it suited Rori. The truck was Rori's baby. She didn't always use it, except when she needed to reach back to memories and Aunt Charley's help. It was like her life training time capsule.

She headed down the highway toward the hospital. She had a hunch. Turning off the expressway, she headed west toward The Black Sow. When she walked in, she gave Bert her sexiest smile, and he instantly reacted by standing up tall and beaming back at her.

"Hey, Bert. Remember me?"

"How could I forget you?" Bert said.

Rori beckoned Bert over to the side of the bar. She held out the photograph of Laura's daughter. "Do you recognize this woman in the picture?"

Bert stared at it for a second and said nothing. Rori's instinct told her he did. "Come on, Bert. You do, don't you?"

Bert was reluctant at first. "This is strictly between us, right? If anyone asked me about this, I'll tell them you're lying."

Rori could sense he was trying to stall. She reached over the bar and put her hand on top of his. "Bert," she said, flashing her eyes.

Bert took one look at Rori and instantly felt a tingle up his leg. He was in love again for the tenth time that week.

"You know I'll keep this to myself. I'm just trying to track something down," Rori said. "She may be able to help me."

"She's the one that gave me the envelope. The one with all the bribe money to keep me quiet after Laura died. But you can't let this get out," Bert said.

"Not a problem, Bert." Rori reached over the bar and pinched his cheek.

Bert smiled and blushed.

"Thanks a lot. I'll be back sometime," Rori said. In a flash she was heading out the door, with Bert staring.

Rori's instincts were right. But she wasn't sure what it all meant. Why didn't Laura's daughter want anything brought out into the open? As she drove to Neil's, she continued to turn the question over in her mind, but she couldn't figure it out. *Was she planning something or did she know something?* Maybe Neil could give her some insight.

Rori got to Neil's house by early afternoon. After giving Maggie a hug, she made her way up to his office. It was a different atmosphere than the previous night. In her hand she carried Laura's letters from her daughter. She was excited to know what was in the rest of them. The two of them could go through them faster together, and maybe get a better understanding of Laura's daughter.

Her editor called her while she was on her way and wanted to know what she was working on. She had filed several articles since the election, but because she was so new, he wanted to keep tabs on her. She stalled, saying she was trying to get an interview with the Vice President and doing a piece on the hospital. She told him she interviewed his doctor (which she had) and would be putting something together and sending it in soon. She neglected to tell him what she and Neil were really working on. He didn't need to know everything.

Rori explained to Neil that Laura's daughter, from what she had read so far, seemed to be a bit a cautious about revealing her identity, and noted she had signed everything as "R. Occupant."

"That is a bit cautious, isn't it? Let's see the picture." Neil examined the photo and then touched it as though he was actually touching her face. He was imagining her mother at the same time. "I wonder if she looks like her mother or father?"

"So how are we going to do this?"

"Why don't we each take a letter and make notes? Then we can put it all together when we get through them. We'll be able to go through them pretty fast. There's only ten or twelve," Neil said.

Rori realized she hadn't told Neil about Bert. "Oh my god, I haven't told you."

"About what?" Neil said.

"About Bert."

"You went to The Black Sow? That's way out of your way," Neil said.

"He told me Laura's daughter is the one that gave him the envelope full of money."

"Why would she not want the truth to come out about her mother? This doesn't make any sense. You know, this is why we journalists have to investigate. We just follow the story where it takes us, no matter where that may be.

"Look what's happened: We were followed to the news conference and the bar, someone may have tried to kill Howard, we saw Vice President Willowdale walking around without a cast when we were told he broke his leg and had surgery, and someone may have killed this lady's mother." Neil held the photo of Laura's daughter up to Rori.

"That's a lot for just a few days. I hate to think what the rest of the year is going to be like for us," Rori said. "I don't see a connection to any of it, do you?"

"The connection is there, we just don't see it," Neil said. "But it may be in these letters."

Rori, not waiting for another word from Neil, grabbed the package of letters and pulled one out. "Let's get to it, then."

With each letter, R. Occupant revealed more about herself. Her name was Rosemary Waterford. She had been adopted by a wealthy family, attended Stanford and became a doctor.

"Looks as though they were going to meet up just before she was killed, according to this letter," Rori said.

Just then, Rori's cell phone rang.

"Hi, Maureen. We're going over the letters. What can I do for you?" Rori asked.

"That picture of Laura's daughter—I said I thought I saw her before, at the cemetery and someplace else. I figured it out. She works at the villas."

Rori was speechless.

"Rori, can you hear me?" Maureen asked.

"What does she do there?" Rori asked.

"She's a cleaning lady, and her husband works with her doing maintenance."

"Thanks, Maureen," Rori said. She was shocked Rosemary wasn't a doctor at the facility, given her degree.

Rori said goodbye, hung up the phone and turned toward Neil. "I think we just got a big break, but I'm not sure what to make of it."

"What's that?" Neil asked.

Rori wanted to just shout it out but she resisted. All this time she worked with Neil, he tried to get her to feel from the gut and let her instinct guide her.

Neil had been part of the interview process when she was hired. He was the one that saw something in her and pushed to take her on. He volunteered to take her under his wing. She knew he wasn't going to be around forever, so she tried not to rely on him entirely. This was different—different than anything else she had encountered. She still needed Neil.

"I don't know what to think of this," Rori said. "Laura's daughter works at the hospital."

"A doctor at the clinic?" Neil asked.

"I would have thought that too, but she works with her husband as a cleaning person . . . down at the villas," Rori said.

Neil looked as surprised as Rori. "Why would a doctor want to work as a cleaning person?"

"We need to find out more about her. Let's do some research," Rori said.

"We need to find out about her life before we approach her," Rori said to Neil. "I think either she's doing the same as we are or she's up to no good. She may be trying to find her mother's killer."

Neil looked at Rori with pride and took a drink from his glass that he poured earlier. "I think you have something there. If she's in there all the time, we may be able to find out all the information we need on the Vice President."

Neil got up and gave Rori a hug. "I think this is the break we've been looking for, and I think it may lead right up to the Vice President's suite."

Chapter Thirty-Four

Medifinne was stronger than previous medicines used with patients who had a nervous breakdown. Dr. Moskowitz had worked with it for several years and had honed its dosage to prevent problems. It was taking hold, or so the doctor thought. To the nurses and doctors who were in charge of his care, it appeared as though the Vice President was sleeping peacefully. He was Dr. Moskowitz's patient. But when he was busy, other doctors would check on Willowdale with the nurses in attendance.

Moskowitz had explained to Ann and Austin how Medifinne treated the brain, allowing it to rest to heal itself. The Vice President appeared to be asleep, but his mind was restless. He had this need of power—this *want* to be president.

On his first night in the hospital, his mind rousted him out of bed. He could think of nothing but his failed attempt to become president. The Medifinne in some way worked as it was intended, but it wasn't supposed to pull him out of bed with anxiety.

It should have settled his mind and organized the neural activity into remedial thoughts, strengthening his brain. The Vice President's thoughts of embarrassment of losing the election were dissolving more rapidly than most Medifinne patients. But he was not at ease. Instead, he became focused on revenge—on the American people who had not made him President.

As he lay in the quiet, his mind was separating his thoughts. They were not benevolent thoughts. It was as though his brain was a filing cabinet, and all negative things and people in his life were placed neatly into a drawer.

One for the current president, who refused to openly support him, another for old friends who didn't stand by him instead worked behind the scenes to undermine him. And one for his wife, who no longer comforted him, but only showed up for photo ops and public events.

They all will pay, he thought in his hazy dreamland.

Slowly Willowdale opened his eyes and stared at the ceiling. Twenty-four hours ago, his mind was confused and couldn't even concentrate on a simple sentence. Today it was clear: he knew what he wanted to do—what he had to do. He would not allow himself to think of all the what-ifs. As far as he was concerned, he had been Mr. Nice Guy throughout the entire campaign, and he vowed he would never take on that role again.

The Vice President reached for the phone, but found it wasn't working, so he rang for the nurse. When she came in, she explained she would have to get permission to have the phone turned on.

"Then get your damn permission. I want this fucking phone on now."

The nurse hurried out to call Austin. It was five in the morning. She was averse to bothering anyone so early, but considering Willowdale's tone, she figured it was worth it.

After the first run in with the doctor, Austin made sure conditions were setup. Austin would handle anything having to do with politics, phone calls, contacts, All other mainly medical issues would go through the doctor.

"Mr. Garcia, this is Nurse Patricia Boothroyd at the desk of Vice President Willowdale's suite. The vice president has asked—no, he told me to get his phone turned on, and according to our records, permission to do so has to come from you."

Austin was alone in bed and had been in a deep sleep. As he put his thoughts together, he reached down under the blankets and grabbed his morning erection. His thoughts ran wild, and wished Ann had stayed overnight.

"Did he sound all right?" Austin asked. "It's only been a few days."

"Other than being very loud when he told me to get the phone turned on, he sounded fine. In fact, he slept all night long. We checked on him several times, and his vitals were normal, especially compared to where they were when he came in the other day."

"How long will it take to get the phone on?" Austin asked.

"Just a few minutes."

Austin rubbed his erection and said, "Go ahead and turn it on, but when it's on, call me back. I want to call Warren to make sure he sounds all right."

As he waited for the nurse to call him back, Austin turned his full attention to his erection. He was approaching completion when the phone rang. He let it ring a few times while he finished up.

"Mr. Garcia, this is Nurse Boothroyd. We have the phone on. I'll transfer you to his room."

"Nurse, once you transfer me in, I want you to go into the room and observe him to make sure he looks all right. When he and I are through, I'll have him give the phone to you," Austin said.

Warren picked up the phone. "Willowdale here."

"Warren, it's Austin. Is everything all right?"

"Austin, everything is perfect. I feel so good this morning. Everything is clear as a bell. Why do you sound like you're out of breath?"

"I was in the bathroom and ran to get the phone when the nurse called me. I wanted to make sure you're okay," Austin said.

"Honest, Austin. Believe what I'm telling you. I feel terrific this morning. I just wanted to call a friend of mine."

"Who do you want to call at five in the morning?"

"Austin, don't you think you're overstepping?"

"Not at all, Mr. Vice President. I'm responsible to take care of your problems. That's why you have me around."

"You made your point. I want to call my old friend Churchill Brewer."

"Warren, is he going to be receptive to you calling him so early?"

"CB and I go back a long way, and he gets up at 4 a.m. He would think nothing of me calling him."

"I think you should be a little careful, considering your situation," Austin said.

Warren was quiet for a few seconds, then said, "I understand what you're saying, Austin."

"One slip up with him and you're done."

"I know, but I can handle it," Warren said. "We've been through a lot, and I think he'd give me a pass."

"He may, but I wouldn't chance it," Austin said. Quickly thinking what the doctor said about the medicine he was giving Warren. *It's going to be much better—faster with the Medifinne than any other medicine.* "Warren—Mr. Vice President, you can make your call, but I want it limited to ten minutes. Can you handle that?"

"Austin, you're starting to act like a son of a bitch too," Willowdale said. His temper was rising. Not wanting to get completely shut off, he relented to Austin.

"I'm just trying to protect you," Austin said.

"You win, but I want complete privacy. I'm not a child. I just wanted to get in touch with him and discuss the future."

"Just keep it to ten minutes. I don't want the doctor coming back to me and giving me hell for getting you all worked up. The nurse will come back in to let you know she is shutting the phone down in exactly ten minutes. Understood?"

"You drive a hard bargain, Austin, but I think I can keep to the agreed timeframe."

* * *

Churchill Brewer backed many candidates running for election, most of whom won. No one knew, although many suspected, how influential he had been in getting people elected. He always made sure to spread out the money he poured into campaigns so it couldn't be tracked back to him. Still, he was the subject of much suspicion because of all of the organizations he backed. Some he openly supported. Others through surrogates. These groups just spread the money around in any manner that supported CB's beliefs. If people didn't see things his way, mysterious incidents would always occur, at just the right time, to snuff out any potential problems.

One of Churchill's mistakes was that of Harriet Blanchard. Blanchard had been a no-name member of the Tennessee House of Representatives. It was said, long before she was elected, CB hired a political group to train and teach her about the law-making process and the way he expected the world to behave. She blossomed, and by the time she was running for president, she had earned the respect of Congress and the country. She won by a landslide, but her one term was riddled with corruption. It was one thing Churchill hadn't taken into account in her training. It wouldn't happen again.

The phone rang, and the Vice President grabbed a pen and a pad sitting on the bedside table.

"CB, Warren here."

"Warren. So sorry about the loss and your fall."

"Thanks for your concern, but as things go, that's old news. I'd like to move forward. Can you get here to see me soon?" Warren asked.

Churchill liked Warren's tone. Just a loss, not a death. "Is tomorrow soon enough? What's this about?"

"Without going into too much detail, I want to talk about the next election. I know you'll think I'm off my rocker, but I'd like to do—no re-do another Harriet."

"What do you mean re-do? You don't want to resurrect her, do you?" Churchill asked.

"No, but I want to find another Harriet-type. I want to make a deal with whomever we choose, so I can take my revenge," Warren said.

Churchill was taken aback. "Revenge? Are you crazy? Politics isn't about revenge—it's about power. If you go around taking revenge on all your enemies, you won't be able to build a powerbase."

Warren understood where Churchill was coming from, but Churchill didn't have his insight. "I don't want revenge on everyone, just the American people. I do keep a scorecard. Do you have a list of names for potential candidates?"

Churchill was beginning to think Warren had lost it, but decided to humor him. "I think I can get you a few names. I have one I think has great potential."

"I don't want anyone that's too nice. Let's give him a fighting chance. I want someone that has ambition," Warren said.

"Well, you have just eliminated ninety-nine percent of the people I've been considering," Churchill said jokingly. "It's all a matter of whether they're willing to listen and stay on message. Most people lose big races because they don't or can't grasp the big picture. They have to realize it's not about them, nor is it about John Q. Public. It's about the message. Find a message that hits most Americans and keep saying it over and over until John Q. doesn't know what they were thinking yesterday and only believes what the candidate says today. It doesn't make a bit of difference whether the candidate believes it or not, he just has to know how to say it."

Warren loved listening to CB. He was so glad he was his friend and not an enemy.

"You know, Churchill, it was my fault and not yours we lost," Warren said.

Churchill knew that was only partly true. "Hey, Warren, we're not perfect. Let's just think about the future."

Warren liked listening to Churchill's philosophy. It was like listening to a rhapsody, his words flowing softly and soothingly.

"Churchill, you know all the right things to say to make me feel good about the American way," Warren said, then he laughed out loud.

Churchill thought Warren's laugh was strange, almost hysterical. "Are you on something?"

"Of course I'm on something. I just broke my leg." He couldn't tell Churchill the truth. He didn't want to lose his respect.

Churchill knew no one could win all the elections, even if everything was in their favor. No, it wasn't losing that bothered Churchill, it was weakness. If he knew Warren had a nervous breakdown, he wouldn't speak to him again. If you wanted to be in Churchill's "church," you had to take losses as a minor blip on life's radar. It was the big picture that mattered to CB.

"I'm on something," Warren said again, "but I have never felt better." That's what Churchill wanted to hear—and Warren knew it. A strong positive spin on life, even if it was a bitter pill.

"Have you thought about who we'd get for a running mate?" Churchill asked.

"I know exactly who will be his running mate." Then with a slight hesitation he said, "Me."

"You? Why on earth would you want to take that silly job again?"

"Whoever we choose to be President has to be someone who can take orders and is willing to work for the party—for me," Warren said.

"Willowdale, I like the way you think," Churchill said.

"There's more, Churchill," Warren said, struggling to find the right wording. "I'm going to be President. Whomever we choose will be there but a short time. Then it will be my turn."

This time it was Churchill who was quiet. The silence was a realization of what Willowdale wanted to do and what was needed in order to carry out his plan.

"Just so your mind is in the right place, if any of this ever gets out, we'll be tried for treason. We must never speak to anyone else about this," Churchill said. "I don't think I'll come there right away. I'll have Terrance to do some research for us. It's best we keep our distance right now."

"Understood. Is it doable?"

"We can get anyone to do anything, but before I hang up, I'm going to tell you that you better think long and hard about this and what you're asking. Once this is in place, there is no turning back. Someone will die."

Chapter Thirty-Five

Rori and Neil sat in Neil's car, about two hundred yards from Rosemary and Gerry Waterford's house. Maureen had told them the type of car they were driving, but didn't know the model. The villa area wasn't a place she cared to even try to see. Rori and Neil didn't want to approach them at the hospital or to even mention their names. They weren't likely to talk there, for fear they would get in trouble or fired. As Maureen told them more, she realized when she saw Rosemary at Laura's funeral, there was a familiarity. But it was a trying time and it never registered. Going through the letters, they found that both Gerry and Rosemary were doctors, which made the whole thing suspicious.

It was a late November afternoon. The sun hung low in the sky, blinding them. It was difficult for either of them to identify cars as they approached the house.

A small ranch in what Neil thought wasn't the most desirable area. Country with a few trailers around, similar to the area where Rori had lived with her parents. It would all change in time this close to the money pit of D.C.

Neil showed Rori how to do some research on city records and found out the deed belonged to an estate. The house was leased for a year to the Waterfords. They had been there for about six months.

"The more I think about it and those letters, I think they both may be doing a little detective work," Neil said. "I can't see any other thing they would be here for. If her mother was murdered, they are way over their heads."

"Maybe that's why they've been here so long. They could be just a couple of bumbling idiots," Rori said.

"They're doctors. How can they be bumbling idiots?" Neil said.

"Just because they're doctors doesn't mean they're a couple of Dick Tracys."

"Maybe we can strike up a deal to help us find out some things about the Vice President," Neil said.

"So what will we have to offer?" Rori asked.

"We can put out whatever we find online. I'm not sure, let's see what's going on first."

Rori tilted her head back and let her mind wander. She thought about Maggie and how hard it must have been to lose a son, especially a little guy. How Maggie told her Neil was better now that he was working on a real case. She looked out the corner of her eye as she saw Neil take a drink from his flask. She was right. He did seem different—better. He wasn't swearing or drinking as much. Sure, he hadn't stopped, but he had slowed down. She sat in the quiet of the surveillance, thinking about Neil and the pain he endured all of these years.

"Maybe if we cracked this story, we could get a Pulitzer," Rori said, as she checked out another car.

Neil didn't respond.

"Look here," Neil said. "Didn't Maureen say it was a mini SUV?"

"Something like that. Or a Volvo," Rori said. "No, that's not it either."

Neil, forever talking about being intuitive and professional, looked toward Rori. "I'm thinking they want some type of revenge, but that could just be the cynic in me."

"You think that's what this is all about?"

"If someone killed Aunt Charley, what would you do?"

"You know what I would do. Only thing . . . no one would know anything about it."

"That wouldn't be too smart," Neil said.

Rori didn't respond.

Neil looked to Rori and knew what she would do but he didn't want to say more. She knew he was leaving when this was over, which is why he kept harping on how to cover a story in an honest way. He felt it was time to change the conversation.

"Just the same, think about what you write as an honest reporter and don't slant it one way or the other. Your readers will know if you do a hatchet job." He pointed his finger at Rori. "Just be honest."

Rori sat listening to her lesson of the day.

"It's difficult to separate your personal feelings when you're reporting on any subject. You have to gather the facts and then create a piece that's interesting but honest. The public knows how to judge an honest piece and one that's biased. Integrity is the word I'm searching for—integrity."

"This car is slowing down," Rori said. "That's them."

"Let them go inside and then I'll pull up into the driveway," Neil said.

They sat in the car for ten minutes while Neil gave Rori more sage advice, and watched her get antsy. "Let's go see if we can help each other."

Neil pulled up and into the driveway. Rori shot out of the car and headed for the door.

Neil raced after her and grabbed her arm. "Take it easy. We need to keep our cool."

Rori looked at him as though she was offended. "Come on Neil, you know I'm just a country girl. I would never offend anyone. I just don't like the dancing that goes on in D.C. Don't worry . . . I'll hold my tongue, as long as they don't act like a couple of Washington *dicks.*"

Chapter Thirty-Six

"Terrance, do you have a list for me?" Churchill asked.

"It's right there on your desk. I felt it best not to leave computer tracks, so I used the library to do my research," he said. He buttoned his double-breasted suit and pulled up a chair facing Churchill.

Terrance was meticulous about his appearance. He wore handcrafted Annunziato leather loafers from the Le Marche region, believed to be the finest in the world—and if it turned out different, then Terrance would find a new region. Whenever he took a trip across the Atlantic, with or without Churchill, he would make a special detour to Italy just to place new shoe orders. His suits were hand-stitched in London and ordered five at a time. It bothered him when he had to do real work for Churchill. Night's he'd have to don his all-black clothing. They had to be just as neat—until he got blood on them. If the blood didn't come out the first time it was washed, he'd burn the clothes. If he got blood on a new uniform, he'd instill extra punishment on his victims.

"Good thinking. How's it look?" Churchill said.

"There are a few relatives of past politicians, including one of the Kennedy's, but they've had enough problems. Did your grandfather have anything to do with any of them?"

Churchill laughed and ignored the question.

"There's one from Indiana and one from Wyoming."

"Who do you think would be the best to use?" Churchill asked, as he spun his large oak framed globe and then looking at the location of each of the states.

"I'd take that cowboy from Wyoming, Hansen Baldwin. He'd be in way over his head before he realized what's going on."

Churchill took a few minutes and looked over his resume.

Terrance reached forward and popped open Churchill's humidor, grabbed a cigar and lit it. Blowing smoke into the air, he turned back to Churchill. "That cowboy has been in D.C. for six years. He's got to be getting restless about now. His grandfather was a sharecropper. Looks like he wants to be governor, but he doesn't have a pot to piss in."

"He's been there six years and he's not a multi-millionaire? Looks like he doesn't know how to play the game. I think Mr. Baldwin is a fine choice, Terrance. Make some arrangements for him visit in the near future. I think we can get him fired up in a day or two. He'll have all these great visions before his world comes tumbling down."

Chapter Thirty-Seven

Neil tried to get ahead of Rori, but she wouldn't allow him to step in front of her. As she put her hand up to ring the doorbell, the front door opened to a man of medium-build with dimpled cheeks. He was clean cut and looked too young to be a doctor. His wire-rim glasses gave him a Wally Cox look, though he appeared intelligent.

"Come in, Ms. Cahill, Mr. O'Connor," the man said and pointed them toward a small front room. "Rosemary has been expecting you."

Entering the room, a short, attractive brunette rose from a wing-back chair and greeted them. "You look surprised we know your names. That has been the easiest part of this ordeal," Rosemary said.

"So you've been looking into us? All you had to do was introduce yourselves," Rori said.

"True, but you didn't have to act like cat burglars waiting down the street," Rosemary said.

"You could have contacted our news office if you wanted to speak to us. We didn't know how to contact you, especially at the hospital. We didn't want to jeopardize your jobs or whatever you're trying to do. We had a friend give us your names," Neil said.

"I know. That's how we found out. Your friend started asking questions and it got back to us. We have friends, too," Rosemary said.

"Mrs. Waterford, there seems to be a misunderstanding here," Neil said.

"All we ever wanted to do is talk to you away from the hospital. We know who you are, and we didn't want to give you away," Rori said.

Rosemary looked over to Neil.

"Don't look at him—I'd like to know what you two are up to," Rori said. "Why pretend to be cleaning and maintenance workers? In your

152

letters to your mother, you said you were doctors."

"Why don't the four of us just sit down and discuss it?" Neil asked.

"Please come into the kitchen," Gerry said. "We made a fresh pot of coffee."

They walked into the sterile, outdated kitchen. Rori gave Neil a nudge in the side. Neil just shook his head.

Gerry had cups setting on the counter, along with cream and sugar. He poured one for Rosemary and turned to Neil and Rori. "What would you like?"

"I'm fine," Neil said. "No, I think I will have one. Make it black."

"Make mine with just cream," Rori said.

The kitchen had dark cabinets and a vinyl floor. There was a center island with white Formica. An addition was built a long time ago, adding a family room that opened to the kitchen. It, too, was dated with dark paneling. At the open side to the family room, five comfortable stools with backs surrounded the island. Rosemary parked herself on one of the stools at the end of the island, away from the rest of them. She placed her cup onto the counter.

Rosemary looked annoyed. "What do you want?"

Neil looked at Rosemary. "First I'd like to say how sorry we are about your mother."

Rosemary raised her left brow. "I see you have been busy, Mr. O'Connor."

"Please, call me Neil. And yes, we have stumbled onto a few things."

Except for Rosemary, everyone stood drinking their coffee. Gerry leaned against the counter by the sink. Neil and Rori surrounded the island.

Rori tapped her foot. "Why are you pretending to be cleaning people when you're both doctors?"

Rosemary had not touched her black coffee. She stood up, turned and stepped away, still clutching her coffee.

"You know about my mother *and* you know I'm a doctor?"

"You're both doctors," Rori said.

"Yes, and you seem to know so much about us, why bother coming here with your questions?" Rosemary said.

"Like I said, we stumbled upon you. We were looking into the Vice

President's recent incident. The more we looked into it, the more we discovered. We were told about a woman, your mother, who worked at the hospital," Neil said, pointing to Rosemary.

"We felt things were a little suspicious when we heard the police say Laura was drunk," Gerry said. "We found information that was contrary."

"You mean when Bert told you she only had one drink?" Rori asked.

"You two *have* been busy," Rosemary said.

Neil reached under the counter and touched Rori's leg in an effort to keep her silent. No small task.

"We're willing to listen," Neil said.

Rosemary's hesitated to speak. She took a sip of coffee then returned to the stool. She leaned back and turned sideways, allowing her right arm to rest on the back of the stool.

"You see, I was happy with my adopted parents. They loved me, taught me good things, helped me find my own way, and never hesitated when I told them I wanted to find my real mother. By the time I started the search, my adopted mother died of cancer, and shortly after my father was in a bad car accident. He hired someone to take care of him full-time. That's when I began my journey to find her. I hired an investigator. I'm sure he did a lot of it on the computer, but our lives were busy at the time, with our jobs and my Dad's problem. When the investigator found her, I wrote my mother a few times and we decided to meet. That was just before she was murdered."

"What makes you think it was murder?" Neil asked.

"Why else would the police cover it up and say she'd been drunk?" Rosemary said.

"So if you thought she was murdered, why not use your detective to find proof the police were lying?" Rori asked.

"I would have, but she was cremated, and the police didn't come out with their official report until her ashes were scattered to the winds. I doubt they were even her ashes. There's no direct way of proving it unless there's some paperwork at the hospital that might help."

"I take it you mean by way of an autopsy?" Neil asked. "Don't they just do that automatically?"

"They said they did an autopsy and found evidence she was drunk.

But the autopsy was performed at MLRC, so I think that was a lie. That's when Gerry and I decided we could afford a hiatus from our jobs as doctors. We developed this plan and hoped to find some records. When we were attending college, we had similar jobs and felt this would be a good cover," Rosemary said.

"Any luck?" Rori asked.

"None. We haven't found the papers—we just don't have the know-how," Rosemary said. "It didn't have to be the autopsy documents. It could have been anything proving she couldn't have been drunk."

Neil had just had a conversation with Rori and what she would do if someone had killed her aunt. He had the feeling these two were thinking the same way. His instinct had never let him down and he was getting a sense what this is all about.

"Are you just trying to find her records?" Neil asked. "Tell me you don't have anything sinister on your mind."

Gerry looked toward Rosemary, then back to the two reporters. "No, nothing sinister. We just want to know the truth."

"The truth about the autopsy or who was involved?" Neil asked.

"Wherever the truth takes us," Gerry said.

"You're a little evasive," Neil said.

Neither of them responded.

"Did you talk to the police?" Rori asked Rosemary.

"We didn't, but our detective spoke to them. He said it was like talking to a wall. They seemed annoyed he even questioned them. They threatened to have his license taken away. After that, he backed off and they left him alone."

"Why not ask the DA to look into it?" Rori asked.

"I did by phone, but the department said they would need more information before they could spend money looking into a questionable murder," Rosemary said.

"I ask again, is it just the truth you're after?" Neil asked

"How many times do we have to answer the same question?" Gerry said.

Neil felt an evasiveness in the way they spoke. He wasn't buying it, but said nothing.

Rosemary looked to Neil. "Of course we did all this by phone with an attorney before we came up with our plan. We didn't want the hospital staff to know what we looked like and spoil our chances of further investigation."

"So if you've talked to the police and didn't like what they said, what will you do when you find the so-called truth?" Rori asked.

"There's always a higher authority," Rosemary said.

Neil felt they wanted revenge, but hadn't heard them say it yet. They were two highly-educated people, and he knew they weren't going to say anything incriminating. But still, he felt he had to bring it up.

"I just wanted to ask you this one question: are you planning revenge?"

He watched their faces for any signs, if they stared at each other or cleared their throat. It seemed they had rehearsed enough that they showed no outward sign.

Rosemary smiled and said, "When I said higher authority, I didn't mean we were playing God. That's what revenge is, and I'm a doctor. I save lives, I don't take them."

"If revenge is not on your minds, would you be willing to help us? Perhaps we can help each other," Neil said.

"I'm not sure how you could help us," Rosemary said.

"If you could help us find out what's going on with the Vice President, then maybe we can do some more digging on the hospital. We want to see any records on Willowdale. Working together, we may be able to help each other. If we pull on a few threads, the whole thing may come unraveled."

"The more we expose the hospital, the more we expose the bad people who work there," Rori said. She understood what Neil was trying to do. Working together, it would be easier to keep an eye on them.

"It sounds like a good idea, but I'm not sure we want our names out in the public," Rosemary said. "This appears to be bigger than us, and I'd be afraid of someone coming after us."

"If you give us information on the Vice President and your mother, we'll protect your anonymity," Neil said. "But we will have to talk to our boss. If he says we can't keep your name out of it, then I'll tell you."

"You would do that?" Gerry asked.

"Absolutely," Neil said. "It's our journalistic duty."

"Give us a number where you can be reached and we'll be in contact with you," Rosemary said. "I want to think on this overnight."

Neil passed a business card to Rosemary and thanked them for their time. He headed for the door and Rori followed his lead. As they left, Neil took notice of their car. "Does that car look familiar to you?" he asked.

"Not really."

"Does it look like the one that was at The Black Sow? You know, when we met Howard," Neil said.

"No, I don't think so," Rori said. "I thought Maureen said it looked like a Mercedes, but that's a Volvo. I don't think it was blue either. It was much lighter, maybe even silver."

"They must have been checking on us to see if we were somehow involved. They know what we're looking for, but I'm not sure they're being totally truthful with us," Neil said.

"How so?"

"Why wouldn't they just hire a good lawyer that works with a detective agency? Lots of security types around leftover from the cutbacks at the CIA. It doesn't make sense."

Rori listened.

"I think they'll help us, but they're not just being benevolent. We have to watch them. We don't want to get in their way and be caught up in it."

Chapter Thirty-Eight

"Come in, come in. Welcome to my home," Churchill Brewer said, as the doorman brought Hansen Baldwin into the library. "Mr. Baldwin, I hope I didn't cause you any concern by asking you here."

"Not concern, although I am curious as to why a man of your stature would be interested in me."

"Would you care for a drink? A little *George T. Stagg?* It's been rated the best bourbon in the world for thirteen years straight."

Hansen was leery about this meeting. He wasn't sure there wouldn't be something in the drink. "Not right now."

"I hear great things about you. I hear you're a smart, intelligent congressman who knows how and when to compromise. A lost art, you know, like so many talents in this country."

"I try to do what's best for the American people, as best as I can."

"I believe you have misspoken," Churchill said.

"How's that?"

"I believe you do what's right for the American people as long as it benefits your future."

"You must be misinformed," Hansen said.

"Not likely," Churchill said. "I believe I'm correct that you've had a few people trying to knock you off pedestal. Trying to take your seat in Congress."

Hansen smiled, knowing Churchill did his research and not wanting to expand what he may or not know. "What's this meeting about?"

"I love it when people like to get right down to business, Mr. Baldwin. A sign of intelligence."

"Call me Hansen or Congressman, please."

"I hear you have aspirations?"

"Yes, I do."

"But no money."

"You could say that."

"I just did."

"Without sounding redundant, what's this meeting about? What are you up to?"

"It's about you. It's about what you are willing to do to see your aspirations come true."

"Do?"

"Are you playing word games with me, Congressman?"

"You send a limousine to pick me up without a word of explanation. I've heard of your reputation, so here I am. I don't want to just *do* anything. I've worked hard to get where I am, even though I don't have money like some of my colleagues."

"Is the House of Representatives as far as you want to go in life?"

"I haven't thought that far ahead."

"Congressman, don't give me that crap. You continue to insult my intelligence," Churchill said. He puffed on his cigar and waved his hands in the air as he talked. "If you have aspirations, then you've thought about it. I want you to tell me what you want. Do you plan on staying in the House? Becoming a senator or governor…or maybe president? Have you thought that far ahead?"

"Yes, but like you said, I have a tight budget. I take it election by election. I see how things are flying, and then I make my decisions. It's not like I want to be jumping around in the federal government. Governor would not be out of the question. Less money is needed in my little state."

"Money is the easy part," Churchill said with a throaty chuckle.

"Are you making me an offer?"

"Depends."

"Depends on what?"

"It depends on you. It depends on your willingness to make sacrifices, your willingness to take orders."

"Take orders from whom?"

"Does it matter from whom? Are you prepared to take orders and not try to be a big shot once we get you into the mix?"

"I'm a big shot in my state now."

"You're a big shot in a state that has a little over a half a million people. Shit, you've got more cattle than people. That isn't piss. Are you willing to take orders in order to get elected?"

"I can take orders, but I'd rather take directions from a team, not from someone who wants to push me around."

"Whether you take orders or directions is a matter of semantics. You'll have to do as you're told, or you just won't do."

"Do?"

"Will you give me a damn full thought?" Churchill's voice intensified. "Do you want more to your life, and are you willing to take orders to ensure success? Are you willing to be in the limelight all of the time? Are you willing to sacrifice in order to be President?" Churchill's cigar spittle splattered the furniture as he grilled Hansen.

"I've thought about being governor, not President."

"You aim too low."

"I'm not the type of person that maps my life out too far in advance."

"That's a common problem. Life is a map. To conjure up the ghost of Frost, you must make a decision as to which road in life you will take. I contend it's too late if you wait for that fork in the road to show its ugly face. What I'm saying is you must design your road, not the other way around. If you wait for the path to present itself, then you're already behind the mark. The fork you take may be one of convenience or necessity, but it may not be the path to your ordained destination. It's all about foresight."

"I see," Hansen said. "You mean if I'm thinking about being governor, I should be laying the ground work now."

"What I think is you should be laying the ground work to be President. Would you like to be President?"

Hansen stood and walked around the room, trying to figure what Churchill had in mind. *Is he offering me the presidency? Is he willing to front his power and money?* He wasn't sure so he decided to be as direct as he could, without sounding like a cowboy.

"Are you offering me the presidency?"

"I am, if you've got the *cojones.*"

"Let's stop beating around the bush. Do you think I could be the next president? Do you think you could help me get the money?"

Churchill laughed. "My god, son, we wouldn't even be having this conversation if I didn't."

"Is it that simple?"

"Simple? Nothing's simple, but if I say it, it's completely doable. There will be many roadblocks down the road. Unforeseen shit. With my power and my people, you'll be protected." Churchill dropped any resemblance of a smile. This had to be a serious choreographed moment. He knew Hansen was running information through his head.

"I'm to believe you've picked me out of the blue? I'm to believe our nation has been so corrupted that with the snap of someone's fingers, any old cowboy can become President?"

"Congressman, you did things to become a representative. You did things to people that tried to block your election."

Hansen tried to determine how much Churchill knew.

"I see that look. I know all about your dealings. Your second term election and that lobbyist. Yes, I know what you did to your opponent. I know about the pictures of your opponent naked, in a boat with someone other than his wife."

Hansen's eyes widened.

"Funny how those things just happen to show up at the right moment," Churchill said. He raised his eyebrow as an acceptable means to an end.

"I don't know what you're talking about, but it is funny how things happen," Hansen said. "So it looks like you've done a lot of legwork. I hope it wasn't wasted."

"I'm sure it wasn't wasted, Congressman," Churchill said. "The truth is I admire you. There are situations . . . things that arise in life requiring special attention. We can't have someone's hard work go up in smoke because some asshole gets in the way. I admire you for knowing when to pull the trigger."

"Not saying I did anything wrong, but now that this conversation is out there, where do we go from here? Obviously you think I have some talent, even though I'm an obscure congressman."

"Obscure enough to capture the ordinary man from Wyoming— and the rest of the country. They love new blood. It makes them feel like they have an ordinary man—like them. Someone they can believe in. Churchill pulled himself out of his leather chair. Do you understand how people will be tripping over themselves just to see you, by the time we get to the election? We'll drive the people into hysteria. With his hand out in the air, as though he were picking an apple off a tree. The people will feel like they plucked you from the political tree."

Hansen had his reservations. *Is this all there is?* He was somewhat scared. "What if I say no?"

"You'd be a fool. But you're not the only clean face that could be President. You're just the one I feel *should* be."

"I'll take that drink now."

Churchill poured Hansen a glass of bourbon, neat.

"You even know how I like by bourbon. You seem to have a handle on me."

"Just doing what I do best. I'm a good judge of men," Churchill said.

Hansen found a leather lounge chair and plopped down into it.

Churchill stood over him and waved his drink around in the air as he talked. "You see, Hansen, on a small scale, you knocked your opponent out for your second term. When it comes to the big time, stuff like that is done every day. And once you develop the reputation, no one will ever fuck with you again."

Hansen took a sip of his drink, letting his mind absorb all Churchill was saying. In addition to filling his glass with whiskey, the man also filled his ego to the brim. Still, he was feeling uncertain about it all.

"When do you need an answer?"

"Can you take orders and do as I say?"

"Maybe."

Churchill was always used to getting his way and hated being questioned. This hick cowboy who couldn't give him a direct answer was starting to get under his skin.

"Maybe I should just get your ass kicked right out of Congress before you ever start your new term. There's no maybe." Churchill yelled as he threw his glass across the room, smashing it against a Monet. The painting was worth millions, but Churchill liked to grandstand to make a point.

"If you want to be President, you must follow the wisdom of those who have come before you. I'll put together a group, but they'll be my team, not yours. If you want to get anywhere, you'll listen, unless you're not who I thought you were. If you're not who I thought you were, then we'll part ways. You have twenty-four hours. If you can't decide by then, you're too indecisive for me."

Churchill pressed a button and a doorman appeared.

Hansen stood when the doorman walked in and assumed that it was the end of the meeting. He downed his drink, and shook Churchill's hand. *Twenty-four hours . . . not much time to decide if you wish to change your entire life.*

* * *

"Warren, this is Churchill. I just met with our next President."

"What do you think?" Warren asked. "Can he handle it?"

"I think he'll do. He only has to keep on script. We'll handle the rest. It's not like he's going to be needed for four years," Churchill said, laughing.

"He'll listen. All we have to do is have the Speaker talk to him, and he'll be with us," Warren said. "It's worked before and there's no reason to think it won't work again."

"He seems to have a lot of reservations. He surprised me. I guess those cowboys are pretty independent," Churchill said.

"Why don't you give the Speaker a cordial call to get her on board?" Warren said. "If I call, it'll seem a little strange, don't you agree?"

"I'm not going to tell Hansen who his running mate is until we're well into the campaign. By that time, it'll be too late for him to back out. I gave him twenty-four hours to make the decision. He'll go home and make love to his wife. She'll tell him she never made love to a presidential candidate before. She won't realize she'll never get to make love to the actual president. He'll be dead before that happens."

Chapter Thirty-Nine

The excitement made Warren eager to get out of the hospital. He rang for the nurse, who showed up almost immediately.

"How may I help you, Mr. Vice President?" Nurse Boothroyd asked.

"When can I get the hell out of this place?" Warren said loudly. "It's been more than two weeks." He pulled himself out of bed, and the Nurse moved to steady him. "I want you to find out when I can get out of here," he said. "I've got important things to do."

He stood demanding an answer, and then began to feel himself sway. He grabbed the side table to steady himself, but his bulk tipped it over. He grabbed the bed, and the nurse wrapped her arm around his waist. She steadied him and helped him sit on the edge of the bed.

"Slide up a little onto the bed," she said. "See? You're not ready to go anywhere. If you don't trust the doctor, you're going to be here a long time. You're taking some strong medicine."

"I just want to get on with my life," he said as the nurse took his vitals. She stepped out and made a call to the doctor.

"Dr. Moskowitz, this is Nurse Boothroyd. The Vice President is demanding to be released, but he just about fainted trying to walk around. His blood pressure is very high. What would you like me to do?"

"Give him another shot," Dr. Moskowitz said in a controlled voice. "Check the chart and give him the same dosage as last time. I don't want to see him up and about. He needs to rest or he's not ever getting out of here."

The nurse returned to Willowdale and told him the doctor wanted him to rest. "When you wake up, the doctor will come and talk to you about leaving."

Warren was agitated and continued to mumble. "I just want to get my life back."

The nurse attached the needle to the IV drip, and in moments the Vice President went into another catatonic sleep.

Chapter Forty

The Black Sow was now familiar and comfortable, despite not being the most antiseptic environment. The beer was cold, and it was a mostly quiet venue to discuss their next move. Rori and Neil sat in the same booth where they met Howard. Rori arrived first and made pleasantries with Bert. He brought over beer for her and Neil and stood talking to her until Neil arrived. Neil sat but didn't seem interested in drinking. Rori wasn't sure what was going on, but she could sense something was on his mind.

"You know, it's been a long time since I felt this good about my job," Neil said. "I don't know how to explain it, but it's all so exciting. It's exciting because you believed in me as a partner. For that I'm thankful."

"No, it's me who's thankful you were willing to believe in this country girl. I know you're the reason I was hired. I've learned so much from you. It would have taken me years to learn on my own. I hope we can work like this for a long time."

"I'm not going to be here much longer. I was going to stay another year, but I can't see that happening. I've made some decisions and up until now it hasn't been that much fun. This is going to be my last big story."

Rori didn't like what she was hearing. She was going to lose her partner. *That's why he's been so instructive lately.*

"There's something I want you to have." Neil reached into his jacket pocket and pulled out his flask.

Rori held up her hand. "No thanks, I'll pass."

Neil laughed. "No, I'm not offering you a drink. I want you to have this."

Rori looked surprised and confused at the same time. Neil recognized her expression.

"What's this all about?" she said.

"There has to come a time when you can look into a mirror without flinching at the sight of your reflection. There has to be a time when you look into that mirror and realize enough time has passed . . . Time to forgive yourself. It's like AA: the pain is still there, but admitting your faults is the first step to healing.

"I want you to take this. I want you to have this as a token of appreciation for what you have done for me. What I'm saying is when you look at this flask, I hope you'll think of me. Think of our friendship. You should know drinking is not the solution. You made me realize that. Take this as my thanks. I don't want it or need it any longer."

Rori was, for once, speechless. She grabbed it, spun the top off, held it up and toasted. "To our friendship, teamwork and faith in each other." She tipped it up and took a good swig.

She didn't always show emotion, but Neil had hit a spot. She could only half-stand in the booth, but she was able to reach over enough to give Neil a kiss on the cheek.

* * *

Rori looked toward the door as it swung open. In walked Rosemary and Gerry Waterford. Rori gave Neil a nudge under the table and whispered, "We've got company."

Neil turned and looked over his shoulder, and returned his eyes to the table, where they met Rori's just as she raised her eyebrows.

"Good afternoon," Rori said and stood up to greet them as they approached. "Nice to see you again. Have a seat."

Rori moved over next to Neil to allow the Waterfords to sit together. She wanted to watch their expressions as they spoke.

As was typical of the couple, Rosemary did most of the talking.

"I—we—will help you. We're looking for some sort of tie-in to my mother's death—that's all we want. You, on the other hand, want to know what all the hush-hush is about concerning the Vice President. You have to promise us one thing: whatever we find, you will expose the whole matter. Expose it enough that they'll have to bring the DA in to investigate."

Neil sat listening, his index finger resting on his temple. "Agreed. I think we're both—all of us are looking for answers and the truth."

Rori's tone was not as harsh as it was at the house. "I'm sorry about your mother, and I hope we can help you get to the bottom of this. We'll do whatever we can. If for some reason we can't, we'll give you the truth."

"Thank you," Rosemary said.

"Do you know anything about the hospital's record-keeping?" Neil asked.

"We've been trying to find things out ourselves, but they have a high-paying clientele, and everything is locked up pretty tight. Gerry has the keys to everything *except* the record cabinets. He's been experimenting with keys, but hasn't been able to create an exact copy. The key to the office is held by the nurses or human resources, but we can't seem to get it long enough to copy it, and even then we'd have to find a way to access the cabinet without being seen."

"What we would like to see are the personnel files of Rosemary's mother. We'd like to see if she was fired, laid off or whatever information was on the record."

"Do you think that information is in the locked cabinets?" Rori asked.

"I have no reason to think differently," Gerry said. "They have to have something. The HR office is locked up most of the time. If we go in there to clean, someone waits for us until we are done."

"During one of our escapades, we watched a nurse play around with something on the bookcase. It was in the living room area, and when she found this *thing*, a drawer popped opened at the other end," Neil said. "She then went over and pulled out some paperwork, went back to the lever or button and the drawer disappeared."

"Next time I go in, I'll see if I can see anything," Rosemary said.

"Be careful—it may have an alarm on it," Rori said.

"The keys are given to us by the nurses. It's not like we could just go in there when they're busy. There are alarms in the office, so even if we *were* able to get in the office, they would know right away," Gerry said. "I could shut it down temporarily, but we still need the key."

"Are there any medical records in there?" Rori asked.

"Only for current patients. Once they check out, their records go with them," Rosemary said. "I hear a lot as to what's going on. A while back I heard the nurses talking about how they have to get the records together to go with the clients."

"What's the reason they have records in the office? Why would they also have some hidden in the suites?" Neil asked.

"I'll bet one's real and one's fake," Rori said. "Just a hunch."

"We better think of a way to get this done before our Vice President flies the coop," Neil said.

"What if we were able to make a copy of the keys?" Rori asked. "You know, like you see in the movies, where they make a wax impression of the key."

"That's a good idea," Gerry said, "but I don't know how to do that. I could try to make one, but then we'd have to try it out, too. And then there's the problem about having the right equipment."

"I may know someone who could help us," Neil said.

Rori gave Neil a look of surprise. "One of your snitches with a nefarious background?"

"Kind of," Neil said, "but he's very good. And cheap."

Rori gave him a wry smile. "If we got the key made, do you think you could get a picture of the Vice President's files? If your mothers are there, just take them. They may or may not be in the same drawer. They're not going to miss an employee's records—but they would miss Willowdale's."

"We'd have to create a diversion, but we wouldn't have much time. You can cut the power or do something crazy when you clean the office," Neil said looking toward Rosemary. "Perhaps both. Whatever gets the job done. Let me talk to my friend, and I'll get back to you tomorrow."

"Would you give us your cell numbers so we can reach you?" Rori asked.

"I'll give you one, but we're not allowed to have them at work, so you'll have to leave a message," Rosemary said.

Looking over to Neil, Rori said, "Can we go see your friend today?"

"No problem. Just let me make a call when we're done. I want you two to figure out some idea on how to create a diversion so you can get time in the office. I'll check with my friend, too," Neil said.

Gerry leaned over the table as though he were a quarterback ready to call the play. "We've been thinking about this for some time and looking for an opportunity. We could take our time, but you can't since the Vice President is not going to be here forever. I've been listening to the nurses, and I think he's getting restless and may leave in the next week or so."

Neil rubbed his hands together, wishing he hadn't given Rori the flask just yet.

Rori could see he was starting to reach for his flask until he realized he no longer had it. She reached into her coat and offered it. He looked at her hand, took a deep breath, and then shook his head no.

The Waterford's stood up to leave and Neil and Rori followed suit.

"We'll get this done and put it to bed," Neil said. "From there we'll let the authorities take over. Understood?"

"Absolutely," Gerry said.

As the couple left the bar, Neil and Rori sat back down. Neil peered out the window. "Do you trust them?" Rori asked.

"Not sure," Neil said. "But we have no choice. If they want to take the risk, I'm okay with that. A little record confiscation is all I'm willing to do. If they have visions of taking revenge by harming someone, then I can't abide."

* * *

Rosemary and Gerry got to their car and looked at each other, each waiting for the other to say it. Rosemary spoke first.

"Do you trust them?

"Not sure," Gerry said. "They're reporters. They want news and who knows if they'll live up to their end of the deal. But we have no choice. If they want to take the risk, let them, but if they get in our way then we'll kill them, too."

Chapter Forty-One

Louise Brownfield was one of Churchill's recruits. He wanted her to run for President, but she had a big mouth and hated to be told what to do. Besides, her husband had too many shady deals to make her a viable candidate. As a congresswoman she was adequate, but she complained too much and her husband had been looked at several times by the Justice Department. Somehow he always seemed to slip through the jaws of justice. She rose to Speaker of the House, but only with Churchill's support. Churchill used her, but as it turned out she was not his type. Regardless that didn't stop him from holding some vague and not-so-vague threats over her head.

Churchill sat in his leather chair in his office, rolling his cigar around in his mouth, contemplating his next move. He was a big man with a robust body and an evil tone to his laugh. He took a puff of his cigar and placed it into his hand, wrapping his stubby index finger around it. He reached over, picked up the phone and called the congresswoman.

"Yes, what is it," a shrill voice said.

"Geez, Louise, do you always answer your phone like a crow in heat?"

"Who is this? I don't have time for stupid phone calls."

"It's Churchill."

Her voice immediately went into submission. "I'm sorry, Churchill," she said, stumbling over her words. "I'm just getting over this stupid election, and I can't think straight. You understand, don't you?"

Churchill was silent a few seconds as he took another puff.

"Churchill, are you there?" she said.

"Yes, yes, I'm here. Louise, it's just an election, not the end of the world."

She stammered more. "But—but—"

"Louise, get a hold of yourself and stop thinking about the past. It's over and done with, and I don't want to hear another thing about it." Churchill's voice resonated over the phone, taking the Speaker by surprise.

"I understand," she said, "but it's just that we had—had—"

Churchill yelled over the phone this time. "Stop. Did you hear a word I just said? Just shut up. I need to get down to business."

The phone went quiet again as Churchill took another puff of his cigar. Louise took the opportunity to pour herself another glass of bourbon.

Churchill left the cigar in his mouth as he began to speak.

"Louise, yesterday I had a conversation with Rep. Hansen Baldwin. Do you know him?"

"Why yes I do. I've moved him onto a couple committees. He's a very knowledgeable man, but a little country for me. We take what the voters give us."

"I want you to talk to him and persuade him to join my team."

"You're team?" she asked.

"Tell him if I say something, it's as good as done."

"Well, what is it you want him to do?" she asked.

"Need-to-know basis and you don't need to know, at this time."

"How can I get him to do as you ask unless I know what it is?"

"Listen, I don't care what you tell him. Tell him he's going to win the damn lottery, but just assure him he can't do anything without me. Got it? And one more thing—I want you to start letting him head some committees."

"What do you mean, move him up?"

"I want to start seeing him on TV. I want to see him investigating some of the new president's men. Get him in the appropriations, maybe head up the ways and means. Get him into the budget process."

"Well, I'd love to, but you know Rep. Shipirro has seniority."

The conversation wasn't going the way Churchill wanted. He didn't like excuses. "Louise," Churchill said sternly.

"Yes, I'm listening," she said.

"Madam Speaker, do you like your job and the benefits that come with it?"

"Why, of course. And I know I have you to thank for it, but it's just—"

"It's just nothing," he said. "I want you to take care of the orders I just gave you, and no more excuses."

The next thing Louise heard was the dial tone. She tipped the bottle up to her lips and downed a couple of stiff shots, then mumbled to herself. "Aw shit."

Chapter Forty-Two

Lt. Snedicker sat in his car across from The Black Sow and saw his two cleaning people enter and leave the bar. His paranoia ran rampant.

Did they plan this meeting, or did they just happen to be in the same place as the two reporters? Why are these two reporters still hanging around?

He picked up his cell phone and made a call to Dr. Moskowitz. "The four of them were at the bar at the same time."

"Is it just a coincidence?" Dr. Moskowitz asked.

"Not sure, but I'll keep an eye on them."

"Should we hire new help?"

"Not sure. They do the job with no problems, and do it unsupervised.

"Don't let that 'unsupervised' go too far. That's when something comes along to bite us in the ass."

"I know. That's why I'm checking on them. All the other clearance I'd have to put new people through would be more work. Unless we get some illegals, but they'd never pass the security checks. Let's not jump the gun."

"Don't worry about how good they are. Just make sure they don't interfere. I've got commitments to people, and they won't like it if people start to talk."

"Understood," the lieutenant said. "It's not them that I'm concerned with, it's those fucking reporters."

Dr. Moskowitz rolled his eyes. "You don't have to use profanity."

"Don't tell me what the fuck to say."

Dr. Moskowitz cringed. The lieutenant was a crude man and the doctor disliked crudeness. He knew in time he'd have to take a Machiavellian approach. He'd let Vitaly handle that. The problem was he'd have to do it before the lieutenant decided to do the same. *His time is coming.*

"If the reporters are gone then the problem is resolved," Dr. Moskowitz said. "Don't let it get so far that it involves the hospital."

"I understand. I hear O'Connor's just a drunk anyway, and things have a way of happening to drunks."

"I repeat, don't let it come back here to the hospital."

"Sure…as you said," the lieutenant said, as though he were really listening, and hung up.

* * *

Snedicker drove down the country road, looking for a particular spot where the hill took a steep decline and dropped into a quarry. He'd followed the reporters on this road before and knew the good spots. He pulled over and walked to the edge. Looking down into the quarry he spoke openly. "This is a good place to end this charade."

He squeezed his fist and then peed down the side of the hill, marking his spot.

Chapter Forty-Three

As soon as Rosemary and Gerry left the bar, Neil made a call to his friend, Bernie Milo. Bernie had been in a little of this and that when he was a young man. A little time in jail for a little too much of that, but now he was too old for even a little of this.

He settled down to showing others how to do what he no longer had the ambition to do—for a price, of course—but he never participated in the dirty deeds himself. Not since Neil got a policeman to look the other way and saved Bernie from a lifetime inside. For that he never questioned Neil's motives, nor was there ever a need for payment. The way Bernie felt, he would never have enough time to repay Neil.

Bernie was a little man, no more than five and a half feet tall. He had a head that appeared too big for his body and a nose to match. He always joked his head was so big because he needed space for his enormous brain. Fellow thieves felt he wasn't too far off from the truth. His cleverness and knowledge kept him as a sought-after planner and helper, as well as in the sights of detectives.

Bernie knew how alarm circuits worked. He knew how to tease alarms, locks, and just about anything else, and make them act the way he wanted. They hadn't made a door, safe or alarm he could not enter, open or disarm. He had a hard time passing up the opportunity to bust open a good lock, which was how the trouble always started. To aid him in his creative habit, he created a workshop where he could practice openly without harming anyone. His workshop contained old and new safes, alarm systems, along with catalogues showcasing the latest and greatest anti-theft technology. He always kept up on the new products coming out, especially with the new controls. He felt equipment today was easier to bust into than the stuff in the old days.

Neil explained to Bernie over the phone what he wanted to do. By the time Rori and Neil arrived, Bernie had already started working on the situation.

Bernie's shop was in an old building off 11th Street, in the Northeast section of D.C. The building was more than a hundred years old. Bernie liked that . . . thicker walls giving him more security from prying ears. Most of the other shops had seen better days, but it suited his clientele. The business was a home alarm company that didn't care if anyone ever called. Most of his business was passing along how-to to whoever needed it and had the money. Other than that, he knew nothing and was happy to tell that to anyone who was curious. As far as he was concerned, his workshop was all hypothetical and there was no crime in that.

Rori stepped into the shop ahead of Neil, and Bernie's face lit up. He had always been a ladies' man, but even though his prime was well behind him, he still appreciated a beautiful woman.

"Neil, my old friend, who is this beautiful lady with you?" He didn't wait for an answer, nor did he put his hand out to Neil. Instead, he took Rori's in his and kissed it. "Bernie Milo at your service."

"Easy does it, tiger. You're gonna scare her off."

Rori looked at Bernie. "Watch yourself, bud, or I'll chew that hand off."

Bernie dropped his smile and pulled his hand back.

Neil laughed. "Hey Bernie you better be careful with this one."

"I'm sorry if I offended you, but I'm an old man and I appreciate beauty," Bernie said, giving Rori a glimmer of a smirk.

Rori looked at Bernie. "As long as you know when to stop. I can handle a little attention."

"Bernie, we're in your shop, not some sleazy bar," Neil said.

"I'm Rori Cahill. If you're a friend of Neil's, then I'll accept you as a friend. Just don't overstep."

Neil turned his eyes to Bernie. "Good to see you're still kicking," Neil said. He stuck one hand out and placed his other on Bernie's shoulder. "You behave yourself with my friend, or I'll send her out to the car to wait."

"No you won't. I can take care of myself," Rori said.

Bernie raised his eyebrows as he looked to Neil for help.

"She doesn't bite—unless you bite first," Neil said.

"I'll keep my fangs in," Bernie said.

"So good to see you. If you could keep your eyes on me, we can get down to business."

Bernie started to reach for Rori's hand again but thought better. "How may I help you?"

"I—we have this situation where we need to make a key, but we only have a few minutes to make a copy. We have some type of high-caliber alarm system too. We can't just break into the room and then into the cabinet. We have inside people, but we're not sure how to get it done."

"These inside people, we're not sure they have a clue what they're doing," Rori said.

"These people inside, what do they have access to?" Bernie asked.

"Just about everything except the room we want to get into," Rori said. "That's why we need the key...or maybe keys, we aren't sure."

"The keys are the easy part; well, it's all easy if you know what you're doing," Bernie said, as he walked over and locked the door, then turned over a sign in the door showing he was now closed. "Come back to my bench."

Rori and Neil followed Bernie to a back room containing a library of manuals, stacked neatly on wall shelves and tools organized as neatly as if it were an operating room.

"Is she okay?" Bert asked, pointing to Rori.

"You just manhandled the woman and now you ask if she's trustworthy? She wouldn't be with me if she wasn't," Neil said. "She's carrying so you better be careful about offending her."

Bernie took a big gulp. He walked over and turned on some music. "You never know," he said in a voice just barely audible over the music, then reached over and opened a drawer where he picked up a metal container of Altoids.

"No thanks," Neil said.

"I'll have one," Rori said.

Bernie laughed. When he opened it up, it was full of wax on both sides, with slots cut out on two sides. He asked for a house key. Rori reached into her purse and handed one to Bernie. Taking the key, he laid it across the wax with the larger part outside the slot. He closed it tightly and then turned the key over and put it into the other slot, repeating the process. When he opened the case for a second time, there were two perfect impressions of the key.

"This is how you get a copy. Then you bring the box back to me and I'll make the key. Piece of cake."

"You are amazing," Rori said. "You can make a key from that impression?"

"With a little work, but shouldn't be too much trouble," Bernie said.

Neil picked up the Altoids tin and looked at the impression. "How do you get the wax off the key?"

"Just a quick wipe with alcohol," Bernie said. "Anything left will come off in the key-slot. Nothing noticeable."

"Here's the problem. A nurse opens the door and waits for the cleaning to be done, so they are being watched," Neil said.

"I'll bet the nurse doesn't want to be there playing babysitter for a cleaning woman. Chances are they'll only have half an eye on them," Bernie said.

"Could be, but we're not sure," Rori said.

"Trust me," Bernie said. "I know human nature, and if you're doing a job that has nothing to do with your job, you're not going to pay that much attention."

"Point taken," Neil said.

The three were quiet for a moment as they tried to come up with an idea.

Neil looked to Rori. "You look like you have something on your mind."

"Kind of," Rori said. "What if Gerry or Rosemary have a real container of Altoids, too? She offers the nurse one and then drops them on the floor. She gets down on the floor on her hands and knees to pick them up. While down there, they crawl behind the desk and make key copies. If the nurse sees the can she'll think nothing about it, especially if she's not paying that much attention."

"Regardless the nurse is still standing there and the keys may be in the door," Neil said.

"Could we create a diversion at the same time?" Bernie said. "Some type of alarm malfunction where she'd have to run off and check on it?"

"If they hear an alarm, they'd have to go check on their patient," Rori said.

"Could you show us how to set off an alarm?" Neil asked.

Bernie smiled. "I can do you one better than that." He walked over to a workbench and took the cover off of a box that resembled circuit-breakers with a red light on the top. Bernie plugged the box into an electrical outlet, then reached into another drawer and pulled out a couple of wires that looked like car jumper cables, but miniature.

Neil and Rori watched Bernie clip the wires onto the circuits.

"Take this device and walk across the room and press this button," Bernie said to Rori, as he pointed to a red button on the device.

Rori looked nervous.

"It's not going to hurt you," Bernie said.

Rori crossed the room, pressed the button and the light came on.

"That light would be the alarm going off," Bernie said.

"Wow," Rori said.

She pressed it again and it went out. She moved around the room and tried it several times more, turning it off and on.

"Will this work anywhere?" Neil asked.

"Anywhere in the building," Bernie said. "Just set the jumpers, flip the switch and the next sound will be the alarm. The jumpers to the circuit where the alarms are connected, that's the secret."

"That takes care of the diversion, but what if the nurse doesn't leave the keys in the door?" Rori asked.

Bernie reached into the toolbox and pulled out another small device about five inches long. It had a round head much like a pencil with a coin stuck to one end.

"Most cabinet locks are the same. Stick this in just like a key, and hit it once. The lock will pop up. When you're done, push the lock back down. They won't know what's wrong and will have to call a locksmith."

Rori picked up the device. "And how do you know all this stuff?"

Bernie smiled again. "I worked hard on my lessons, so I could have money to buy jewels for beautiful women like you."

Chapter Forty-Four

"Rosemary, we'll meet you at your house tonight. We have too much to talk about to do it at the bar. We've got tools that are going to make this much easier," Neil said, leaving a message on the phone.

"So what's the plan?" Rori asked.

"I wish I knew."

"You just *said* you had a plan."

Neil smiled, reached into his pocket for his flask, and came up empty.

"Do you have the flask?" he asked. Without waiting for an answer, he said, "Give it to me. I need to think."

Rori handed it over, and Neil quickly spun the cap off, as he'd done so many times before. "You know, I can't ever remember taking the cap off before. It's like the flask was always open. Always open so I could drown my sorrows."

Neil just stared at it and passed the flask back to Rori. She started to put it away, and Neil said, "What are you doing?"

"I'm putting it away."

"Take a drink, I need to think."

"Then you take a drink," Rori said laughing.

"No, I don't need it anymore, and if I don't need it, I don't want it." Neil smiled. "Go ahead and have a sip for me. It'll help us think."

Rori tipped it back.

"Okay, that's enough. We want to think, not stink."

Rori put the flask away.

* * *

"You were right," Neil said. "Bernie showed us how we can make a wax copy of the keys, but how do we go about this is the real question? Maybe we should have pressed Bernie a little more for ideas."

"Neil, this isn't rocket science. Why don't we just create a diversion? Listen, when she drops the mints, she presses the button to make it look like the Vice President's alarm has gone off. I'm assuming some red lights go off or something. When the nurse runs off, Rosemary can make the copy with the fake tin. If she doesn't leave the keys, she can just break in and grab the folders. If she's got the time, she can photograph the Vice President's records. Most of Willowdale's records, I suspect, are in that secret drawer, so whatever we get we'll sort out after.

"We may have to create the same diversion a second time? Maybe with *us* at the door instead? Whatever we have to do to get what we're looking for," Rori said.

Neil looked at her. "How'd you get to be so smart?"

"I had a good teacher. I'm glad we had that drink. Maybe we should have another?" She popped the flask out and took another swig then shoved it back into her jacket without offering to Neil.

He licked his lips.

Chapter Forty-Five

"I'm feeling great," the Vice President said loudly. "I'm sure there must have been improprieties, or I would not have lost the election."

Austin said little, not wanting to get Willowdale riled, but his thoughts were harsh and he felt it best to keep them to himself. *You couldn't even carry your home state.*

The door opened and Dr. Moskowitz entered. Everyone stood. "I hope we're all doing well on this fine day."

"Cut the crap and let me know when I can get out of here," Willowdale said.

"Please, let's all have a seat and talk this out," the doctor said. "I have you on a drug called Medifinne. You seem to be doing remarkably well, but it does mask things, and there's the problem. Even if we cut the dosage, you will still need to rest. Rest is what will get you back to normal. Little by little, you can re-enter the real world."

"How long?" Ann asked.

"A month or two, maybe less, maybe more. Everyone is different. When you have a nervous breakdown, you have to dig into the causes. We have to determine if additional medicines are needed."

"I can't stay here that long," Willowdale said.

"In a little over a month, you will no longer be Vice President. You'll have plenty of time to rest," Dr. Moskowitz said. "You don't have to stay here if you stay out of the spotlight. That's all I ask. Short days, rest, and keeping up the treatments."

"And he'll be fine?" Austin asked.

"This medicine helps heal the brain faster."

"But..." Austin said.

Dr. Moskowitz stood up and walked around the sitting area. "What

I'm saying is this is not black and white. In the old days, you'd take antidepressants, rest and have regular visits with a psychiatrist for years. Not to say that you shouldn't talk to someone, Mr. Vice President, but this medicine is not just avant-garde—it's a healthy alternative. It takes you out of that place where life is meaningless and gives you a euphoria and enthusiasm."

"Sounds like I should have had this before the election. Then maybe we wouldn't be here," the Vice President said.

"See, Mr. Vice President, that's it, you joke. That's the medication talking. Behind the medication, you are still very sick. Rest is what's needed," the doctor said. As he talked, he circled around the couch then returned and sat in a chair in front of them.

"There's only so much time one can stay in the hospital with a broken leg," Ann said.

Dr. Moskowitz checked the chart again. "I can write up paperwork to make it look legit. I could make it so he could stay here through the end of the year."

"What do you mean?" Austin asked.

"Perhaps an infection delaying things without causing suspicion."

"The hell with that. I don't want to stay here another six weeks."

"You're not hearing me, are you?" Dr. Moskowitz said.

"I'm hearing you, but you're not hearing me. I'm not the type to just hang around. I still hold the office of Vice President for a time."

"I'm going to say one thing, and then I'll tell you when you can leave. If you don't give yourself enough rest, you'll be back in here before the end of your term. That being said, how about you ship out next Friday?" Dr. Moskowitz said. "But only under the condition I continue to give you shots after you leave."

"How often would he need the shots?" Austin asked.

"At first, every week, and then we'll taper off to every two or three weeks. We'd have to see as things go. One week from today, you can leave."

"Good," Willowdale said. "Let's get this thing rolling."

Austin looked over to Ann, and she stared back at him intensely. *Better enjoy ourselves.* He still couldn't separate the messages coming from his head and those coming from his groin.

Chapter Forty-Six

"The Vice President will be released on Friday. Make sure all is updated at the end of your shift. As always, we will give them their chart and all other documents in our normal folder. The one in the drawer will be given to them when I make arrangements for future treatments. Once they are out of the building, make sure all computer records are cleared. I will have security check them on Friday afternoon," Dr. Moskowitz said. "Please make sure you go through the checklist."

The nurses stared at each other. They had heard it all before.

When the meeting was over, Moskowitz paid Lt. Snedicker a visit in his office. "Have we seen those reporters around?"

"Not lately, other than when I called you."

"Was that a coincidence?"

"Not sure. I've been keeping an eye on the cleaning people. They haven't done anything suspicious."

"Well, if necessary, have a discussion with them. Don't take any chances. This is a big payday in so many ways. The Vice President has provided a lot of information and we may have to create a relapse if more is needed. If not here, I could do it at his house when I go to give him shots. It has proven to be even more lucrative than we originally thought. Just the same, keep an eye on everyone. I'll make sure you get a special bonus when this is all done."

Dr. Moskowitz had no intention of passing more money to the lieutenant. He had extracted enough out of him already and it was getting near the time for Vitaly to put an end to it.

Chapter Forty-Seven

"I've been thinking about why all the hush, hush," Neil said as he drove out to the Waterford's' home. "There's more to all this broken leg stuff. There's more to it, and I have a good idea why they won't let us in to see the Vice President."

"Are you planning on telling your partner any time soon?" Rori asked.

"You might think I'm nuts."

"I know you're nuts. Just tell me."

"I think the Vice President had a nervous breakdown. Everything has been a scam right from the beginning."

"How so?" Rori asked.

"The world saw Willowdale give a concession speech—remember how he stopped mid-sentence at one point? He gathered himself, but he wasn't the same man we saw on the campaign trail."

Rori turned slightly in her seat. "You may have a point. You know, without a medical record, we couldn't prove a thing. I couldn't understand why it was such a big deal. Why we couldn't talk to the Vice President just because he broke a leg."

Neil pointed his finger at Rori. "That's just it. These bastards have been lying all along. The older I get, the more I recognize the same old patterns. Politicians never learn the public copes better with truth than lies. Nixon never did a thing except lie."

"Nixon? Sounds familiar, but don't know anything about him," Rori said.

"Didn't you learn anything in college? That was one of the biggest scoops in the last hundred years. *Kids,* " Neil said with casual disgust.

"Anyway, all Nixon had to do was let the law take its course and he could have finished his term. They just never get it. The cover-up is often worse than the crime."

"How are we going to prove all of this? We can't just accuse them of lying without solid evidence. Even our bosses wouldn't let us file anything," Rori said. "Can't we just ask the question?"

"Let's talk to our other partners first," Neil said.

Just then, there was buzz from Rori's pocket. "Is that your phone or your flask?" Neil said, licking his lips.

"Very funny," Rori said as she answered the phone.

"Hi, Maureen. Okay. Do you know which day for sure?"

"Friday," Maureen said, and then added, "let's meet at the Hotel Kirkwood tonight for a few drinks and dinner."

Rori looked at Neil and thought for a second. "Yeah, I can do that," she said with a smile. "Meet you there at six."

Rori closed the phone and held it with one hand on top and one on the bottom and drifted in thought. She turned to Neil. "The Vice President is being released Friday."

* * *

They sat in the kitchen drinking coffee. Neil was doing well without his flask, although reaching for it often. This time the conversation with Rosemary and Gerry was not as contentious—instead Neil thought it seemed as though all parties decided it was time for trust. Rori was not as sure, but she relied on Neil's instincts.

Rori looked at Neil and Neil returned the look. They hadn't decided who would explain the plan. Since she explained it to Neil, she decided to take the lead. She went over the various scenarios and what they discussed with Neil's friend, Bernie. Neil got up and walked into the open concept family room as he listened.

"Is this something you two feel comfortable doing?" Rori asked Gerry and Rosemary.

Gerry took a deep breath. "I think 'comfortable' is not the word I would use. Rosemary and I have talked, and we would like to just get this thing done. We've been digging at this long enough, and if it weren't for you two, we wouldn't be at this point today. Let's end it, and we can get out of this nightmare."

"That place isn't a hospital, it's an ATM for the doctors," Rosemary said. "Let's get this done."

"Gerry, you know how to attach this device to the alarm system?" Rori asked.

"Not a problem. It seems pretty basic," Gerry said. "I worked my way through college helping out an electrician. Learned some things."

"Rosemary, you carry this switch with you in your smock," Rori said. "All you have to do is to flip the switch to sound the alarm. If you are not ready when the nurse returns, sound the alarm again. Once the key is formed in the wax, you can get out of there."

Neil listened to Rori's explanation. He listened to the nervousness in Gerry's voice. Most of all, he listened to his gut.

Just as Rosemary was asking about how to make the keys, Neil held up his hand.

"Stop." His voice was intense. "We can't do this more than once. On the way over, we were told the Vice President is leaving on Friday. We can't expect to repeat this two days in a row. And if the records are there one day, who's to say they'll be there the next? It's just too risky."

Rori understood what Neil was saying. "What are you suggesting?"

Neil walked away from the three of them and stood looking out the window.

"Neil, what's going on? Are you okay?"

Neil stood there for a few seconds longer then, without turning around, he said, "Take it all. Take every record on the Vice President and your mother. Don't waste your time worrying about these fucking thieves and murderers."

Gerry and Rori looked at each other. Rosemary understood what he was saying. She stood up and walked toward Neil. He turned around and took her hand.

"You know I'm right, don't you?" Neil asked.

"Yes. You're right. What do we care about these bastards? I know they killed my mother. And you were right about something else," Rosemary said, looking at Neil. "I wanted revenge, and I was willing to do anything. And if you got in our way, I was prepared to…"

"That crossed my mind," Neil said.

"My revenge can end with the records. If not, where does it end? The lieutenant? The doctor? The police? No, it would never end if I did it my way. We'll do it your way," Rosemary said, as she hung her head and settled into a chair. Looking up at him she said. "You are a great man, Neil. You read me all the way. In the long run, I probably couldn't have done much. I think it's really beyond my makeup."

Gerry said nothing.

Neil reached into his pocket and pulled out the little gizmo they'd use to break into the filing cabinet. "Rosemary or Gerry—whichever of you two decides to take the records—just use this. It's simple and quick. "What do you use to clean the office?" Neil asked.

"It's a roller cart with a small trash barrel. The trash container has a bag for collection. I keep clean bags inside the barrel," Rosemary said.

"Take all the records you want, then stick them between the trash bag and the trash container," Neil said. "Get the records and get the hell out of there."

A smile came across Rosemary's face, but Rori's eyes were bulging like a bullfrog's. "They'll know it was Rosemary and Gerry. They'll know we were behind it."

"Who cares?" Neil said. "Do you think they want that much publicity? I don't think so."

"Won't they come after us? We know what they're capable of," Rori said.

"Once we get out of there and get this reported, we shouldn't have anything to fear," Neil said, feeling oddly satisfied. Something he hadn't felt in years.

"Gerry, you attach the wires and then go into the Vice President's suite. We know there's something in there too. Perhaps you could pretend to be fixing something," Rori said.

"What about the heat? Can you adjust it on the computer?" Neil asked. Gerry nodded. "That's it. Turn it down, and then go in with some tools and pretend you know what you're doing."

"I do know what I'm doing," Gerry said.

"Well pretend anyway even if you do know. Make it look good," Neil said.

"When you're in the suite, go to one end of the bookcase and look for a lever or a button. It should be on the left side, underneath. I'm pretty sure that's where it was," Rori said. "If you find something, you should see a drawer pop open at the other end. Grab what's in there and get out."

"One more thing," Neil said. "Make sure you shut the camera off. Can you do that at the computer, too."

"I'll put that on my list," Gerry said.

Neil looked to Gerry and Rosemary. "Have all of your personal effects out of there and your house. You may not be able to come back, at least not right away. Grab the records, walk out to your car, and get out. You can meet us at The Black Sow, and we'll take the records and create enough stir and hassle for them that they wouldn't dare touch us. They'll be too busy with the Feds."

Rori looked to Rosemary. "We'll make sure your mother's honor is restored."

Chapter Forty-Eight

Maureen looked over her shoulder as she hung up the phone with Rori. Lt. Snedicker was watching. Maureen knew she broke the rules and she didn't try to hide it. She turned around and looked directly at him.

"Hi, Lieutenant. How are you doing today?" Maureen said with a smile.

"I hope that wasn't a personal call," the lieutenant said.

Maureen looked him straight in the eye and said, "It was."

"You know you can get fired for things like that."

"Ah, come on, lieutenant. Don't be a prick. My little sister is in town and I wanted to let her know when I get off."

"And when is that?"

"In a few minutes," she said. "I'm going to take her out to dinner."

"Don't make it a habit, and have a good time," the lieutenant said, his face still stony.

The lieutenant entered his computer password—MONEYFORLIFE—and then put his eye to the scanner. When the computer allowed him to log in, he pulled open the employee files. Finding Maureen's file, he looked it over until he found what he was looking for. "An only child," he said to himself. He logged off and shut his computer down. "Bitch." His adrenaline was kicking in.

Snedicker went to the bathroom to take a piss, then ripped some paper towels out of the machine and walked to another urinal where he grabbed a couple of random pubic hairs, placing them in the paper towels. He wanted nothing that could point directly to him.

The lieutenant went back up front, turned the back camera off, locked everything up and left. He walked out the front door and followed the walkway around back to wait.

Maureen came out and jumped into her car. It happened so fast, she didn't see it coming. She was pulled into the back seat, punched in the face and knocked unconscious. The lieutenant duct-taped her hands behind her back, then he taped her mouth. He ripped her blouse off, cut off her bra, then her panties. He pulled the paper towels out and wiped it on her, leaving the pubic hairs behind. The lieutenant took a deep breath and smiled to himself. He wanted to take time to enjoy this.

He could have put a condom on and raped her, but that wouldn't satisfy him. Teasing someone knowing they were going to die is what satisfied him. Sex was not what he enjoyed. As she started to recover from the punch, she realized she was naked and being played with. She tried to scream, but the duct tape suppressed her words. She struggled to pull her hands loose, but it was useless.

The lieutenant climbed on top of her and looked into her eyes, allowing his hot breath to crawl across her neck. She could see his craziness. He watched her eyes follow his movements and smiled after he pulled away. Maureen watched with terror at the silhouette of the lieutenant. He licked and manhandled her while she squirmed to try and break free. The lieutenant made sure she knew he was enjoying himself, even though he had no intention of penetrating her. The fact she was no longer unconscious made it more enjoyable. He leaned down and whispered in her ear.

"I have something special for you. You should not have lied to me." He rubbed a gun along her neck, then the side of her face to make sure she knew what it was. He put the gun to her forehead, and she tried to move franticly. In an instant, she was dead. Her vivacious, active body disappeared into the night, leaving behind her crumpled frame in a blood-stained backseat.

The lieutenant climbed out of her car, took a look around, closed the door, walked to his car and drove home to dinner.

Chapter Forty-Nine

"Neil, drop me off at the Kirkwood Hotel," Rori said as they drove back to D.C. "I'm supposed to meet Maureen for drinks and dinner."

"Not a problem," Neil said. "I've been thinking about tomorrow."

"And?" Rori asked.

"Instead of meeting me at The Black Sow, I'd like you to get in touch with Austin."

"Don't you think we should stick together?"

"We are. What I'd like you to do is to go directly at Austin and tell him we know he's been lying. Get in his face and make him feel uncomfortable."

"Do you want me to do that tonight?" Rori asked.

"No. Wait until I call in the morning to tell you what I have. Make an appointment for around eleven. Don't just do it by phone, tell him you want to meet him in person."

"You know I'm dying to be there with you. I want to see the records for myself, and the blowhard doctor and his evil twin Snedicker or whatever his name is."

"Let's get our ducks in a row, and then the two of us will go see both of them together," Neil said. "Just remember, I don't think Rosemary would have stayed unless she was sure about her mother's death. If the records establish when she was fired, we can pin down the time she was at the bar, what she drank and prove she couldn't have been drunk."

"Whatever you say, but I'd rather be with you."

"I understand, but let's keep separate on this in case we get in trouble. We may have to call on you in case we need an attorney.

"I'd rather be there with *Jack.*"

* * *

Rori sat in the hotel lounge at the end of the bar, positioning herself so she would see Maureen when she arrived. She was already thirty-five minutes late. Rori just assumed she ended up working a little later or got caught up in traffic. Rori tried her cell phone and got no answer. She laid her cell down onto the bar.

A man sat near Rori and said hello.

"Hi, " Rori said.

Rori checked the time again and decided that she didn't want to start a conversation so she pulled her tablet out and started clearing her email.

Rori glanced up and saw Austin approaching as she looked to the door.

"Rori, nice to see you. How are you doing?" Austin said, as he approached with a big smile.

"I'm fine. You must have been reading my mind. I was going to call you tonight," Rori said.

"What about?"

"Can we get together tomorrow?

"How about right now?" Austin asked.

"Doesn't work for me. Besides, I'm waiting for some information that's not available until tomorrow. I'd like to set something up…say around eleven?"

"I can do that," Austin said, shutting his phone calendar.

"How about I just stay until your friend shows up?" Austin asked. "Maybe we can talk a bit in the meantime."

"Sure, have a seat. I've got to go to the ladies room." She grabbed her phone and headed to the bathroom.

Austin stared at Rori's ass as she walked away.

While in the bathroom, Rori thought it seemed a bit too coincidental. It was as if Austin listened to her conversation with Neil, telling her to set up and appointment with him. She shook her head. *Nah, that's too much to consider.*

"What's new?" Rori asked when she slid back onto the stool next to Austin.

"You mean officially or in my life?"

Rori laughed. "Who gives a damn about you? I want official gossip. I'm a single girl. I have to support myself somehow. Give me some news about the Vice President."

"Things are a little quiet since the election," Austin said.

Not wanting to miss a shot Rori said, "Oh, I forgot. You lost, didn't you?"

"Nice," Austin said as he clutched at his heart dramatically. "I don't take it personally. I don't get caught up in wins and losses. Could I have another bourbon and water?" Austin asked the bartender as he passed by.

"I hear the Vice President is getting out at the end of the week."

Austin almost choked on the ice. Clearing his throat he said, "Maybe I should ask you what's new."

"You'd be surprised at what I know. He's been in the hospital an awful long time for a little broken leg." It was half-statement, half-question.

Austin coolly took a sip of his new drink. "The doctor said there was an infection, but he's much better. They want to make sure it's all cleared up before letting him go back to work."

As Austin spewed his propaganda, Rori undressed him with her eyes. *Not bad.*

"Can't we get away from all this political stuff? I would like to get to know you better," Austin said.

"Wouldn't that be like a fox in a hen house?"

"We're not working together. We're both in the political arena, but it doesn't mean we have to be enemies."

Rori glanced at her watch.

"Do you want me to leave?" Austin asked.

"Yes—I mean no. I don't know. I'd like to get to know you too. Right now I'm wondering where my friend is. It's been more than an hour since we were supposed to meet. It looks like I've been stood up. I'll let you buy dinner. If Maureen shows up, she can join us."

"You're on. Let's just have our dinner right at the Corner Bar," Austin said.

It was a nice meal, and Rori enjoyed the banter. However, she still couldn't take her eyes off of the entrance. Every time a woman came through the doorway or walked around the corner, Rori looked up thinking it was Maureen. She knew she dropped her guard as a reporter, but Austin dropped his, too.

"You know, we're not all that different," Austin said.

"I'm not so sure about that. I'm much cuter." Rori gave him a flirty laugh. "We both may have the same training, but you went after money and I went after principals. You spin the truth until it's no longer recognizable as the truth. I just try to find the truth."

"Really?" Austin said. "Look, I just took a different path. Now my main job is to protect my boss. Don't you do the same?"

"I guess you're right there," Rori said, and excused herself to call Maureen again. The phone went directly to voicemail.

Walking back to the table, Rori had a thousand thoughts running through her mind.

Austin took one look at her. "You look concerned. Something I can do?"

"This may be a little too much to ask, but would you consider taking me by her apartment? If she's there, I can at least talk to her and I'll know she's okay. You don't have to. I can drive myself, but I'd need a ride to my place first. I had Neil drop me off here and I was going to have Maureen take me to my place. I hate to be a pain," Rori said and gave him a smile. "Oh, and thanks for dinner. Maybe I can make it up to you somehow."

* * *

Austin pulled into the parking lot of Maureen's townhouse and slowed down as Rori pointed toward her unit.

"Down further. A little more … here. Right here," Rori said. "I don't see her car."

"Try the door and see if she's here. Maybe her car broke down and she got a ride home."

Rori rang the bell. There weren't any lights on. Rori walked back to Austin's car and sat in the passenger's seat. "Could you do me one more favor?" Rori asked.

"Anything. I told you I wanted to get to know you and being your chauffer is one way with no strings."

"Would you be willing to take me out to the hospital?"

Austin thought about it for a minute.

Rori saw the consternation in his face. "I understand if you feel uncomfortable taking me out there."

"I don't. I mean, I'm working for the Vice President. I don't want anyone from the hospital or other reporters to see us together out there. Maybe another time."

"I didn't think it was a great idea either . . . at least for you. Will you take me to my place? I should have had you take me to my truck from the start," Rori said.

"It's okay. I have to head back toward the bridge to get home anyway."

"Thanks," Rori said.

Austin talked as they headed back toward D.C., but Rori's mind was wandering. She was wondering where Maureen was and thinking about Neil. She was having a strange feeling. Maybe it was all the things Neil had been discussing. Maybe it was her instinct kicking in. Whatever it was, she felt she was in the wrong place.

"Right here's good," Rori said. "Drop me off on this corner and I can walk down the street. My condo is right down there and it's one way."

She opened the door and closed it quickly. Turning to head down the street Austin dropped the window down and yelled.

"Hey, don't run away so quickly."

"I'm sorry I was thinking about some things," Rori said.

"I understand. When things settle down, can we get together? Have dinner again when your mind's not preoccupied or watching a doorway?"

Rori walked back and put her hand on the side of the doorway. "I'd like that." She gave a little smile and walked away again.

* * *

A guard met Rori at the hospital door. His chest puffed out and he tried to stand a little taller as Rori approached. Unfortunately, neither move of vanity did anything to help his overhanging belly.

"I'm looking for Maureen Lexington. She was supposed to meet me after work, but she didn't show," Rori said.

"Let me check the electronic sign-out sheet." The guard glanced down and said, "It looks as though she signed out several hours ago. I'm not supposed to say more than that," he said apologetically.

"Where would she park?" Rori asked.

"That would be out back, but I can't allow you to go back there by yourself. Let me get someone to cover and we can walk out back," the guard said.

When they got to the back lot, Rori noticed there was less light for the employees' cars than the well-lit visitors' area.

The guard with his flashlight led the way. There didn't seem to be much light as they crossed the parking lot. The guard's chest was still puffed up as they walked. He was standing as erect as his stomach would allow him.

"That's it, that's her car," Rori said. "It's an Altima." Her stomach started churning. She put her hand to Jack.

"Are you certain?" the guard asked.

"Yes, yes that's it," Rori said.

Rori stood next to the darkened car as the guard aimed his flashlight into the front seat. As he moved the light around to the backseat, he spotted something. He backed away from the front and then opened the back door. The guard's big body blocked Rori's view as he looked into the car. The light shined directly onto Maureen's naked body. Her dead eyes pointed toward the roof of the car, and her mouth was wide open. Blood was everywhere. The guard retched and heaved. He dropped the light, spun around and immediately vomited into a crop of bushes.

Rori picked up the flashlight and looked inside. She screamed, dropped the light and reflexively pulled Jack. She grabbed the car door, and walked around to the back of the car, leaning against the trunk. She held the gun out in front of her and moved it in a semi-circle. "You better get your shit together and get someone out here," Rori yelled.

* * *

Rori's mind was racing. While she was at the scene waiting for police, she grabbed her tablet. She typed away and filed an article, along with pictures, about Maureen's death. She had taken some quick pictures of the car, Maureen's body and of the guard as he bent over dumping his dinner, and then called Neil. His phone went straight to voicemail. After leaving a message, she said she'd call again in the morning and explain what happened. During the drive back home to her condo, her mind searched for a reason why anyone would kill Maureen.

Despite her toughness the situation affected her. She had never seen anything like it before.

* * *

After dropping Rori off, Austin went home and decided it was time. He poured himself a tequila and tried to settle his mind. He pulled his cell out.

"Ann, this is Austin."

"Where are you? You're supposed to be here beside me," she said in her typically soft, sexy tone.

"I've been busy," Austin said.

"That's exactly what I planned for you."

Austin took a gulp of his drink and said, "You know, I think it's time to put this to an end. I've been thinking about this for a while. I'm ending it now." Austin could feel the silent tension on the phone, the daggers.

"Listen, I'll tell you when it's over. You sure wanted to fuck the First Lady, but not the wife of the loser. Is that the way it is? How would you like me to tell the Vice President?"

"That would hurt you more than me. How do you think the public would look at you in the future after the news media dragged you through the mud?" Austin knew he had to take the offense with Ann. Give her no alternative.

"Why don't you just bite my ass," Ann said, then threw the phone across the room.

Austin hung up, finished his drink, showered and went to bed. He felt cleansed.

Chapter Fifty

"Are you on crack or just an idiot?" Dr. Moskowitz yelled over the phone. "On the hospital grounds? I'm beginning to think you're losing your touch."

The lieutenant listened but didn't care. He was the one who took all the chances. He was the one who got his hands dirty. "You know, Doc, I think you're the one losing a little nerve. I've made it look like someone else was involved, and I shut off the camera near her car. Someone's going to get blamed, but it's not going to be us."

"Don't use the term 'us,' you stupid son of a bitch. Think twice before you do something like this again," Dr. Moskowitz said.

"You listen to me. I do your shit-work every day, just so you can keep your hands clean. That is unless some birdie turns me in, and then you're just as guilty as I am. Have a nice day."

Chapter Fifty-One

Rosemary and Gerry both woke up earlier than usual. The chance to find out the truth and to get back to their real lives was more important than sleep.

They sat at the breakfast counter discussing the plan. Gerry was to connect the jumper wires to the alarm. Rosemary had to activate it. They both had to be actors this morning, but then they had been for six months. Today they would be thieves, too. It was a big step.

"Just stay calm and be yourself," Gerry said.

"Don't tell me to be calm," Rosemary said. "So much could go wrong. All you have to do is check some stupid damn wires."

"You were willing to kill people at the hospital *and* the reporters if you had to."

"That was different. We didn't want to."

"But you would have if you had to. You'd give anyone a needle to avenge your mother's death if they got in your way."

"Just shut up. I don't want to talk about it anymore."

* * *

Neil had listened to Rori's voicemail and gave her a call.

"Neil it was unbelievable. There was blood all over the place," Rori said. "You can check our site and see what I wrote."

"I did earlier. I had trouble sleeping so I got up and did some writing myself. Quite a mess. Howard's going to need some comforting. I'll give him a call later."

"Do you think this has anything to do with the Vice President?" Rori asked.

Neil hesitated. "I thought so at first, but he's not going to get mixed up in a murder. I'm thinking they'll find it was just a random thing."

"I hope so. Are we still going through with this?" Rori said.

"I don't see why not. I think it's today or not at all. With this crime, they're going to want Willowdale out ASAP."

"I'm meeting Austin at eleven, so give me a call after you meet with the doctors. Talk to you later, old man." Rori let the phone fall onto the bed and thought how Neil's voice was chipper this morning. It was good hearing him like this. She was going to miss him when they were done with this job.

* * *

After Neil hung up, the Waterfords called to firm up their meeting. They were to meet him at The Black Sow around 8:30 a.m. Neil decided not to say anything about the death of the nurse. They were nervous enough as it was and one more thing might stop them.

"Once we're sure what we have, you'll take care of the rest?" Rosemary asked. She discussed this the day before with Gerry, but both were nervous and needed support.

"Absolutely," Neil said. "And if you're arrested, ask for your lawyer and then call me. I'll get it written up online as soon as I get you out."

There was silence on the phone for a second.

"Neil, I'm really scared. I feel like they're waiting for us. I have this feeling this is how my mother felt just before she died."

"Don't talk like that. They have no idea who you are. Besides, nothing's going to happen to you," Neil said.

"When we're done with this, we're just going to disappear," Rosemary said.

"I have your number if I need to talk to you," Neil said. "Don't worry. You'll have done your job. Then you can go home and do some good for the children."

Neil hung up and reached for his flask. Coming up empty, he grabbed a pencil and began playing with it.

* * *

Rosemary and Gerry stood in the maintenance area. Gerry was busy gathering his equipment. Rosemary paced. It wasn't a big area, and every time Gerry turned, Rosemary was there next to him.

"I don't think I can do this," Rosemary said.

Gerry grabbed her arm. "You're being foolish." Normally a quiet man, who followed his wife three thousand miles to aid her in a quest to find a killer, Gerry became a pillar of courage. He had to take control or she would be too nervous to follow through.

"You take care of sick kids, this is nothing. In fact, it's kids' stuff. No one's going to do anything to you even if we get caught, other than getting fired."

"I know, but I just want to get this done," she said.

"Then let's just do it. If anyone questions us, tell them we've got a personal appointment and have to do some of the work early. Say that we're coming back later to finish up but we needed to get a head start."

Rosemary gave him a look, took a deep breath, grabbed her cleaning cart, turned and walked out into the corridor.

Gerry went over to the computer and dropped the temperature down in the Vice President's room. In a few minutes, the nurses would notice the temperature change. By the time Rosemary got to the nurses' station, they'd be looking for him.

Rosemary approached the nurses' station, took another deep breath and tried not to show how nervous she was.

"I need to clean the HR office."

"A bit early, aren't you?" Nurse Boothroyd asked.

"Yes, but I've got an appointment. I have to split my day up," Rosemary said with an easy smile.

"You *do* look a little pale. Would you like me to check your vitals?"

"No, I'll have all that done later. I just need to get going."

"Give me a minute and I'll be right there. Is Gerry here too?"

"Yes, he is. Do you want me to get him?"

"I'll just page him on his radio," Nurse Boothroyd said.

Rosemary moved down to the business corridor, smiling to herself, and stood waiting for the nurse. While she waited, she reached her hand into her smock and pulled out her mints.

"Gerry, Nurse Boothroyd here. Will you go into the living area of the Vice President and see what's going on with the heat? It's down about twenty degrees."

"No problem. Just let me get some gauges to test the thermostats."

"You sure you don't want me to check you out?" the nurse said as she walked up to Rosemary.

"No I'll be fine."

Rosemary waited until the nurse opened the door and was halfway through the threshold. Then she turned and offered her a mint.

"Oh, thank you. I just love these, but boy are they strong," the nurse said.

"I know, but I love them, and I'm always worried I have bad breath," Rosemary said with a nervous laugh. She let the can of mints fall. The dull tin can sound hit the floor, and the tiny mints scattered like cockroaches to all corners of the office.

"Oh my god," Rosemary said as she pulled her cart halfway into the office. She was shaking as she fell to her knees and proceeded to pick them up.

Nurse Boothroyd rolled her eyes and let out a gasp. She looked back toward her area, knowing she had work to do. Rosemary crawled around on the floor pretending to pick up the breath mints. Once under the desk, she reached into her other pocket and took out Bernie Milo's device. She flipped the switch and nothing happened. "Oh shit."

"What's that?" the nurse asked.

"Oh, I just banged my head picking these up," Rosemary said. She flipped it again and nothing happened. *This is bad.*

She turned the device around as though she knew what to do. Looking blankly at the device, she noticed a little red button. The top of the button was marked RESET. She pressed it and then turned it back to the original position and flipped the switch again.

The blare of the alarm put the nurse into panic.

"I have to go," Nurse Boothroyd said. "Don't touch anything and stay here until I get back."

The moment the nurse left, Rosemary was up and at the filing cabinet. She went to the one marked "employees" and took out Bernie's other device. *Stick it in the key slot and pop it,* were Neil's instructions. She stuck it in and popped it. The lock came up as though she just used the key. It was an orgasmic release. She went through the folders then saw her mother's file. She grabbed it and resisted looking. She then looked around for the patients' cabinet. She couldn't find one, and then she remembered the desk, where she used the device again. She reached down, opened the drawer, and found nothing. She opened the second drawer and saw a file marked PATIENTS ONLY. She pulled it out and glanced at several folders inside. She looked at the last folder and saw the name "Willowdale." In her haste to grab the folder, she grabbed someone else's, too.

Rosemary looked up to see if anyone was in the corridor. No one. She took the folders and shoved them into the trash bin, on the inner side of the plastic bag lining it, just as she had been instructed. She shut the alarm off after the nurse left, but while putting the folders into her trash carriage, she accidentally hit it again. The moment it went off, she dropped to the floor and started to pick up the mints. She glanced over her shoulder to see the nurse rushing in.

"I need to get you out of here. You can come back later to vacuum," the nurse said quickly.

"Okay," Rosemary said. She pulled her cart out and rushed back to meet Gerry. He wasn't there. She looked around their work storage area, but he wasn't around.

"Gerry, this is Rosemary," she spoke into the radio. "You remember we have that appointment, don't you?"

"I copy, but I'm having a little trouble with the temperature control *lever.*"

Gerry connected the meter to the thermostat then went over to the bookcase. The nurse had just left and he knew she was going back to see Rosemary. He dropped to the floor looking for the magic that would open the secret drawer. He slid his hand along the bookcase edge until he got to the far end and found the button. Having heard the alarm go off the second time, he knew the nurse would be back soon. He got up and went back to the meter as though he was observing a reaction. Just as he got back, Nurse Boothroyd walked in.

"Did you find the problem?" she asked.

"Not yet, but I think we have a bad thermostat."

The nurse went into check the Vice President. He was asleep, having just been administered his morning Medifinne. Returning to Gerry she asked, "Is that hard to fix?"

"No, just let me check out a couple things and confirm it, and then I can change it if necessary."

"Why is his room comfortable and the sitting area freezing?" she asked.

"They're zoned so that each one is controlled by its own thermostat," Gerry said, trying to sound as technical as possible. He could see the nurse's eyes start to glaze over.

"I trust you know what you're doing," she said, and then returned to the Vice President. "One more thing," she said, returning to the living room. "When you get that fixed, can you see why the alarms were going off? The cameras are off too. The Vice President is fine, so they must be on the fritz."

"Can do," Gerry said. "You know, it may have something to do with the temperature change."

Nurse Boothroyd's eyes glaze over again. "I'm going back to my desk. It's too cold in here."

The moment she was gone, Gerry was at the button. One touch and the drawer opened. He rushed to the other end, grabbed the files inside and shoved the drawer in. Grabbing the gauges, he hurried back to his work area, got the jumpers and went to the computer. He adjusted the temperature to one-hundred degrees.

"That'll warm them up," he said to himself.

Grabbing his personal stuff, he turned to Rosemary. "Did you get the device off of the breaker?" Rosemary asked.

"Yes. Did you get everything?"

"Yes," Rosemary said, and then a look of horror came over her face. "I didn't lock up the cabinets. I was too nervous. I'm sorry."

Gerry looked at her. "Who the fuck cares? Let's get the hell out of here."

Chapter Fifty-Two

Nurse Boothroyd expected Rosemary to come right back and vacuum up the mints. When she didn't return, she paged her. Then she paged Gerry, because the Vice President's living room was too hot. She was going to page them again when the front guard came in and asked if she had paged the Waterfords?

"Yes I did," the nurse said.

"I saw their car leaving. They didn't even sign out. They just about ran over a guard."

The nurse ran down the corridor to the HR office and opened the door. She bent down and looked under the desk to see the pile of mints. It didn't look as though any of them had been picked up. She put her hand on the drawer to help herself up. The drawer opened. "That's not supposed to be open," she said to herself. Once she got up, she looked the office over and realized the employee cabinet was also open.

Nurse Boothroyd ran to the Vice President's suite and went over to the button. She put her hand to it, but nothing happened. She went back to the drawer and touched it, and it popped open. Then she saw it was empty. Picking up her radio, she called Lt. Snedicker.

* * *

"Looks like we have a problem," the lieutenant said. He could imagine the doctor's strained face.

"Tell me what happened," Dr. Moskowitz said.

"Our cleaning people broke into the files in HR and it looks like they took some employee records. They took the Vice President's records, too. There may have been others."

"Which employee records?" Dr. Moskowitz asked.

"We don't know. That's not all."

"What else?"

"The files from the Vice President's room too—excuse me doctor. What is it, nurse?" the lieutenant asked.

"Eisenblatt's folder is missing too," Nurse Boothroyd said.

The lieutenant came back to the phone and was about to tell the doctor, but the doctor heard.

"Didn't I tell you to keep an eye on them?" Dr. Moskowitz yelled over the phone. "Just get to fixing it and find those bastards. Leave no loose ends. And make sure none of it happens on hospital grounds."

Chapter Fifty-Three

Moskowitz sat behind his massive desk and fumed. He grabbed his cell phone and dialed Vitaly.

"Are you nearby?" he asked.

"Not far. I'm heading toward the Waterfords' house. I've watched the reporters with them and thought it'd be a nice time to revisit it. What can I do for you? Do you have some new patients?"

"No. The lieutenant just called and said the cleaning people stole some records."

"I told you we should have gotten rid of that druggie lieutenant. He doesn't know how to watch situations. Never trust an addict."

"I know, I know. I should have trusted your experience. If you can find them, do as you see fit."

"Very well. It's about time to have some fun. I'll be in touch," he said. "I'll continue out to their house and see if they're there." Vitaly pressed the pedal and flew through a yellow light.

Chapter Fifty-Four

"I know where you're going," Lt. Snedicker said to himself as he got into his car and drove to The Black Sow. He slowed up as he drove past and saw two sets of vehicles he recognized.

"Those fuckin' reporters," he said. "They must be selling it to them. I'll take care of them first and get the folders back. Then I'll take care of the other two." He smiled as he thought of the horrific fun he was going to have.

He pulled into a driveway and turned around. Parking behind another vehicle, his view was good as he waited to execute his damage control.

* * *

Vitaly drove out to where the cleaning people lived. Being Russian, he always needed to know situations and people. You always need a backdoor—for your life. In Russia, you always had to be on guard if you wanted to survive. He made a point to know where everyone who worked at the villas lived, including Dr. Moskowitz, the lieutenant, the nurses and the cleaning people.

The Waterfords house seemed different than the last time he was there. He let himself in and walked around the home, his gun (silencer attached) hanging at his side. The refrigerator was empty, except for some condiments and a pickle jar, with a single pickle suspended at attention in liquid. The bedrooms and closets were empty, along with the dresser drawers, too.

Vitaly stood looking around for a clue as to their whereabouts. In the kitchen on the counter, he noticed a notepad with an imprint from a

210

previous written note: B-SOW 8:30-9 a.m.

He thought a few seconds. "Ah," he said. He jumped into his silver Mercedes and headed to The Black Sow.

Chapter Fifty-Five

Neil waited for them at what had become his usual booth, enjoying a cup of black coffee. He watched Rosemary come through the door first, looking pale and grim, followed by Gerry.

"Can I get you something?" Neil asked as they both fell into the booth.

"I need a drink. Make it a double. I don't care what time it is," Rosemary said. "Scotch and water."

"I'll have the same," Gerry said. "But just a single."

Neil got up and went to the bar to order the drinks. "Put it on my tab," he said to Bert.

When he returned to the table, Gerry asked, "Where's Rori?"

"I needed Rori to do some other investigating for us. I've asked her to meet with someone this morning. As soon as we get out of here, I'm going to call her and feed her questions."

Neil reached over and picked up the folders Gerry dropped onto the table. The first one was the Vice President's. As he scanned the file, Rosemary downed her double scotch.

"I've never been so nervous in my life," she said. "I kept thinking we were being followed. I checked and didn't see anyone, though. I had to let Gerry drive because I was shaking so badly. I think it was just an adrenalin rush."

"And you think I was much better?" Gerry asked. "The nurse kept coming into the room. Why'd the alarm go off twice?"

"I accidentally hit it, and the nurse almost caught me."

"I'm not seeing any surgery here on this file," Neil said as he leafed through Willowdale's file.

"You sure you have the right one? I just grabbed what was there.

212

You may have more than one. Let me look at it." Rosemary took the file and flipped through it. "You don't see anything because he never did have surgery. See this medicine, Medifinne?" Rosemary pointed to the page listing medications Willowdale was taking.

"What's it for?" Neil asked as he peered over his glasses.

"I'm not sure, but from all indications, I think it's for nerves. I remember reading something about it. It's only been on the market a few years. You'll have to research it."

"Let me see," Gerry said. He looked it over. "I know about this stuff," he said. "Before it was on the market or just after it came to market, a few years ago, some subjects got sick and one or two died. From what I remember, it had something to do with the dosage."

While Gerry was looking at the folder, Rosemary picked up the other one she grabbed. "This one was given sodium pentothal, and he didn't have any surgery either.

"What would surgery have to do with sodium pentothal?" Neil asked.

"It was used for patients having minor surgery," Gerry said.

Let me see the Vice President's folder again." She looked at the list of medications again. "Look, he was given it, too."

"Given what?" Neil said. "And who are we talking about?"

"Eisenblatt, Dietrich," Rosemary said.

"Let me check his name," Neil said. Neil pulled his phone out and punched in Eisenblatt. "It says he is a leading researcher with laser technology, some kind of weapons specialist. We'll have to look into this. One investigation at a time."

"Willowdale had sodium pentothal too," Gerry said.

"What's this stuff for?" Neil asked.

"It can be used as a pre-anesthesia for minor procedures, but you know it as truth serum," Gerry said.

"So you said Medifinne was for nerves. Is that a big deal?" Neil asked. "Wouldn't anyone go into the hospital be given something to calm them?"

Gerry looked to Rosemary and then said, "He had a nervous breakdown."

"I knew it," Neil said. "I told Rori I thought they were hiding something. Wait till I tell her my gut was right. Speaking of gut, what was Eisen—what's his name?"

"Eisenblatt," Rosemary said.

"What was he in for?"

"Pneumonia," Rosemary said. "There wouldn't be any reason for sodium pentothal."

"I think a lot of people would pay a lot of money for what this guy knows," Neil said.

"What about the Vice President?" Gerry said.

"I'll bet he knows a few secrets, too. It's just a hunch, but we need to look into this further. This goes beyond what happened to your mother," Neil said.

"A little research and you may get more than a murderer," Gerry said.

"Have you looked at your mother's file?" Neil asked. "Once I go through the original police investigation and do some back tracking, I'll put a piece together. It'll take some legwork but we'll get it done. Hopefully, then we'll get the case reopened. Maybe get the DA involved. Did you find what you wanted? "

"I only glanced at it, but I think you can do my mother justice if you just print the truth. It shows the date and time my mother was fired. There's no way she had time to get drunk. She was only gone forty minutes, and fifteen of that was to get to The Black Sow. She couldn't have gotten drunk in that short of time," Rosemary said as she took another stiff drink. "Do me a favor when you write your piece?"

"And what's that?" Neil asked, as he put all the folders together and wrapped a couple of large rubber bands around them.

"Make sure what you write is incriminating enough to get them all—every last one of them. Make sure you take care of that freak Lt. Snedicker."

Chapter Fifty-Six

"We've got the bastards," Neil mumbled to himself, as he walked out of The Black Sow with a big smile. He knew it would take weeks to get all of the alcohol out of his system, but he felt good today. He put his face to the sun and thought it was a fine day to be alive.

"Shit. There's only one of them," the lieutenant said.

Closing the door, a thought crossed Neil's mind. He'd come full circle, with the help of Rori, Rosemary and Gerry. Maggie will be glad. With their support, he'd been able to re-capture some of his former self. He knew he could never be the man he once was, but he hoped this story would show the Washington world Neil O'Connor was still a man. If nothing else, he would be able to hold his head high before he walked away. And when he looked at himself in the mirror, he'd see a different man.

He failed to notice the car pulling out behind him as he left The Black Sow.

"Rori, I was right. We've got everything we need," Neil said to Rori's voicemail. "I knew they were lying. The Vice President had a nervous breakdown and has been taking some kind of new medicine. I'll show you at the office. I think they are involved in some type of espionage, too. Hope you'll be able to talk to Austin today. We did it. *We did it,*" Neil said. "I'll give you a call shortly and we can setup a line of questions." He was yelling like a schoolboy who just won a gold medal. He hung up and tossed the phone into the passenger bucket seat. For his own self-worth, it felt like he had.

* * *

Rosemary and Gerry were coming out of the bar and saw the lieutenant's car follow Neil.

"Did you see that?" Rosemary said. "That was Lt. Snedicker's car. They must have noticed the missing files."

"Why would he follow him and not talk to us?" Gerry asked.

Rosemary watched intently. "I believe he thinks we gave the records to Neil. We'll be next. Get into the car. I'll drive. Come on Gerry, get your butt moving. We've got to cover Neil's ass."

Rosemary would normally never think of protecting a reporter, but she gave Neil the records that would clear her mother. Besides she had started to like Neil. She wasn't so sure about Rori.

"Be careful. You've had a couple of drinks."

Rosemary ignored Gerry and threw the car into reverse. Loose stones slammed against other vehicles in the parking lot, as Rosemary pressed down hard on the gas. By the time they drove out of the bar's driveway, Neil was already a good two miles down the road.

* * *

For the lieutenant, death was an amusing part of the job. He thought about his past often, but never allowed it to affect this part of his job. When he was hired, he knew what it was all about. The doctor knew, too. Dr. Moskowitz had learned of his past in their private sessions. He had thoughts of his wives, who had all disappeared mysteriously. How the drugs made him feel better. It was time to move on, but first take care of loose ends, and the first one was right in front of him.

They just wouldn't leave it alone. They kept nosing around.

Neil was only thinking about how this story had to be written up. *Pulitzer.* When the lieutenant's car came up to Neil's, he snapped back to reality. He hadn't realized the car behind him was getting dangerously close—and it wasn't slowing down.

Neil braced himself. The sudden bump from the car hurled his vehicle forward and to the left side of the road. A second bump sent him back to the right. His white knuckles squeezed the wheel tightly.

His phone rang. He looked over and reached to grab it, but it slid to the far edge of the seat beyond his reach. He assumed it was Rori. "It'll have to wait, Rori. I'm a little busy right now."

Hold tight, he thought. *It's that shit-head Snedicker. I wish I had my flask.*

The next hit was harder. Neil felt his car surge off the ground, fishtailing when it came back to the pavement. His phone flew up into the air, bounced once on the top of the passenger seat and landed on the floor in the back.

Snedicker yelled at the sound of the two vehicles kissing. "God, I love this."

He gunned the engine again, and hit Neil's car so hard it went airborne. The nose of the car came down first. Neil lost control and flew over the embankment. Surprisingly, he found himself calling out his son's name as he flew through the air. When his car landed, Neil was thrown through the windshield. The lieutenant's car couldn't stop soon enough either. The nose went over the edge of the bank of the road past where Neil went over. He laughed loudly looking down at the heavy smoke. He knew the fire would start soon. He jumped out of his car and worked himself down the ravine, moving quickly. He could smell the gas leak and knew at any moment the whole area would be in flames.

He located the folders on the floor of the backseat of Neil's car and grabbed them. The rubber bands kept them together. He didn't bother looking to see what happened to Neil, instead quickly working his way back to his car.

Rosemary and Gerry saw the lieutenant smash into Neil's car. They saw him run down the ravine as they drove down the hill. As they approached the scene, the lieutenant was carrying something as he got back into his vehicle. Rosemary saw the taillights come on as the lieutenant shifted into gear.

"Hold on, Gerry," Rosemary said, and then smashed into the lieutenant's car, pushing it over into a deeper part of the ravine. As it tumbled down, something gouged the gas tank, ripping a hole and starting a gush of gas. It exploded as it hit the bottom of the ravine, sending a firebomb a hundred feet in the air and up the side of the hill. The lieutenant and the records were both burning and would be totally consumed in a matter of minutes. Part of the fire shot over to Neil's car, lighting another spot of the dry weeds and grass.

"Careful," Gerry said to Rosemary as she hurried down the hill.

Rosemary and Gerry fought their way through the smoke and pieces of torn metal looking for Neil. They checked the car and found it empty.

"Over there," Gerry yelled, pointing off to the side-hill bushes. Neil was laying half in the bushes surrounded by rocks. Gerry got to Neil first and started checking his vital signs.

Rosemary rushed over and took one look at Neil and knew they were too late. His face was bleeding in what looked like a dozen places. Blood was coming out of his ears and mouth. Rosemary knelt next to him, looked to Gerry and shook her head.

Neil opened his eyes and looked out into space. Then he let out a deep rattle and was gone.

* * *

Vitaly was coming from the opposite direction, certain Lt. Snedicker would attack his prey at the same hole. He saw Snedicker's car going into the ravine.

"Finally he's met his match," Vitaly said to himself. Times like this, his Russian words would come out. "He always has been such an *eblan* (dumbass). I was so looking forward to the pleasure of taking care of him myself."

* * *

"There's nothing more we can do here," Rosemary said. "Check to see if the files are there." Rosemary leaned over and kissed Neil.

Gerry spent a few minutes searching the car and the surrounding area. "I don't see them anywhere," he said.

"I saw the lieutenant with something. They must be in his crematorium," Rosemary said. "I think it's best we get out of here. There's no way we're convincing the police this was an accident. Not if they see our busted fenders."

They both took one last look at Neil, and started to work their way up the hill.

* * *

Vitaly stood at the top of the ravine, watching. He stepped below the road grade ten feet to conceal himself from the roadside.

Hidden by smoke, he observed Gerry searching for the stolen records and Rosemary cradling Neil as he died in her arms. They hadn't seen him until they decided to leave. They stopped when they finally noticed him.

Vitaly pulled his gun up from his side and shot them both through the head. He hurried down and put both bodies into the flames. Quickly he made his way up the hill and then got into the Waterfords' Volvo. Aiming it down the hill, he put it in neutral and hurried around to the side of the vehicle to take the gas cap off. Then he pushed the car over to join the rest of the fiery boneyard. He got into his Mercedes and disappeared.

Chapter Fifty-Seven

It was a windy, bone-chilling and rainy November day in Washington, D.C. A nasty drizzle persisted for a week. Rori felt the rain and cold deep in her body. It made her wish she could be in a warm, comfortable place. She didn't care where so long as it was dry.

She found all cold, rainy days to be unbearable, but this one was the worse because it happened to be the day of her best friend's funeral. As her tears intermingled with the rain on her face, she wished she were someplace getting drunk and laughing with Neil again.

Rori didn't have many friends, and in the past week she lost two of them, along with a couple of new acquaintances. Murdered by power and greed. She stood under a dull-looking tent with raindrops dripping off the edges, arm and arm with Neil's wife, Maggie.

Rori stared at Neil's casket, her mind drifting off to his phone message. *We got them. The VP had a nervous breakdown.* The word *espionage* repeated over and over in her head. The rain seeped into every part of her body. But Rori was a sponge. At this weakened moment, she was getting stronger and had choices to make.

* * *

Washington Independent Review Online
By Rori Cahill
Staff Writer

WASHINGTON—Officials say Maureen Lexington, found brutally murdered in the employee parking lot of the Maryland Rehab and Life

Health Center on Tuesday, was shot in the head by Simon Snedicker, an employee of the same facility. Snedicker was killed the next day in a car accident on River Road, which also killed Neil O'Connor, a reporter for this paper.

The camera nearest Lexington's car at MRLC had been shut off, police said. However, when the police examined other cameras, they were able to make out a man's image. With the help of the latest satellite technology and the NSA, the police were able to enhance the pictures to fully identify Snedicker.

Officials are still piecing together details, but they believe O'Connor was hit by Snedicker's car from behind. It's unclear whether Snedicker intentionally pushed Mr. O'Connor's car over an embankment, killing him.

Two more bodies were found at the scene but have not been identified, police said. Another vehicle, recently burned, was also found at the bottom of the ravine, officials said.

Chapter Fifty-Eight

Rori got out of the car, walked over to the edge of the embankment, and stood looking down at the pit of rock, dirt and leftover car parts where her friend's life came to an end. She held her hands over her eyes to block out the sun. As she peered down a gust of wind came up and gave her a gentle push, taking her off balance. She looked around, but saw nothing. She backed away, wiping the moisture away, got back into her car, and headed to the MLRC.

* * *

"I'd like to see Dr. Moskowitz. Tell him it's Rori Cahill, from the *Washington Independent.*"

The guard picked up the phone and relayed the message. "Please put this badge on and wait over there," he said, pointing to a waiting area. "Someone will be here in a minute."

"I know the drill. I've been here before," she said.

Rori found an opulent chair where she could view the hallway. As she sat there, she started to second-guess her presence at the hospital. The last time she was here, she was with Neil, and they talked to Dr. Moskowitz. Neil had noticed how intently the lieutenant watched them.

Would Neil approve of me being here, by myself? He's gone, and I have to do what I feel is necessary.

"Miss Cahill, Miss Cahill. Hmm, Miss Cahill, would you please follow me?" the secretary said.

Rori looked up and realized the woman was talking to her. "I'm sorry."

The secretary took her to the third floor where the doctor's main office was, then closed the door.

Dr. Moskowitz was standing by the window, eating popcorn. He watched her drive into the hospital parking lot. The fireplace in his office was smoldering, as though someone tossed a wad of paper into the flames. He stepped around the massive desk and looked her over like she was a new car. Rori shook with anger and tensed up as he approached her. He held out his hand. "How may I be of assistance?"

Rori ignored his hand.

"I'm sorry about your friend—or should I say, friends."

"You son of a bitch. You're just as responsible for their death as that crazy lieutenant of yours. I just haven't figured out you're involvement yet." Rori gave a wry smile. "Let me tell you something. You can bet your ass that I *will* figure it out."

Dr. Moskowitz looked at her with a degrading smile. His movements were slow and deliberate as he moved closer to her, until they were face to face.

"I'm afraid you have things confused, because if you could prove anything, you wouldn't be here."

"I know you covered up the Vice President's nervous breakdown and you may be mixed up in espionage," Rori said.

The doctor looked over to the fireplace and then walked over and stirred it up. The papers the doctor tossed into the fireplace were beginning to smother the flames. The doctor stood watching it, making sure it would consume it all.

"You see," he said, turning to Rori, "you could never prove anything like this, because everyone takes their own records with them."

"You must keep some, because we had them—at least before you killed everyone."

"Theoretically speaking, let's say, if this were true, it would have been a little dumb on my part. I doubt you would find any now," the doctor said, as he looked toward the fireplace.

Rori stared at him as she tried to hold back her simmering anger. "You'll make a mistake sometime. It may be a simple mistake a doctor or nurse makes with paper, but you know what? I'll be right there to nail your ass. People like you are a sickness to society. You're nothing more than a greedy bastard."

Dr. Moskowitz's smile disappeared, and he dropped his popcorn to the floor. He had a madman's grin on his face. He rushed to Rori and pinned her to the wall, holding her with his forearm against her throat.

"You better be careful, you little tramp, or you could end up like your friends. What were their names? Oh, yes, Maureen. The lieutenant told me he had a great time with her. And what were the other ones? Neil? Yes, Neil the drunk, and those other two cleaning people."

Rori wasn't sure what happened to Rosemary and Gerry. At one point, she thought they killed Neil and the lieutenant, but when two unidentified bodies were found in the wreckage, she knew it must have been them. In her grief over Neil's death, she hadn't taken the time to think too much about the Waterfords.

Dr. Moskowitz's body was now pressing up hard against her, keeping her from moving at all. His breath stank of popcorn. Rori's face was getting redder, as he applied more pressure against her throat. She was starting to feel lightheaded and knew in a few minutes she would pass out. She squirmed as much as she could, searching with her right hand until she found Jack. She gave the doctor a push with her shoulder and twisted, and then kicked his shin. When the doctor flinched, she pulled Jack, jamming the gun into his side.

Moskowitz froze and eased up, looking down to where the barrel of the gun was pointed at his side. It was aimed upward toward his heart. He released his grip and backed away.

"You know if you shoot me, you'll be arrested for murder," Dr. Moskowitz said, his voice shaking.

"I'll tell them you attacked me," Rori said. "A little rip here and there should be enough to prove that. They'll give me some shit, but I'll get through it, and you—you'll be dead."

The doctor backed farther away from Rori. "They'll think it was revenge for your friends," Moskowitz said.

"How would they know anything about that? And if they did, I'd just turn it around. Get on your knees."

Dr. Moskowitz did as he was told. He was sweating under his clothes but tried not to show any outward signs how terrified he was.

"Turn around," Rori said.

The doctor struggled to turn while on his knees. "This isn't as easy as you think. Especially at my age."

"Shut the fuck up. Just do it."

When his back was facing her, she placed her pointed boot in the middle of his back and pushed his face to the floor. "I'll get you. I'm not about to go to jail for it. You just try and come after me, and I swear to God I'll shoot you on sight."

"I have no reason to come after you, because I have done nothing and you can't prove I have," the doctor said, his voice muffled by the carpet.

Rori put her foot on the doctor's back and kicked the back of his head with her heel then walked out.

The doctor struggled to get up, but was able to pull himself to his chair. He wiped the sweat from his face and brushed himself off. Eventually, he got up and went over to the window. He put his hand to the back of his head and touched the spot where Rori kicked him. When he brought his hand down, it was covered with blood. He put the bloody hand to his mouth, licked it and began to laugh. Watching Rori drive out of the parking lot, he picked up the phone and called Vitaly.

Chapter Fifty-Nine

Rori pulled her pickup into the empty lot of The Black Sow and sat there for a few minutes thinking about Aunt Charley. She always told her she could shoot the pains in the ass. But it wasn't that time yet. First, close some doors and then talk to Bernie. Maybe he knew something that could help clear things without too much effect on her conscience. She knew it would come to her, but she needed time. Maybe it was time for a vacation, a trip to see Aunt Charley?

Rori got out of her car and took one last walk into the bar to say goodbye to Bert. She avoided looking at the booth, as she entered the bar, where she and Neil spent time together talking. Where she developed a friendship. Something she tried not to do. Friends made things complicated.

"Where are all your customers? Did you scare them away?"

"Nah, it's just early in the week. Shit, most of them spent their weekend here and need to give it a rest, before they start up again. Nice to see you, Rori," Bert said.

"Thanks," Rori said. "Were you here…that morning?"

"Yeah, like I said when you called."

"That's right. My mind—I'm just not with it."

"That's okay," Bert said. "I understand." He stood there awkwardly for a moment. "Your friend, Howard, was in here a few days in a row. Drunk every day. He said he got fired. He was so drunk I called a cab one day. Haven't seen him since."

"Let's toast our friends," Rori said.

"Beer?" Bert asked.

"No, Jameson. Neat. Get whatever you want, too."

Bert poured a Jameson for Rori and a beer for himself. Rori picked

226

up her glass to make a toast. Bert grabbed his mug of beer, but as he started to speak, blood began to spurt from his jugular.

Bert dropped his mug and put both hands to his throat, trying to stop the spurting. The blood sprayed Rori's face, but she didn't realize what was happening until the second bullet hit Bert in the forehead.

She reached over the end of the bar to grab Bert, but was hit in the shoulder and fell to the floor. She remembered how she and Neil noticed the grime coating the floor when they first came to The Black Sow. Here she was, lying in it and bleeding. She looked under the bar and saw Bert was dead. The spark always there whenever he saw Rori was gone.

She heard the door open and knew she would be dead in minutes, too. She crawled under the saloon doors into the kitchen. The pain in her shoulder was something she had never felt. *Is this what Neil felt as he fell into the ravine?* She banished the thought and focused on her survival training.

She dragged herself around a prep table and stuffed herself underneath. The smeared blood trail was easy for the killer to follow. She laid her head down onto the tile floor, expecting to die at any moment. The blood loss was starting to make her woozy. She closed her eyes and thought...survival.

Vitaly moved slowly into the unsavory room and moved to look over the tacky bar. Bert lay with his face completely obscured by blood.

A smile came across Vitaly's face. "Child's play." He turned and walked to the end of the bar, stepping over a barstool and around the blood as best he could. He followed the blood streak into the kitchen. *I must be getting old or out of practice. I usually don't need more than one shot to put them down.*

Stepping off to the side, he bent down to see what was ahead of him. It was darker in the kitchen. Staying low, he entered the kitchen cautiously, following the bloodstain streaks. At the end of the table, he could see a pair of boots sticking out from under a workstation. Vitaly knew he had her.

He kept his gun in front of him and bent down. He shot twice under the table in the direction of Rori's body. Not seeing her move, Vitaly knew she was dead. *Not so old after all.* He chuckled.

He walked over to the stainless steel table and kicked at one of the boots. It slid across the floor. Two shots echoed from a corner across the room. Vitaly fell to the floor with a thud.

Rori leaned against the gray Rubbermaid trash barrel she had been hiding behind, then fell and hit the wall.

The End

The Willowdale Conspiracy continues
Book II coming early 2015

Acknowledgements:

Throughout my life, there have been numerous people that have influenced me. Some have just provided the stories while others have influenced my thought pattern. To those that remain nameless thank you very much. Thank you Mrs. Stone, my High School English teacher. I should have followed your direction. To Linda Hughs who typed my stories 35 plus years ago, long before the computers were invented. Others who have pointed me in the right direction: Joan Lee Hunter of the Fifth House Lodge Retreat, Laurie Lamountain, Kim Linehan, Mary Linehan and Susan Kohlback. Thank you Rebecca T. Dickson for your guidance and kick-ass editing.

ABOUT THE AUTHOR

Thomas D. Linehan

Thom Linehan is the youngest of fifteen children. He grew up in Waterloo, New York, on a farm that is still in the family. The country life gave him the freedom to develop his own adventure. That freedom lent itself to stories, which after written were put into a box.

After retirement from a career as an Industrial Engineer Supervisor with a major corporation in Connecticut, he and his wife, Judy, moved to Denmark, Maine.

The stories have crawled out of the box.

Drop me a line at tdlmaine@gmail.com or on Twitter at tdlmaine

Thomas D. Linehan